THE TRITON DISASTER

Hard Science Fiction

BRANDON Q. MORRIS

Contents

PART 1: THE JOURNEY	1
PART 2: THE DESTINATION	189
Author's Note	333
Also by Brandon Q. Morris	335
A Guided Tour of Neptune	345
Glossary of Acronyms	357
Metric to English Conversions	359

Part 1: The Journey

5/23/2080, VSS Freedom

"What is that?"

Startled, Nick turned towards the sound of the voice. One of the passengers, the skinny bald one, was watching the radar image over his shoulder.

"During the flight, you should..." Nick began, but then shook his head. *Here we go again,* he thought. There wasn't really anything wrong with people asking him questions during the flight. They were, in the end, paying for him to entertain them.

"Let me see..." He looked for the bald man's name tag and read it. "Mr. Wiseman. We'll find out shortly."

He shifted the radar image to center on the shadow the man had spotted. Usually the autopilot handled the radar and Nick didn't have to check it. The pilot only had to step in if something was endangering the ship's flight path and the autopilot hadn't determined a detour. In other words, never. Whatever was casting the shadow must have been rotating, since the intensity changed at a rate of approximately once per minute. Nick retrieved the orbital data and nodded. It was probably one of the Spacelink satellites a crazy billionaire had paid to have fired into low orbit, way back when, only to just leave them up there when his company had gone bankrupt.

"Mr. Wiseman? This looks like an old Spacelink satellite. It's a miracle it hasn't burned up yet."

It was strange, though. At such a low orbit, the atmosphere would have caused so much deceleration that the satellite should have fallen long ago. But during one of the launches the satellite deployment hadn't gone as planned, so four of them had ended up in higher orbits. Nick remembered this only because it had delayed his own first launch into space by a month. NASA had wanted to be sure that the private firm had its technology under control.

"Spacelink?" the curious passenger asked.

"Yes, that's what the low orbit suggests. If it were an active satellite, the radar would issue a warning."

"Then that thing is worth a lot!"

"Well, after so much time it's become electronic waste."

"Didn't you hear that one of the company founder's vehicles was auctioned off at fifty million the other day? A salvage company brought it back from its Mars orbit."

The man was right. The Spacelink founder's fans still adored him, and the fact that most of the other satellites in the series had burned up would increase the value of this specimen significantly.

"I think, Mr. Wiseman, that we should note what the exact path of this gem is. Then, later on we can—"

"But why *later?*" interrupted the passenger. He had become so loud that four of his five fellow travelers stopped photographing from their portholes to look up at him.

"We should discuss this in private," said Nick, raising his arms.

"I've got an idea. I've booked an EVA with you, anyway. We'll just use our time out there to bring this thing in."

"We'd have to change course," Nick replied. But he no longer protested, only searching for possible objections so the man could help clear them out of the way.

"You're the pilot. But it looks to me like that thing isn't that far off."

"Up here, that's relative. It's above us. We'd need to decelerate to get into its orbit, then accelerate again to recover the lost time in a lower orbit. I have to get all of you back to New Mexico, preferably with a couple of gallons of methane left in the tank, or else my boss will give me the sack."

Which might not be so bad, Nick thought. Then he'd never have to get back on this space bus and make stupid passengers with no training into astronauts.

"You'll have to figure that out on your own. I can't help you with that," said Wiseman. "But I assume we have reserves on board. What if you lost me during the EVA?"

Nick sighed. "True, we have about twice as much methane in the tanks as we need. This is regulation in private space travel, and that's what makes the tickets so expensive."

"Just check it again. But let's suppose we could bring in ten million for this thing there, then you'd get three million. Of course, since I discovered it, I get a little more."

"No way. We'll go fifty-fifty, or it's not going to happen," Nick replied.

"So you're in?" asked Wiseman.

The bald guy had fallen for it. Nick gave a short laugh. "Are you a politician or something?"

"No, I'm a real estate agent," answered the passenger. "Let's just split the proceeds. It'll bug me, but so be it. I'm Walter, by the way."

Wiseman held out his hand and Nick gave him a palm slap.

NICK PRESSED A BUTTON ON HIS CONTROL PANEL. AN automated voice announced, "Your attention please. Orbit correction. Please ensure that your safety belts are securely fastened."

The same text appeared on the displays adjacent to every passenger porthole. Everyone reached for their seatbelts except for a blond woman in her mid-40s, sitting on the right-hand side in the back, who ignored the announcement. She had headphones on and was bobbing her head back and forth with her eyes closed. When they'd crossed the Karman Line, she'd paid attention to outer space for just a moment. Nick figured her husband had given her this flight so he could screw his secretary in peace.

Nick sighed, lifted himself up, and floated over towards her. He knocked on the casing of her headset. When she opened her eyes in alarm, he pointed to the warning on her screen.

"Oh, excuse me," she said loudly, buckling herself in.

Nick returned to his seat. Meanwhile, the computer had calculated the new course and all he had to do was press the start button. It was a good thing he'd had such thorough training in orbital navigation. But would he really still be able to calculate the necessary deceleration phases on his own? The thrust of the engines pushed him into his seat, and he closed his eyes and surrendered to it.

His seat was shaking. Nick winced. Had he fallen asleep? He checked the display. The ship had reached the pre-calculated position and was hovering, adrift in space.

Nick turned to the passengers. The blond woman with the headphones appeared to be asleep. The others were glued to their portholes.

"Time to get out," he said, nodding to Wiseman.

"Get out?" asked the Japanese woman.

"Mr. Wiseman here booked an EVA," Nick replied. "He wants to take a look outside."

"Oh, I'd like that too," she said.

"I'm sorry, but you should have specified that when you made your reservation. It costs $5,000."

"Can I pay now?" The woman grabbed her purse, presumably in search of her wallet.

"Unfortunately, no. We only have equipment for one guest on board. Planning, you know?"

Part 1: The Journey

She sank into her seat, disappointment written all over her face.

"Come with me to the back, Wiseman," Nick said.

The realtor followed him to the rear of the ship towards the airlock. Nick activated the outer door, which opened laterally to reveal what looked like an oversized chocolate box. To save air, there was a pair of three-dimensional forms, vaguely human-shaped, made of soft but very durable material. The spacesuits were inside.

Nick took out Wiseman's spacesuit first. "Slip it on," he said. Then he donned his own.

The suits were so uncomplicated that even a layperson could put one on quickly. Most importantly, it was possible for someone with no previous training to fill one up with air. Nick still remembered the old NASA suits and having to cycle for half an hour to avoid getting the bends.

"It worked," said Wiseman, smiling at him.

Nick checked the fit of the suit, tightened the buckles on the belt, and then put his hand on Wiseman's shoulder approvingly. "Good job." He pointed to the helmet. "When you close it, Wiseman, radio communication is activated automatically."

"Roger that. And outside?"

"You don't need to do anything. My suit controls yours, which automatically follows me wherever I move. Do you see the jets on the belt? They take care of everything."

"What if you get hit by a meteorite?"

"First of all, they're asteroids as long as they're still out here. Second, the risk is very, very low. You'd more likely get hit on the head by a coconut in New York City. And third, your suit would automatically bring you back into the airlock. FYI, this also happens when there's a risk of running out of fuel. Nothing can happen to you."

"Very reassuring," said Wiseman.

"Then we'll squeeze into the pack," Nick said, closing his helmet.

Now he went forward. It was always quite an effort to

7

move into the narrow cavity. The less space between suit and wall, the less air they wasted. A status display in the helmet visor told him that the bald guy was ready.

"Close inner airlock door," said Nick.

The inner door shut behind them.

"Watch out, Wiseman, you're in for a shock. But nothing can go wrong."

"Thanks for the warning."

"Open outer airlock door," Nick commanded. He knew what was going to happen, but he still instinctively looked for a strap to grab.

The metal plate that had been blocking the view to the exterior slid briskly aside. He was hanging with his head downwards over the Earth, which filled his entire field of vision. The sensation of freefall was overwhelming, and Nick felt sweat break out. *No*, he told himself, *you're not falling*. It would only take him a few seconds to adjust to this perspective. He mentally rearranged his orientation, and closed his eyes to better do so. When he opened them again, he was lying back and staring up into the sky, where the Earth was suspended above him. Enormous. *Much better.*

Wiseman was breathing heavily.

"Everything okay? Close your eyes. The Earth is above you, you hear?"

"Everything—"

"Listen! Nothing can happen to you, Wiseman. There is no down and no up here. Close your eyes and picture the Earth up in the sky."

What Nick had said wasn't exactly true. If Wiseman needed to throw up, the trip would be over. This was also somewhere in the fine print he'd signed.

The outer door automatically closed behind them.

"Okay," the realtor finally said. "Now everything's fine."

"Great! You're a natural astronaut." These were the first words he'd learned when he was in training to be a tourist pilot. Because they worked.

"Thank you."

Part 1: The Journey

"We're going to separate from the ship."

"Roger."

Nick pressed his thumb against the side of his index finger. As a result, the jet on his back emitted a pulse that pushed him slowly forward. He exited the narrow alcove and detached from the spaceship. The passenger suit copied his every move.

Wiseman's breathing was audible again.

"You all right?" Nick asked.

"Yes. Weird, but okay."

"Good. I'm looking for the satellite. You can change your position in space with your left hand. Did anyone explain that to you?"

"Yes, I remember."

"And don't worry, you won't get away from me."

"Very reassuring."

Nick navigated the menus in his helmet with his eyes. First he received the radar display, followed by the infrared view. The satellite they wanted to capture was already on the same orbital plane. The computer had calculated an almost-perfect course. Nick masked the menus and looked around. There was a shadow in front of the sun. That had to be it.

Nick reached into his tool belt for the regulation nylon cord for emergency use. "Got it," he said. "Come on, let's go."

He set course for the satellite by stretching his right arm out towards it. He always felt a little like Superman at this point, with his spacesuit serving as his cape.

Wiseman cheered, and his suit followed Nick automatically. His passengers almost always adjusted quickly to the conditions in orbit—Nick had a natural talent for this. But the profits they were eyeing might have had something to do with it, too.

AT FIRST GLANCE, THE SPACELINK SATELLITE LOOKED LIKE new. It had a few minor scars, but its solar cells shone as if freshly cleaned. Nick floated around it. He'd have to fold in the solar panel. But when he tried to do so, the satellite only turned.

"Wiseman?"

"Yes?"

"I need your help over here. You're going to have to press against the right panel while I fold in the left one."

"But how? I have no control over my suit."

"Now you do. Point your right arm towards the right panel and gently tap your index finger with your thumb."

"Okay," Wiseman replied, slowly starting to move.

When he was right about at the level of the panel, Nick took command of his suit again, and it stopped immediately. "Nice job," he said. "Just hold the panel now."

Nick had his own suit exert forward pressure. Wiseman's suit copied the movement so they were pushing the panels inward simultaneously. It worked. After about 15 degrees of rotation, the solar panels automatically began moving into their safety position and folded up completely. Nick fixed Wiseman's position in space and moved towards the satellite. He took the line out of the belt pack and fastened it between the two panels, then took Wiseman back in tow.

"That's it," Nick said. "We're returning to the ship. We can pull in the lifeline from the inside."

"That was fast," said Wiseman. "Can't we break any rules while we're out here?"

"We've already lost time. If we're really late, there will be trouble. The ship still has to be prepared for another launch tomorrow."

Meanwhile, they had started moving back to the spaceship. After Nick attached the line to a reel on top of the capsule, the outer door opened, and they floated into the airlock. The two men made their way back into the narrow gap, the outer door closed, atmosphere flowed in, and the inner door opened.

Part 1: The Journey

"Congratulations, Mr. Wiseman," said Nick. "You've completed your first EVA."

"Thank you."

Wiseman took off his spacesuit and an unpleasant odor reached Nick's nose. He politely ignored it. Sometimes people relieved themselves in reaction to the adrenaline kick when the external airlock opened, but everyone was required to wear a diaper since there weren't any toilets on board.

Nick floated back to his command chair and pressed the button for the 'Fasten Seat Belts' sign. He realized there was something else to do, so he searched the menu for emergency operations, which he could use to control the reel on the roof and draw in the line. The satellite began moving towards them, but the ship was also changing its position slightly. For every action, there is an equal and opposite reaction—you can't escape Newton. Finally, the satellite landed on the roof.

Nick drew the cable in as tightly as possible so their prize wouldn't escape. He entered the modified data, including the total mass of the ship plus the Spacelink satellite, into the control computer. They were going to land in the Spaceport 40 minutes late. His boss would not be pleased.

ANOTHER 40 KILOMETERS TO GO. IN THE PAST, HE'D COVERED that distance in just a few minutes.

Afterwards, he could sit himself down in his car and have it drive him home. He hoped Rosie wouldn't be back yet. He wanted to rest, just half an hour. Sit on the sofa in front of the house and stare into the desert. Come down.

Suddenly there was a drumming sound from above. *Crap.* Nick braced himself against the seatbelt and straightened up.

"Mr. Abrahams?" asked a female voice from behind.

Yes, he was taking care of it. Nick closed his eyes for a moment. There was an impulse to just do nothing. Wouldn't that be the best for everyone? His wife would get the mandatory insurance his boss had taken out for him, and he'd be at peace.

"Mr. Abrahams?" The Japanese woman was worried.

A hand touched his shoulder and Nick turned around angrily. Had she gotten up? The realtor was kneeling on the floor and pointing upwards.

"You got that under control?" he asked.

"Of course."

He nodded. It was entirely clear to him what was going on. The fucking satellite wasn't fixed tightly enough, and now it was thrashing in the wind. He should have fastened it in at least three different places. Why had he forgotten that? Had he perhaps wanted to bring this situation onto himself? But it was too late now. He couldn't exit during the descent, and a go-around was out of the question.

Nick released the straps to reach the command screen more comfortably. He was looking for the emergency program. He couldn't cut the line, but he could push off the reel that was holding the line and, along with it, the pricey souvenir he wanted to sell off to Wiseman.

"Sorry, my friend," he said, tapping the button that released the reel. The drumming didn't stop. "Crap!"

"Mr. Abrahams? What's going on?" asked the woman from behind.

"Doesn't sound like things are under control to me," said Wiseman.

I really don't need this, he thought. "Please, all of you, just be quiet. I have to think!"

It worked. Nobody uttered another word. The only sound to be heard was the drumming, which was getting louder and louder. What would happen as the density of the atmosphere increased? How many impacts could the roof of the spaceship sustain? The bottom was reinforced for reentry, but the top didn't have to be equally robust, so the design engineers had certainly saved some weight there. Every gram cost a few dollars per launch.

Nick pulled himself toward the ceiling. The emergency

Part 1: The Journey

release could not be controlled electronically, but it was designed to work even in the event of a power failure. He was going to have to eject the reel by hand. If only he could remember that training! But that had been eight years ago, and there hadn't been an emergency since. *Crap!* This was sure to send his boss off the handle. The fact that he was proceeding manually would necessitate a multi-day repair.

Nick hoisted himself up. With a folding knife he pushed the ceiling panel to the side. Just past it was a dark cavity. "Wiseman, give me light here!"

The bald guy reacted quickly. Good man. Now Nick could see the levers and switches in the false ceiling. They were labeled with abbreviations that he'd had to memorize long ago but had since forgotten. What he did know was that the name would have to end with Ej for Ejection. But there were four candidates. MSEj, LEj, and CEj numbers 1 and 2. He ruled out the last two because there was just one reel.

What could MS stand for? Should he try it? He touched the lever with his right hand. What if the 'S' was for 'seat?' If he were to fling them out of the ship at 35 kilometers, they would all die. No, it had to be the L. Maybe it stood for 'Line?' His mind was blank. He really shouldn't drink so much.

Nick looked down. A look of farewell? Wiseman moved his lips, but the drumming was now so loud that Nick couldn't understand a word. He pulled on the LEj lever. There was resistance, but Nick kept pulling. The lever gave way and moved down a few inches.

And the drumming stopped. *Whew—lucky.* Nick's heart rate started slowing back down and he took a deep breath.

"Thank you, Commander," the bald man said, returning to his seat.

"Everyone buckle up. Landing in twenty minutes," Nick ordered.

5/24/2080, Socorro, New Mexico

Nick threw his jacket over his shoulder. When he had left the house that morning, the thermometer wasn't yet at 16 degrees. Now the sun was shining, and it had surely broken into the 30s. He approached the gate and then passed into the lobby.

His boss was standing in the doorway to his office. "Come here for a minute?" Had Bill been there long? He hadn't noticed.

"Can we do it tomorrow, Boss? I'm sure Rosie's already waiting for me so we can have dinner." Rosie in fact would never wait for him before eating, but his boss's wife, Solveig, cooked for him every night.

"No. Now." He was noticeably abrupt. Bill was generally affable. He stepped out of the doorframe and let Nick go in first. He didn't ask Nick to sit down, however, but instead went to stand behind his desk.

"What's going on?" Nick asked.

"You're fired," Bill replied. "I can't leave the passengers with you anymore. You're unfriendly. I've told you so many times. But what you did today really takes the cake."

"This guy Wiseman wanted—"

"It doesn't matter what he wanted. You're responsible for their safety. If things had really gone wrong, the company would have ended up broke and everyone here would've been out of a job. Who do you think you are?"

"Astronaut Nick Abrahams, the world record holder for most launches into space?"

"You were a good astronaut once. I suggest you take a year off, have a rest, and then come back. I'll see to it that you get an office job here. You can guide the visitors through our museum. That'd be interesting, right?"

"Shit, man. I'd rather kill myself, Bill."

"I didn't hear that just now. Otherwise I'd have to get you committed."

"And the flight tomorrow?"

"We have to cancel for tomorrow. The whole rest of the week we're closed. That's your fault."

"But after that—"

"Now it's Mike's turn," his boss cut in.

Of course. Mike, who'd been interning there for half a year. They'd just been waiting to replace Nick. Mike would undoubtedly be cheaper, plus he was 20 years younger and not as defiant.

"Oh, just bite me," said Nick. He turned to leave the room. He tossed his employee badge at the woman behind the reception desk and she caught it deftly. Was this the new one? Maybe he should take her out sometime.

Oh, shit, they won't be seeing me back here anytime soon. Out of here!

'YOU ARE NOW LEAVING TRUTH OR CONSEQUENCES.'

The city where Spaceport America was located had a stupid name. Nick turned around and looked back at the last of its houses. As if there was really a choice between truth and consequences! Truth *and* Consequences would have been more logical. They only came in a twin pack.

Semi-desert started to appear along the roadside as he drove the four-lane highway to Socorro. Nick took the

Part 1: The Journey

steering wheel in both hands and the car realized that he wanted to take control. He stepped on the accelerator. On the I-25, the speed limit was 120 kilometers per hour, so in autonomous mode the car wouldn't go any faster. Now he got it up to 150.

Maybe he'd manage to get home before his wife. Their commutes were about the same distance. He had to go north, and she went east, with Socorro as home base. It had seemed practical to them at the time. His wife worked at the Very Large Array, or VLA. She often put in overtime, and lately even more than before. Evidently she did not long for his company. Nick shook his head and pushed the accelerator up to 160 kph, causing the car to issue an alert. The speed lock would turn on at 175 kph.

He moved into the right lane and passed a truck, then weaving back to the left. The local sheriffs weren't very active around here. Really, he couldn't get away from his old job fast enough. And there was also a little part of him that wanted to get caught.

THE CAR SLOWED DOWN INDEPENDENTLY, TWO KILOMETERS before reaching Socorro. The speed limit in the city was 50 kph, enforced by a GPS system mandatory for all vehicles. Socorro was proud to be among the first three cities in the U.S. to adopt this technology, and the mayor even appeared on the national news about it. *What had become of the American dream, the idea of freedom?* he mused. Nick glanced at the glove compartment. At least they hadn't taken his Smith & Wesson away from him yet.

The car turned onto a side street. The median strip had still been a fresh green when they'd moved here. It had seemed almost artificial to him, but Rosie had explained that it was an extraordinarily resilient species of grass. Now, ever since the city had prohibited the watering of gardens and green spaces, everything here was gray, from one bungalow to the next. Nick couldn't even tell which one was his, but the car knew. It signaled, stopped briefly, and then turned into the driveway.

There was already a vehicle parked in one of the spots in the garage. Rosie must have gotten off work early. She'd left the trunk open, and he slammed it shut without looking inside. So she'd been shopping, that was good. Maybe there would be something other than frozen pizza. Or was there a special occasion he'd forgotten? Rosie's birthday was in November and their anniversary was in February. He couldn't think of anything he'd done wrong.

He opened the door leading directly from the garage into the kitchen.

"Rosie?"

There was no answer. He walked through the kitchen into the hallway, then stopped at the entrance to the living room. Rosie was sitting on the sofa across from where he stood. In front of her were two suitcases. She smiled shyly, almost awkwardly. That was the smile he'd fallen in love with more than 20 years ago. He smiled back. But what were the suitcases for?

"Hello, Darling," he said.

Rosie's smile faded. "Hello Nick," she said. "Have a seat."

He didn't want to sit down. Even though his flight instinct had been triggered, he stayed put. He even managed to formulate a question but suspected that he wouldn't want to hear the answer. Those suitcases... "What's going on?"

"I... I'm leaving you."

"I see. That explains the suitcases." Shouldn't he have felt something? Sadness, perhaps, or anger? He paced up and down the living room.

"I packed everything I need. Most of it is already in the car."

"So you'll be living somewhere else?"

"Yes. Jim has a room that's free, so I can move in." Jim, who had been her PhD supervisor, had retired a long time ago. He was gay.

"Is there... is there someone else?"

"That's not what this is all about."

So there is someone else! Who can it be? Dave? So that's why she's been putting in all that overtime lately. It was an explanation that seemed to make a lot of sense. Regardless, he felt no anger, no annoyance. It was no different from what had happened earlier in his boss's office. He just wasn't needed anymore. Such was the march of time.

5/25/2080, Socorro, New Mexico

Brrrrrrriing!

Nick reached out with his right hand. "Sweetheart, the alarm clock... so evil..." But next to him, the bed was empty.

The previous night came back to him. Rosie had told him she wanted a divorce, and she'd moved to Jim's place. Nothing like 'taking a break.' No, what she wanted was a divorce, plain and simple. He had asked her why. She had given her reasons, and he'd had to agree with every single one. He really had grown cynical. At some point, the enthusiastic astronaut he'd once been had gone on an EVA and never come back. Nick the cynic had climbed into his spacesuit to take his place. *Nick the drunk.*

He opened his swollen eyes. The sun was casting hard, white rays into the bedroom. It looked like it wanted to force apart the slats of the blinds. The New Mexico sun is harsh. Nick was actually from Seattle, where sunlight was always welcome. Here, people had to protect themselves the best they could.

Brrrrrriing! Brrrrrriing!

The alarm clock started up again. He rolled over to Rosie's side and reached his hand to the alarm clock. But the stupid thing fell to the ground, where it kept on ringing. He crawled to the edge of the bed and groped around the floor.

He found Rosie's slippers and let out a moaning howl. He suddenly realized that she was his last link to reality. His face was wet.

He kept fumbling around until he found the alarm clock. He opened the back cover and removed the batteries. The noise stopped.

Nick remained in bed for an hour, exhausted, on Rosie's side, with his arms and legs stretched out. He breathed in her scent because he knew that once it disappeared it would be gone forever. Then he got up. Enough already. He couldn't live without his wife. He'd have to get her back.

He went into the kitchen and made some strong coffee. He needed a plan. Somehow he had to manage to get back to his old self again, the one that Rosie had fallen in love with, a college baseball champion on his way to becoming an astronaut at NASA.

Rosie, on the other hand, had been aspiring to a career in radio astronomy. Their friends had always called them the perfect couple. And then they had moved to Socorro. They'd wanted kids, though not at first—and Nick more so than Rosie, so he'd quit his job at NASA and played the part of the well-paid private pilot for wealthy space tourists. He hadn't thought about how much giving up on dreams could change a person.

But this was all in the past now. He'd win Rosie over, though he wasn't sure how. He tripped over Fraser's empty bowl on the way to the toaster. Fraser the cat. Shit, he'd forgotten to feed him last night. But people did those kinds of things after getting such news, right? Presumably, the cat was sulking somewhere—or had gone over to their friendly neighbor, an older black lady living alone in her bungalow, to get fed. Nick had always imagined his kids calling her Grandma.

Maybe he should have talked to Rosie. Not about the job or his stupid boss, but about their lives, their desires, and the

Part 1: The Journey

fact that even though they'd tried for a few years, they'd never had kids. It was easy enough to say they should have talked it over, now that it was too late.

Nick got some cat food out of the fridge and dumped half the can onto Fraser's plate. Then he let some water run into the sink. Fraser never drank from a dish, only from the sink. Then he put the phone in the pocket of his pants and left the kitchen through the garage door.

LOOKING ACROSS THE PLAINS OF SAN AGUSTIN, LOCATED AT least 2,000 meters above sea level, it was easy to see why this was the prime location for the VLA. Socorro was the last town before the hour-long drive led through an awe-inspiring landscape. The plains were dry and covered by low-lying shrubs, fascinating in their desolation. Agriculture was hardly worth the effort here. There were a few farmers with extensive livestock, but they got more from leasing their land to the institute.

As Nick let his car drive, a thunderstorm seemed to be brewing over the high mountains on the horizon. The astronomers wouldn't be pleased, since lightning and humidity disrupt their observations. Most of them worked in Socorro itself and just had the data sent remotely from the telescope. But not Rosie, who wanted to be on the front lines. If she found something, all she had to do was go to Rob in the control center, kindly ask him for a tiny observation slot, and she'd have the data she needed. Rosie didn't like to wait.

The first antennae appeared in the distance. Outwardly, they were indistinguishable from the 27 dishes built here in the 1970s, but the electronics made all the difference. There had been three waves of renovations, meaning that Rosie had still been able to do world-class research. Otherwise they wouldn't have continued living in Socorro. Nick counted the dishes and evaluated the distances. Every four months, they would move via a network of double-lane railway tracks.

When had he been there last? Two years ago? Now they were probably arranged in the A-configuration.

A, like the beginning of the alphabet. And where was he going to begin? Rosie didn't make spontaneous decisions. She was very different from him, and he'd always liked that about her. He couldn't imagine planning out an entire year. Rosie, on the other hand, was the type of person to have her whole life planned out, and now he was no longer a part of her plan. How would he be able to get himself back into it?

It was impossible. She'd probably made her plans months ago. It was a coincidence that she'd told him just the day before, the very day his boss had sacked him. It was a good thing they owned their house. Half of it belonged to Rosie, but she certainly wouldn't force him to sell. That just wasn't her style.

Nick hit the stop button as hard as he could, with no reprimand from the car's automatic system. Once there had been a product series with control software that would gently scold human drivers. Then an owner pulled out his gun and shot his mouthy vehicle, and the industry realized that including this feature was a mistake. Without complaint, Nick's car squealed to a halt, bumped off the asphalt, and came to a standstill on the hard, crusty surface of the desert, right in front of a mighty cactus.

Nick leaned back. Without a strategy, he shouldn't visit Rosie at all. She would probably have the security guards send him away. He closed his eyes.

There was a knock on the glass and Nick jerked upright. Outside was a man in uniform. His smile was friendly but he had his right hand on his weapon.

Nick held up both his hands, then used his right hand to press the button to lower the window. "What can I do for you?" he asked.

Part 1: The Journey

"Are you okay, sir? Your car reported to us an emergency stop, and an owner in questionable condition."

Questionable? So that's how my car perceives me? "Thanks for your concern, but I'm fine. I just had to rest a bit."

"Sir, if you'd like, I can get an ambulance. I see on my screen that in thirteen minutes, a vehicle..."

"No thank you. My car was a little overzealous."

"Would you do me a favor, sir, and put your hands on the wheel? I hope you can understand. I'm responsible for this stretch of road, and even if you're traveling with the automatic system, you could still do some damage."

"Of course." Nick did as requested. His car measured his heartbeat, oxygen saturation, and skin resistance to generate an ECG.

The officer looked at the display on his arm and then nodded. "This is reassuring, sir," he said. "Thanks very much, and enjoy the rest of your drive. But if you don't mind my saying so, you look awful. You should definitely take a day off."

Nick laughed. "I'd like to, but I lost my job yesterday."

"Oh, I'm sorry." The policeman looked genuinely concerned. "I hope that your wife Rosalie has been able to cheer you up."

Nick twitched as the officer said her name. But of course his data was linked to his car's computer and license plate. "Rosie," he said. "Rosie left me yesterday, too. Just my luck."

"Oh, you poor guy. I'd say that I could relate, and maybe that would make you feel better, but I can't."

"You're not married?"

"No, sir."

"Consider yourself fortunate."

"I couldn't say, sir. Well, if you really don't need me, I'll leave you be now."

"Of course. I'm sure you've got other things to do." Nick searched for a nametag somewhere on the uniform but didn't see one. "What's your name?"

25

"Automatic unit 3BT6, sir. It was a pleasure to chat with you. Call 911 if you need help."

That night, shortly after ten, Nick returned to his bungalow. He had spent the day at a casino on a reservation near Socorro, where he'd found some comfort in the rhythmic blinging of the machines. He looked around the kitchen. Fraser hadn't touched his food, and the water in the sink had completely drained.

"Fraser?"

It would certainly be the first time that the ginger-colored cat answered to his name, but he could give it a try.

No answer.

Nick checked the litter box. It appeared to be completely clean.

Well, Fraser, did you leave me too, you traitorous pal? Honestly, I don't blame you.

5/27/2080, Socorro, New Mexico

A POLAR BEAR WAS MOVING WITH NO APPARENT DESTINATION across a frozen landscape that reminded Nick of the freezer compartment in their fridge. On the television, a seal was sitting on the edge of an ice floe, grooming its fur, just like Fraser. *That traitor!* he thought. Nick filled up the bowl with fresh food every day, but the cat still hadn't returned. The polar bear approached the seal as if it just happened to be in the area. The seal raised its head briefly, did an about-face, and dove into the black water. The polar bear sat up on its back legs, its face showing no emotion. *The polar bear, that could be me,* thought Nick, switching to another channel.

Nature documentaries, boring. Talk shows, the same. He kept switching. The selections seemed endless. He could get his own personal program arranged, but he'd have to know what he wanted, which he was simply unable to decide. Linear television had been created for people like himself. He took some comfort in the thought that he was not alone in his total misery. All over the world there were men—and certainly also women—with a can of flat beer on the table, clicking mindlessly from channel to channel.

An old woman was pleading in her own defense before an austere, black judge. She had been feeding pigeons, which was illegal in her town, and hadn't been able to pay the fine, so now she had to go to jail for a week. She thought this was unfair, but the TV judge swung the gavel as if at an auction and sent her off to the slammer. The audience in the courtroom grumbled.

What crap! Why am I watching this?

Because he had nothing else to do. Fine, he could tidy up the kitchen again, vacuum the house, mow the lawn. *But why?*

There was a ringing sound.

"Alexa, reject call."

"Reject call."

He could at least ask who'd been trying to reach him here. "Alexa, who called?"

"The caller is listed as Bill Asshole in your address book."

So it had been his boss calling. What could he have wanted? Had the company changed its mind? Had the kid who'd replaced him been unable to handle the passengers? Some experience was needed to turn Midwestern housewives and car salesmen from Illinois into astronauts.

"Alexa, call back Bill Asshole."

"I'm calling back Bill Asshole."

"Alexa, change the address book entry to Bill."

"I'm changing the address book entry to Bill."

Nick heard a connection signal, and then his boss answered. "Hi, Nick. Thanks for getting back to me. How are you?"

"Oh, I'm fine."

"I heard about your wife."

So word had gotten to Truth or Consequences. Nick wasn't especially surprised, since Spaceport America and the VLA, as the only two high-tech employers in this region, were quite well-connected.

"Yes, she's gone. But it was foreseeable." That was a lie. Nick had been caught entirely by surprise. But saying it was expected certainly made it sound better.

"Still, it must be a shock. If you need someone to talk to..." Bill's voice trailed off.

Sure thing. The prick probably felt complicit somehow,

Part 1: The Journey

and now he had a guilty conscience. Nick realized he was being unfair. He kneaded his hands together to calm himself down. Bill wasn't all that bad. He was just doing his job. He himself was a danger to the company. What had become of him?

"Thanks, Bill. But I don't think you can help me. I may have to revisit some of my old dreams again. Did I ever tell you about the winery?"

For a while, Nick had dreamed of retiring as a winemaker. Of course Rosie had played an essential role in this future, but did he really need her for this?

"Winery, no," says Bill. "It sounds crazy, and that's why it suits you. I just can't imagine where you expect to get the millions from."

"Yes, that's the problem. Maybe I'll rob a bank."

"Shh, don't say anything else. A criminal's first rule is no confidantes," Bill said with a laugh.

But Nick had already thought it through, including how to escape with the spoils. But the chances were minimal. He needed another way.

Ding-dong. It was the doorbell.

"Nick, your neighbor is on the doorstep," Alexa announced.

"Bill, I've got to go, I've got a lady visitor," Nick said.

"Chin up, kid. My offer still stands." A pleasant sound signaled that the connection had ended.

"Alexa, please let the visitor in."

Nick looked down at himself. He was reasonably presentable. He quickly closed the door to the kitchen. The chaos in there was nobody's business. He opened the living room door and went into the hallway. The outer door was open, with the neighbor standing just outside. She was whistling a song he didn't know.

"Come in, Mrs. McIntosh," he said.

She smiled, revealing a row of shiny white teeth. How old could she be? Her face was as wrinkled as an 80-year-old's, but she walked with the energy of a young woman. She made no move to enter his house, but extended a dish towards him.

"I baked you a savory pie," she said by way of greeting.

"That's really nice. What's the occasion?"

"Well, it's clear you need something. Your wife moved out and you hardly leave the house. So you probably lost your job. You seem to be in crisis."

"Is it *that* obvious?"

"Listen, I have nothing to do but look out the window, so of course I notice. By the way, your cat is also with me. So you don't have to worry about him."

"Thank you. That's very kind, Mrs. McIntosh."

"Please call me Daisy. If you need someone to talk to, just come and pay me a visit. And here, take this dish. Be careful and just touch it along the rim on the top. It's still scorching on the bottom."

Mrs. McIntosh extended the dish towards him, and he took it from her gently. The rim was cool. Though he'd been expecting hard plastic, it must have been ceramic.

"Thank you," he said.

"Enjoy your meal. Life goes on."

Mrs. McIntosh turned with almost military precision and headed back towards the street, waving at him again from the garden gate. He brought the dish to the kitchen and the front door closed behind him. He searched for a clean plate and utensils, then brought everything to the living room.

He removed the lid from the dish. It smelled delicious. He piled about half of the contents on the plate and ate. There was pastry, small chunks of meat or tofu, and vegetables. It was al dente and she'd seasoned everything, so the ingredients hadn't lost their flavor. He couldn't remember the last time he'd eaten so well. He reached for the bottle of beer and smelled it. He took it to the kitchen and got himself a glass of water.

Part 1: The Journey

It was early evening and there were no dirty dishes left in the kitchen. He had vacuumed the whole house and even cleaned the bathroom. He really hated such chores. If he'd still had his job, he could have paid for a housekeeper.

Nick collapsed onto the sofa, exhausted. He looked for the remote control, which he found hiding in a crack. He pressed the power button, then changed his mind and turned the TV back off.

"Alexa, can I buy a vineyard?"

"Shall I search vineyard listings for you?"

"Yes."

"There are precisely one hundred and eighteen vineyards and wineries in the United States for sale. What criteria should I use to list them to you?"

"Cheapest first."

"A winery in Minnesota. Round Lake Vineyards, for a hundred and twelve thousand."

That was suspiciously cheap. "Is there a description?"

"Yes, Nick. I'll read it to you. Due to a serious fire that destroyed both the vines and the buildings, unfortunately our beloved winery must—"

"Alexa, stop." He could get maybe $150,000 for the house if Rosie gave up her half. He'd need it, since a new building on the winery wasn't included.

"Alexa, how much is the cheapest winery that has hours of operation available?"

"Nine hundred and fifty thousand."

So more than a million with taxes and fees. For the moment, nothing would come of his dream. He needed a different plan. Maybe he could hire himself out for a few years on an oil rig? People had made good money in the oil industry. But was that still the case, now that most of the oil fields had been depleted?

"Alexa, look for a job that fits my profile. Access to my personal data granted."

"Which fields should I search?"

"Intergalactic fields. Ha!"

"I do not understand."

"Search all over the world, without any restrictions for location."

"Okay. I have found seven descriptions that match your qualifications. What criteria should I use to list them to you?"

"Highest salary first."

"The RB Group is looking for a pilot for a long-term mission."

"And the salary?"

"It is equivalent to seven point four million dollars."

"Excuse me?"

"It is equivalent to seven point four million dollars."

"Display the offer on the television."

Alexa answered with a pling, and the television turned on. Nick soon saw a lion gnawing on a gazelle, and then the text of the job offer appeared.

Experienced pilot wanted for long-term mission

Do you have stamina and extensive experience controlling spacecraft of all kinds, with standout performance in extravehicular activities? Are you physically healthy, with an extremely high level of psychological stability and no family ties? Are you available immediately and for at least four years? If so, you (m/w/x) are our ideal candidate.

We need somebody to pilot one of our modern spacecraft who is technically savvy but can still thrive during long periods of isolation. We offer extraordinary pay for this extraordinary assignment. In addition, there will be food and lodging for the entire duration of the assignment, as well as medical care, insofar as is possible within the scope of the job. Please note that it is technically and legally impossible to terminate the assignment before it has been completed. The contract is concluded in accordance with Russian labor law. The RB Group, a world leader in asteroid mining, is a private conglomerate with headquarters in Akademgorodok, Russia.

In an anonymous survey, our employees praised our working conditions as outstanding.
If you are interested, apply online immediately with the standard documents.

Nick leaned back. $7,400,000! He wouldn't just be able to buy a vineyard, he could live out the rest of his life comfortably if he budgeted adequately. Who paid a pilot so much money? This job had to be one unlike any other. There must be something else to it. Was the mission especially dangerous, perhaps? Well, he'd probably be gone for a while, but that wouldn't be a problem for anyone right now. Even the cat had moved to Mrs. McIntosh's. Mentally stable? Well, when your wife runs off after so many years, shouldn't you suffer from a little shock? Otherwise, he had pretty much come to terms with himself, though strangers had been annoying him all his life. So why not? Even four years would go by eventually. He'd spent a whole year longer than that with the Marines, and it hadn't been especially exciting—but it had passed.

"Alexa, put my records together and send an application to the RB Group."

"Would you like me to read the other listings?"

"What's the second highest salary?"

"One hundred and thirty thousand dollars a year, limited to six months."

"No thank you. I'll be applying for the RB position."

5/28/2080, Socorro, New Mexico

"Nick, there's a call for you."

What did she say? Nick rolled to his other side.

"Nick, there's a call for you."

Leave me alone, Alexa, his brain commanded. He knew it would do no good, but he pulled the pillow out from under his head anyway and put it over his one free ear.

"NICK, THERE'S A CALL FOR YOU."

Now she was turning up the volume. Nick flinched. The pale light of the streetlamp was filtering in through the blinds. *It's still dark outside!*

"NICK, THERE'S A CALL FOR YOU."

"Yeah, I heard you, Alexa. Who's calling so early in the morning?"

"The phone number is not in your address book and cannot be traced. I only recognize the country code for Russia."

"Why didn't you say so? It's someone from the RB Group. Answer it, fast!"

Nick jumped up and opened the closet. He needed a fresh T-shirt, underwear, and clean shorts.

"Good morning, Nick," a female voice greeted him in English. There was no hint of an accent. "I see you wanted to show us what good physical shape you're in. Very admirable." The woman sounded amused.

Nick quickly shut the closet door behind him. "Alexa, turn off the camera," he shouted. "I'm sorry, Ma'am. I did not mean to shock you."

"Don't worry, Mr. Abrahams. You aren't the first naked man I've ever seen. And it wasn't such a horrifying sight."

The Russians seemed to be cut from a different cloth. If a potential American employer had caught him like that, his chances of getting the job would have instantly been zero. Nick quickly put on underwear, T-shirt and shorts, and went into the living room. The TV was already on, with an elegant woman in her early 50s on the screen. Her style was conservative, a blouse and skirt, but something told him that this didn't match the woman's character.

"Alexa, turn on the lights and the camera," he said, taking a seat on the sofa.

"I'm Valentina Shostakovna," said the woman. "Nice to meet you."

Alexa had heard, and beneath the image of the woman his digital assistant displayed the information that she could find out from the name. Valentina Shostakovna was apparently the daughter of the company's founder and had taken over as the owner. This was certainly no ordinary job.

"A pleasure. Nick Abrahams, but you knew that already. I was expecting a call from Human Resources."

Valentina smiled. "I have to apologize for disrupting you so early in the morning. But I have an appointment later, and then it will already be nighttime. Mr. Abrahams, you have applied for the position that we advertised. I assume that you've read it through and meet all the requirements."

"Correct. Do you need any additional documents?"

"Not at this time. Of course we've checked your background, which is more efficient than exchanging documents. You can already tell that this isn't your average trip that we'll be sending you on. The payment is so liberal because we expect unconditional confidentiality. Half the sum is therefore

Part 1: The Journey

paid to you as an interest-free loan, which is due immediately if you violate the confidentiality part of the contract. So that you have some peace of mind, we'll pay you one million dollars before you leave."

"That only sounds fair," said Nick. "You need security, too. But what is it all about?"

"I'll have to ask you to turn off all recording devices."

"Alexa, sleep mode."

"Thank you, Mr. Abrahams. You will have to visit one of our installations, which isn't working as expected. Your job is to find out the reasons why this is the case and to restore its functionality."

"The description mentions a duration of four years. So the installation must be very far away?"

Nick quickly calculated some distances. With the current technology, it wasn't possible to travel to Uranus and back in four years. It had taken the *ILSE* two years to fly to Saturn.

"Correct. But details can only be revealed after you've signed the contract at our facility in Akademgorodok."

"Understood. What makes you so sure that I can fix the mistake? Although I'm no slouch when it comes to fixing things, I don't have any special training in space technology."

"We don't think you need such training. What you need to know, we'll teach you. What's important to us is that you're a professional, and you've proved that with your 2,267 launches."

"But 2,254 of those were with tourists in space."

"You alone were responsible for the state of the spacecraft for 2,254 days. That's a good six years. You'll be traveling for just four years."

"That's not a problem for me."

"I hope so. Anyway, the ship we provide is equipped with all the amenities."

"Sounds good. So what's next?"

"You'll understand, Mr. Abrahams, that we need to protect ourselves. Therefore I need a power of attorney from you so we can view all your private data—bank accounts, medical reports, et cetera. As long as we don't find anything that works against you, my assistant will send you the plane tickets for the job interview. But it's all just a formality."

"Got it. How much time do I have to take care of everything here?"

Valentina looked down and tapped something, then looked back up at him again. "The next flight leaves Albuquerque tomorrow at 9:38 AM. You'll be with us about twenty-four hours later. Or is that too soon?"

Nick rubbed his eyes. Tomorrow morning—that was fast! Rosie could take care of the house, and perhaps she'd even want to live there while he was gone. He'd have to pack some personal belongings in boxes. Nothing else sprang to mind, though wouldn't he need a visa to visit Russia?

"I can do that. My wife is... never mind." The RB Group would find out when they reviewed his records anyway. "What about the visa?"

"No problem, Mr. Abrahams, we have good relations with the authorities. Your visa will be entered electronically when you arrive."

"Great. See you the day after tomorrow. What's the name of your headquarters?"

"Akademgorodok, which you could translate as 'the academy town.' But it's a full-blown city now. The day after tomorrow our driver will be waiting for you at the airport. Now I will need you to say, on camera, that you give us full power of attorney."

Nick swallowed. What if this was a large-scale attempt at fraud? Alexa had confirmed that the woman's voice and appearance matched the data about Valentina Shostakovna. But that could be faked. On the other hand, there was nothing left to steal from him. His accounts were overdrawn, and the bank was going to start threatening to seize the house that he and Rosie co-owned after the next credit card statement came due.

"I, Nick Abrahams, grant full power of attorney to the RB Group, represented by Valentina Shostakovna, to inspect

Part 1: The Journey

all my personal information," he said. This way, the banks and insurance companies would at least check whether the request really came from RB. These big companies had better resources at their disposal than he did.

"Thank you, Mr. Abrahams. I hope to see you again in my office."

"I'm looking forward to it," Nick replied.

THIS IS NUTS. NICK CHECKED AGAIN TO MAKE SURE HE HAD locked the door, then shut it behind him. Now he needed a little exercise. He had just consumed three large cups of black coffee and shoveled in some of the cereal his wife had left behind. There were a few remnants caught in his teeth that he tried to dislodge with his tongue. It was still early in the morning, but the sun was already shining down mercilessly.

The sprinkler was just turning on in the yard of the house to the right, where a man named Miller lived. Nick walked down the street. There was no sidewalk, but the road was so wide that you could easily play a great game of catch there. In the past, he'd sometimes imagined having a son to teach how to throw the ball there. That had been another life.

He waved to old DeWitt, who was raking the driveway to his house, just like he did every day. The bungalows all looked the same, but it was possible to tell them apart if you paid attention to detail. DeWitt was the only one with a raked driveway, Miller was the one with the green lawn, Gump had giant cacti growing in front of his house, and Dillinger's property was decorated with his young Thai wife, who had suddenly appeared two years ago and always seemed to be relaxing on a lounge chair under the Coca-Cola umbrella by the small pool.

It was a tiny cosmos he'd be leaving soon. Tomorrow. Maybe when he came back, DeWitt would have already died. But then again, the first to go could be Dillinger, who had hinted at a serious illness the last time they'd had a neighborhood barbeque.

Of course, it was also possible that he'd be the first one the universe called back. Just because anybody could fly into space didn't mean that space travel had become particularly safe. Once he was beyond the orbit of Mars he'd be on his own. It was somewhat comforting to know that the RB Group specialized in space transport over long distances, since it was involved in asteroid mining. But even RB ships had experienced accidents.

Where were they planning to send him? With four years of space travel, it would have to be limited to the outer solar system. Hardly any expeditions had been made there since the *ILSE* flights in the 2050s. Economically, this area was uninteresting because distances were just too great, and space agencies had to mind their tight budgets. There were still many exciting destinations. All the better for him. No matter where RB sent him, it would probably be a first. *Perhaps I won't have to go down in history with my spotty record.*

Nick walked down the street, which smelled of hot asphalt and dust. He searched his memory for any snatches of Russian. A language course had been part of his NASA training. According to NASA specifications, an astronaut should be able to communicate with a cosmonaut. This had been important when there had been a common space station. Today, in the area close to Earth, Mandarin Chinese would probably come in more useful.

"Menja sawut Nick," he said softly, then repeated in English, "My name is Nick."

"Gówno." *Shit.* This was the word that he'd be likely to hear the most often in Russian. But he would be traveling alone. What luck! So he wouldn't have to talk to anyone, in Russian or in English. Valentina Shostakovna seemed to speak English very well. He'd noticed from her lip movements that she had not been using a simultaneous translator.

"Hey, Nick!"

He turned around. It was Tedesci. He was of Italian

Part 1: The Journey

descent but born in the U.S. His wife Maria had immigrated to the States from his family's home region, Sicily. She was a real sweetheart.

Nick waved. "Hey, Paolo!"

"How are you?"

"Doing fine." At the moment, he didn't feel like going into any further detail.

"Do you have any plans tonight? We'll be throwing burgers and brats on the grill."

"Thanks, Paolo, but I have to pack up and leave tomorrow morning."

"Oh, okay. Are you going on vacation?"

"No, I'll be meeting with a new employer."

"Cool. That's good to hear, Nick. Will you be gone for a long time?"

"About four years."

"Ha-ha, good one. Well, have a nice evening. This won't be the last barbecue we have."

Nick felt no desire to correct Paolo. He himself couldn't quite believe that he would be gone for four years.

"Yes, thanks for the invitation. Another time," he said.

5/29/2080, Socorro, New Mexico

"Good morning, Nick. Today is Wednesday, May 29, 2080. The weather forecast for Socorro, New Mexico, shows that it will be sunny, with temperatures reaching thirty-two degrees. The taxi you reserved will be here for you in forty-five minutes. The plane ticket has also been arranged from Russia."

"Thank you, Alexa."

Nick jumped up. He'd already laid out his travel clothes. Since it was going to be quite cool in Siberia, he had pants, a long-sleeved shirt, and sneakers. He'd carry his jacket with him. The suitcase was already in the kitchen.

"Can I do anything else for you?"

"Thanks, Alexa. Please tell Rosie 'Hello' when she comes in the house. You'll probably be alone for a few days. If any neighbors come to the front door, please let them know that I'm on an extended business trip."

"That's too bad, Nick, I enjoy your company," Alexa said.

He shrugged. This chatty feature still struck him as a little strange, but he'd never found the settings menu where he could have turned it off. "Maybe Rosie will move in here then," he said. At some point he'd have to let Rosie know, but he could just as well do that from Russia.

He walked into the bathroom and brushed his teeth.

Alexa's voice followed him. "That would be nice," she said. "Rosie still has the highest authorization level."

He spat into the sink. "Yeah, great. There shouldn't be any problems then."

Nick pulled down his pants and sat down on the toilet. It was funny—even though Rosie wasn't there anymore, he still peed while sitting down. It took a few seconds to get started. He somehow had the feeling that Alexa was in the room, which of course was silly. He'd always had trouble taking a leak when there were other people around.

"You can count on me, Nick."

"Thanks, Alexa."

The taxi door opened to let Nick out at the airport drop-off area. He approved the fare total with a voice confirmation.

"We hope you will be our guest again soon," said the automated voice.

Someone had drawn a penis in black ink on the lower part of the seat. Nick briefly considered how the artist might have accomplished this without being filmed by the security cameras that monitored for such vandalism. Then he got out. The trunk opened automatically, allowing him to remove the suitcase and backpack. He reached back inside to grab his jacket before the automated system closed the lid. So far he hadn't had to speak to anyone today, but this was about to change.

The Albuquerque airport reminded him of a museum. The walls were decorated with folk-art motifs. It was surprisingly empty and smelled like popcorn.

In the entrance hall there was an ancient plane, and directly behind it was an elderly, dark-skinned woman selling candy at a small booth. She held out a bag with unidentifiable contents. "A present for someone special?"

Nick shook his head.

Part 1: The Journey

At security, the border official told him, "You don't have to unpack anything and you can leave on your shoes."

Nick looked at his nametag. 'Automatic unit 4ZZ2.' The border guards wore ponchos, tattered leather pants, and cowboy hats. It was an odd combination, but automatic units rarely complained. The state was proud of its past, even though it had not always been peaceful. Nick suddenly froze —he would never see all this again, that was for sure.

His backpack was waiting for him past the security checkpoint. He put it on and looked for his suitcase before remembering that it was being transported automatically to the plane. He spotted his jacket in the plastic bin on the conveyor. He had almost walked away before noticing it. As he walked down the concourse he kept his eyes fixed straight ahead, though there really wouldn't be anyone else who'd talk to him.

The doors were already open at Gate G8. Cameras captured images of his face. If he hadn't had a ticket, the door in front of him would have closed automatically. He headed down the dark, long, and hot boarding chute that led into the plane. Unruffled, he tossed his jacket into the empty seat beside his, sat down, and clicked his seatbelt.

Ha! he said to himself with a wry grin. Once again, he'd managed to avoid talking to anyone. Rosie would have thought it was bonkers, so he'd never told her about this rather bizarre hobby. But she was no longer with him. His new life awaited him at the other end of this journey. He reached into his backpack and found his passport. Valentina's assistant had reminded him that he'd need a physical passport to enter Russia. Nick hadn't even been excited when he'd received the tickets. He'd been counting on it.

He leaned back and closed his eyes. It was strange, but he missed the sound of Alexa's voice. She would have noticed that he was tired and wished him sweet dreams.

45

5/30/2080, Akademgorodok

"Tired?" Raissa, as Valentina Shostakovna's assistant had introduced herself, bent over the flat coffee table to serve him an espresso.

Nick noticed her low neckline and quickly averted his eyes. He put his hand over his mouth and yawned. "Yes, it was a long flight," he said.

"Were you unable to sleep, Nick? May I call you 'Nick?'"

"Of course you may. And yes, I can never sleep on a plane."

"What about in a spaceship?"

This was actually pretty bizarre, and he'd never thought about it before. The engines of a brand-new aircraft were mere whispers in comparison to a spaceship's rocket engines. But he'd never had trouble sleeping in space. "Yeah, that's funny, I sleep fine then," he said with a shrug. "Maybe it's because I control the spaceship myself, or at least I feel like I do, and I'm just a passenger on the plane."

"I can understand that," said Raissa. "I also prefer to be in control." She remained standing in front of the coffee table and seemed to be thinking.

He looked at her. She was an attractive woman, blonde and long-legged, dressed conservatively in a sort of corporate uniform consisting of a dark skirt and white blouse with the company logo. Raissa didn't say anything. It seemed as if she had been briefly deactivated. Was she an automatic unit like the border guards in Albuquerque? If so, then the technology here was quite advanced.

Raissa took in an audible breath, then pinched her nose and sneezed. So, she was a flesh-and-blood human being. The technology here hadn't gone that far yet. Nick was relieved. "Sorry," she said. "The boss should be right here."

With that, the door opened. The door's lining was impressively thick, presumably as a security measure. As the heir to and head of the company, Valentina Shostakovna was probably a target of interest for many criminals. She smiled welcomingly. She actually looked even better than she had in the camera image, though she'd obviously already passed the 50 mark.

Nick compared her with Raissa. They could be mother and daughter. But he'd encountered other Raissa look-alikes as he'd made his way down the long corridors. The recruitment requirements appeared to include a particular look, though RB seemed so modern otherwise.

Valentina approached and Nick got to his feet.

She shook his hand. "Glad you made it so quickly."

"Thanks to your impeccable preparations."

"Thank Raissa. She's the one responsible."

Nick smiled at Raissa. Valentina then made the universal shooing gesture and Raissa left the room. Allegedly there was still corporal punishment here. It was said that the RB group was not squeamish in the treatment of its enemies—and employees who didn't do their jobs were presumably classed among them. But he only knew that from hearsay. Perhaps RB was in reality quite different.

"Take a seat," Valentina said.

Nick sat down on the sofa again, and the head of the RB Group chose an armchair across from him. *Where else would the boss do the hiring herself? This assignment must be a very special one*, he concluded.

"I don't want to keep you from your well-deserved rest,"

Part 1: The Journey

said Valentina. "However, I still have a few questions. But before I go into further detail—you haven't changed your mind, have you?"

Nick shook his head.

"Good." Valentina leaned forward and tapped the table, which then transformed into a screen.

Nick focused on her fingers so as not to stare at her neckline. Such situations had made him blush ever since he'd been in high school, and even now he felt his face growing hotter.

"Look, here," said Valentina. With a swipe she rotated the display.

Nick's eyes widened. One million dollars had just been deposited in his account. That's what it said, anyway. He couldn't really believe it.

"That's our agreed-upon advance payment," said the RB owner.

"Thanks."

"We can now move on to the confidential part," said Valentina, leaning back again.

"My assignment."

"Right. The RB Group has an important installation on Triton."

"The Neptunian moon?"

"Exactly."

Neptune was the outermost planet of the solar system. It couldn't be reached in two years with conventional technology, which is why Nick had been thinking of Saturn or Uranus as destinations.

"I can see that you're skeptical," said Valentina, "but you can trust me. We'll be putting you in a ship equipped with a bundle of ten direct fusion drives. Since we only need to transport one person along with supplies, we were able to reduce the mass of the ship to one-sixth of what it was for the most famous expedition into the outer solar system, the one made by the *ILSE*."

"I followed that story when I was a little boy," Nick said. "Back then there were six astronauts who went on that voyage, if I recall correctly. But aren't certain components still the same size, even if there's just one passenger?"

"Ah, you're referring to the ring, or the garden module. Well, you will accelerate in half the time, since others would slow you down. This way, you actually have gravity all the time. So we don't need the ring. And our mechanism for making food, which uses nanofabricators, has become so sophisticated that you don't have to grow food."

"That makes sense. But what's my job?"

"The installation on Triton no longer responds to our commands. Something must have happened. You have to check into it for us and get it working properly again."

"So what kind of installation is this, and who or what is no longer reacting?"

"That far from Earth, we can't use humans—apart from you, clearly, but this is an emergency-level situation. For this reason, the device is controlled by artificial intelligence. Its job is to give a final boost to the Starshot Gamma spaceships."

"'Starshot Gamma?'"

Starshot... That name rang a bell in the back of his brain and then his memory kicked in.

Several years ago, an international committee had sent micro-spaceships to the nearest stars with the help of giant lasers. The probes only had a few miniaturized measuring instruments on board, and it had been possible to accelerate them to tremendous speeds, even to within several fractions of the speed of light, because they were so lightweight.

"It's an evolution of the Starshot Project, purely in-house. The project was especially important to my father, so I am determined to complete it successfully."

"And what's so special about it?"

"Well, our spaceships grow with time. There's human DNA on board, and after a few years' flight time, two children are born, and by the time they reach their destination, they will be adult, well-trained scientists. Honestly, such a tiny probe doesn't do much. Two human researchers are capable of so much more."

Part 1: The Journey

"Your father didn't ask the two passengers, did he? That seems morally questionable."

"It's hardly possible to ask two strands of DNA for their consent. But did you get to choose if you wanted to be born? Did your mother ask for your permission before she gave birth to you?"

"Well, she didn't have me light years away from everyone else." *Maybe that wouldn't have been so bad*, he thought. But of course that was an entirely personal problem.

"Fundamentally, I agree with you. My father's ideas were often less focused on what was ethically acceptable than what was technically feasible. He was a researcher, mind and heart and soul, and he had the means to implement these ideas without asking anyone. But the situation is different now. The spacecraft in question are already underway. Still, they're progressing relatively slowly in the solar wind. If they don't get the final nudge from Triton, they won't reach their destinations in twenty or fifty years, but thousands of years."

"Would that matter?"

"The development of the two human embryos begins following a predefined time so that the two passengers will be ready to go when they reach their destination. Without the boost from the Triton station, Adam and Eve will grow up, get older, and eventually die, never having seen anything other than the blackness of space, locked for their entire lives in a two-bedroom house they can't leave."

"That sounds awful," Nick said. "Adam and Eve, was that your father's idea?"

Valentina nodded.

"It seems that he was a bit..." What word could he use without offending his new boss? "... a bit ambitious."

"Megalomaniacal is more like it," she answered. "But that's just how he was. I loved him and would have done anything for him. The genes of the women on these ships are based on my genes, which he had technically altered and improved. But still, those Eves are all my sisters. I don't want

51

them to just waste their lives away." With these words, Valentina's cheeks reddened.

This issue is really important to her. This isn't about money, that much is clear. "I understand," Nick said. "Isn't there a way to stop the development, some kind of kill switch for the whole experiment?"

"My father was too careful to let that happen. After his death, someone might have come up with the idea of sending out this death signal and destroying his legacy."

"How many of these ships are out there?"

"A thousand have been launched. We expect a natural attrition rate of less than ten percent due to collisions and the like."

"So, in a few years, there will be human spaceships reaching nine hundred nearby star systems?"

"Nine hundred systems with confirmed exoplanets in the habitable zone. Actually, my father had planned a second wave with ten thousand ships, but the whole thing has already attracted too much attention. The public doesn't know yet, but there are very talented people working for the secret services. In the long term this would mean losing our autonomy, and I would like to keep RB in the marketplace as an independent player."

"You're very smart, Ms. Shostakovna."

"Please... Valentina."

"You're very smart, Valentina."

"Thank you. I am my father's daughter. What else can I tell you about your job?"

"How much time will I have on Triton?"

"One month after your expected arrival, the laser has got to send out the boost."

"Okay. I take it you've thought of everything I'd need there?"

"Yes, we've been preparing the flight for months. Triton is an ice moon with hardly any atmosphere. You'll be getting a vehicle and, of course, appropriate spacesuits."

"Well, then I can't think of anything else."

Part 1: The Journey

"You'll be traveling alone, Nick. Is that okay with you?"

"Yes. That's what makes your job so attractive to me. I like traveling alone."

"Well, if you don't want to be so entirely alone, I could offer you an HDS android from one of our employees' workshops. The HDS models can be switched off at any time."

"HDS?"

"Home, Defender, Sex. The android can provide every service and is visually difficult to distinguish from a human woman."

Nick felt his face turn red again. That would be the day! Now, with the chance to be alone for four years, and then sharing the cabin with someone? He thought about Alexa and knew for sure that he would never have the heart to turn this HDS robot off.

"Thanks, Valentina, but that's not necessary. I can cook pretty well, and I can probably do without a defender because of the lack of attackers in the middle of outer space."

"As you like. Should I perhaps still have Katharina come in? Just to have a look?"

Nick shook his head. Then he remembered the state of his house. He really liked cooking, but found it challenging to clean up afterward. "Could we get a cleaning robot to go with me? I'll admit housework is a struggle for me. But not one that's anthropomorphic."

Valentina looked around the room, then got up and walked into one of the corners. She squatted down, opened a door, and took out a disk about 10 centimeters thick and 40 centimeters in diameter. She came back to the sofa with it and pressed a few of its buttons. Nothing happened.

"This is Oscar," she said, holding it out to him. "It's a household robot. It cleans, washes dishes, and dusts."

Nick took it and pressed some of the buttons on the disk's top, but still nothing happened. He turned the robot over in his hands and discovered four wheels that rotated 360 degrees.

"You have to plug him into a standard power port for a

while. He must have run out of power overnight. Yesterday he was still scurrying around in here."

"And he washes dishes, too? How does he do it?" Nick asked.

"Oscar has an arm made of a sturdy, lightweight alloy that he can unfold from the disk if necessary. Don't underestimate him. He's not as universally useful as an HDS model, but he could take down an attacker."

"Luckily that won't be necessary."

"Of course, Nick. I do hope that's the case."

What does she mean by that? Are there possible attackers we haven't talked about yet? But Valentina had just said it dismissively. His assignment seemed straightforward enough. Fly in, repair the AI, restart the laser, fly back.

"I don't want to keep you any longer. Will we see each other at the launch?"

"No, that would draw too much attention. We'll see one other again in four years, when I transfer the remaining sum to you. I wish you great success!"

"Thank you, Valentina."

They stood up almost simultaneously and shook hands. Then Valentina left the conference room through the heavy door.

Nick was tired but unable to fall asleep. He was thinking about old Shostakovich's plans. What else might he have done in secret, with nobody monitoring his activities? Nick wasn't particularly squeamish and had enjoyed his time with the Marines in his youth. There hadn't been a war during his service period, but he wouldn't have had any problem shooting enemies who'd had him in their crosshairs, or as ordered by a superior.

But to cram 2,000 people into tiny spaceships and send them to other stars? What if it turned out the destination was uninhabitable? Just because a planet was located in a star's

Part 1: The Journey

habitable zone didn't mean it would be a good place to live. Then, Adam and Eve would be doomed to carrying out their entire lives in a spaceship. If he didn't fulfill his task, this would be the case for all 1,000 Adam-and-Eve pairs. Where did Shostakovich get the genetic material of the man? Would he have been crazy enough to use his own DNA? He should have asked Valentina.

The door squeaked and Nick sat up. He dropped himself down next to the bed, just in case someone was coming for him. Then a dim light came on. He could see the intruder was a woman, standing naked at the foot of his bed, holding a hand over her mouth.

It was Raissa. She was stifling a laugh. "You don't have to run away from me," she said.

"You never know," Nick said.

"I heard you didn't want the HDS android," said Raissa. "I thought that was sweet. And then I thought I could be the last woman you'd hold before your long flight... unless you're gay. Which is fine by me. I have a nice colleague, Pavel, he's five years older than me, but he looks good. I'm sure he'd be happy to pay you a visit."

"I'm not gay, though there have been times I've wished I were," said Nick.

"What do you mean?"

"It's a long story. But I would certainly like for you to keep me company."

"It's been a long time since I've had such a charming invitation," said Raissa, smiling.

"I promise you that over the next four years I'll always remember this last embrace."

5/31/2080, Vostochny Cosmodrome

HE REALLY HAD TO HAND IT TO THE RUSSIANS. IF THEY HAD A plan, they'd get it done, no matter what. Just three days ago, the boss of the RB Group had woken him up. Now he was $1,000,000 richer and strapped into the reclining seat of a two-person capsule at the tip of an Angara rocket about to put him into Earth's orbit. The seat next to him was empty, and a CapCom named Yuri was giving him instructions over his headphones. But it was really just information about the flight, since the rocket was controlled from the ground and he was just a passenger. He wouldn't be his own commander again until he was back in a spaceship.

A shiver ran down his spine. He'd really missed this feeling. On the *VSS Freedom* flights, they'd been launched from a plane. It had been 15 years since he'd experienced the mighty roar of a rocket engine. Now it seemed to move each of his body cells individually. It was incredibly loud, but yet such a dull, deep sound that he could still easily hear the beeping of the instruments from the cockpit. He could probably even have talked to his co-pilot if he'd had one.

"Launch!" said CapCom.

Nick felt the pressure in his stomach first, and then his whole body was pressed into the seat. He yielded to the acceleration. He couldn't fight it anyway. Two, three, four, five g's weighed on him, and for a moment he even had to endure six times the force of Earth's gravity. But it passed and then came his reward, weightlessness. CapCom Yuri counted off the seconds. After about two and a half minutes, the first stage, and then the second, would have to be cast off.

He closed his eyes. The pressure made reddish patterns dance on the insides of his eyes. This seemed to be associated with age, as he hadn't seen it before. He was getting older, but when he came back, he'd still be under 50. But then he'd be a millionaire or the owner of a vineyard, and—if he economized and shopped around—maybe both. That would be a good idea, given that he would never get a job like this again.

What had he promised Raissa? He would remember holding her. Now he was thinking of her firm breasts and the way she'd ridden him. And Rosie? *Who?* Nick laughed. He was held captive by the acceleration, but he felt free. And suddenly he weighed nothing. His heart was beating like never before.

THE SPACESHIP WHERE HE'D BE LIVING FOR THE NEXT FOUR years was called the *Eve*. This had been Valentina's decision, probably in honor of her many sisters in space. It didn't have a coupling device for the capsule he'd been in while reaching orbit, so extravehicular activity would be required to make the switch. Nick put on the spacesuit. The technology had long been standardized worldwide, but the RB model had convenient power boosters on the joints.

A virtual user interface inside the helmet picked up the functions offered by the capsule now, and later by the *Eve*. This way, he could control the functions while he was wearing the helmet. He checked the oxygen and nitrogen levels in his blood and the values matched the specifications. As he looked at the inside door of the hatch, the helmet tracked his gaze. He stared at the lock and a virtual circle lit up around it.

Part 1: The Journey

Okay, let's do this! Nick set the lock in the crosshairs. The ring turned with a gorgeous display of colors. The designers had really outdone themselves, but he thought it took too long. He was tempted to turn the lock by hand in the old-fashioned way, but Yuri warned him against it. There was no need to cause the CapCom any unnecessary problems. Finally the door opened. Nick hoped they hadn't equipped the *Eve* with such optical gimmicks. He climbed into the airlock, the air pumped out, and the way outside was clear.

Below him was the Earth. It was huge and he was falling towards it. Nick thought of Wiseman, the realtor from the *Freedom* with whom he'd gone on the spacewalk a week ago. What was the date today? It was the 31st, so it had been eight days. Nick ended his fall by briefly closing his eyes and hanging the Earth up in his head. When he opened his eyes again and turned around once on his longitudinal axis, he was floating above the tiny-looking capsule.

The *Eve* was waiting for him about 20 meters away. This ship would be his home for the next four years. If there were spaceship races—*come to think of it, why aren't there any?*—the spacecraft would probably look like this one. The living area in the central axis looked like a long barrel. The ten DFDs, which looked like slender torpedoes, formed a circle around it. They mainly worked with the rare isotope helium-3, which was why they were so expensive to operate. To propel the spaceship they needed reaction mass, which was stored in an outer circle of ten tanks. Each engine had its own tank, but the tanks could also share their contents with each other.

It was not a beautiful spaceship, but it was very special. No other spacecraft in the world could have kept up with it. Probes had reached higher speeds by cleverly building up momentum from planets, but thanks to its powerful engines and its relatively low mass, the *Eve* sped directly towards its destination. With this ship, reaching Neptune in two years seemed possible. The scientists' numbers were one thing, for sure, but the sheer appearance of the spaceship gave Nick the reassuring feeling that all the prerequisites were there to fulfill this mission.

"Nick? Ja shdu tebja." *I'm waiting for you.*

Oh! He'd forgotten about Taras, the engineer waiting for him in the *Eve*.

"Iswini, ja pospeschu," he answered. *Excuse me, I'll hurry.* Nick steered his suit in the direction of the spaceship. It was farther away than it looked. The closer he got, the bigger it seemed. The DFDs were 3 meters in diameter by about 15 meters long, or about the height of a 5-story house. Nick approached the ship from the side, as was the rule, even if the engines were completely off.

He estimated the dimensions of the spaceship. The inner circle with the engines must have measured about 60 meters in circumference and about 20 meters in diameter. The outer circle formed by the tanks was about 40 meters tall. The tanks themselves were shaped like pillows and were slightly curved so that they almost form a closed circle around the *Eve*. Nick suspected that the designers had arranged it so that the contents of the reaction mass tanks protected the individual passenger from cosmic radiation.

Nick stopped before one of the tanks and touched its shell. It was rough, and it appeared to be made of metal. *Wouldn't it have made more sense to use carbon nanofibers for weight reasons?* he wondered. He'd ask Taras. Nick squeezed through the gap between two tanks.

The circle of fusion engines below didn't look so impressive in comparison to the tank ring. Fragile struts extended outwards at 90-degree intervals. If the *Eve* had to fly in a planet's atmosphere, these delicate struts would snap quickly, but in the vacuum of space there would no longer be any need to keep the tanks in place. Thick fuel lines were running along the four sector struts. They were placed so that the struts were located in front of them in the direction of flight, probably a minimal protection against micro-asteroids. Nick corrected himself—they were, of course, support lines. The fuel storage would have to be inside the DFD housing.

Part 1: The Journey

Taras was waiting and Nick sped up a little. All of this for one astronaut—him! And who'd been the one to organize it all? Valentina Shostakovna. What power a CEO like Valentina had! But he didn't envy her, because with all that power came so much responsibility—and loneliness. He'd been able to read it on her face. Did she have any real friends at all? But that didn't matter. In the end you're always alone. He had no friends.

Nick flew between two DFDs. The *Eve's* core was now in front of him. She looked vulnerable. It was strange, but for him a spaceship was always female. The *Unity*, the *Eve*. In the plans he'd gotten prior to the launch, the core had been called the 'transport module.' In fact, they were barrel-shaped modules hanging in a row. The rear twelve contained food and spare parts, and the front four were living spaces. He would spend the next four years in an area measuring about 80 square meters. That the *Eve* would never be weightless while traveling was a disadvantage here, because without gravity, he could have used the entire volume of the modules. But at least his bones, muscles, and joints would remain functional.

"I'm over here," Taras said in Russian.

A round hatch opened on the module that was fifth down from the bow.

"You didn't have to come outside to get me," Nick said.

Taras waved a hand. "I've just inspected the *Eve* and had to go outside anyway."

Nick reached him and took hold of a ladder.

Taras pushed off and embraced him. "That's the way we do it," he said. "But we'll have to forgo the fraternal kiss."

"A pity," said Nick.

"Come in. I'm jealous of you getting to take this journey. The *Eve* is a monster. I've never built such a powerful spaceship."

They floated into the chamber, and Taras closed the outer lock.

"You're the engineer?" Nick asked.

61

"The designing was left to others. I am the site manager. I was up here from the first module."

"When did you start?"

A red light blinked and the airlock filled with air.

"Pretty much half a year ago. That was an intense time, I can tell you."

"Why don't you fly yourself?"

"I'd like to, my American comrade, but four years? No, my wife won't wait that long."

"Ah, love is what stops you."

The red light turned off and a green light came on.

"Yes, love and family. Very important. You can take the helmet off now."

Nick opened the helmet fasteners—first left, then right—to take off the helmet and let it float in the air next to him. Then he took a deep breath. There it was, that familiar smell, a mixture of machine oil and sweat, as distinctive as a new car smell. In spaceships, he had experienced this only once—when he entered the *VSS Unity* for the first launch.

"People slept in here while we finished up with the *Eve*," Taras said apologetically.

"How many of you were there?"

"In the end there were twelve of us. Eight men and four women. A few robots, but they had to stay outside."

Of course, if a dozen people sweating in their spacesuits for the entire working day had spent half a year here, there was nothing left of the new car smell. But that wasn't a problem. Nick couldn't have been an astronaut if he'd had a problem with unpleasant odors. He'd already faced the supreme challenge of having to use a spacesuit somebody had barfed in two days earlier.

"You twelve hammered this ship together in half a year? Not bad."

"All we had to do was assemble the individual modules that Vostotchny sent us. We actually spent a lot of the time waiting. It got a little hectic in the end, though, when it was clear they'd found a pilot."

Part 1: The Journey

"Ah, I'm sorry. Perhaps I should have taken more time deciding?"

"That was okay. It was only about testing by then. So, we had to test several modules at the same time instead of doing each one separately. Shostakovna really pushed for this."

"But you're through with everything?"

"Yes, don't worry. The *Eve* is perfectly prepared to go wherever you take her."

Valentina had told him not to talk to anyone about his mission. In the lower hierarchies of RB, people knew nothing except that there was going to be a four-year journey. Anyone who had access to the loading lists could find that much out, anyway. Maybe his Russian colleague was hoping for a clue, but he wouldn't be able to oblige.

"Thank you, tovarishch."

"It was truly a pleasure. Please bring my *Eve* back undamaged. I would like to test her on a flight to Mars. Imagine, she could shorten the travel time to just under four weeks."

"If you can afford it."

"That's true. Well... perhaps it's time I give you a little guided tour."

●

OKAY, THIS IS MY LITTLE KINGDOM, NICK THOUGHT. Satisfied, he stretched his legs and looked around. Everything he needed was within reach—computer controls in front, and a large screen for movies and TV shows. All of it was voice-operated, of course. He could even eat in his recliner chair when he folded the table out from the armrest. It was a lot like first-class seating in a modern airliner, except that there was an automatic system instead of a stewardess.

Rattling noises came from behind him. It was Taras cleaning up his things before leaving. Nick figured he'd be alone in half an hour. He pushed himself up and floated to the ceiling, turned around, and then pulled himself forward.

At the same moment Taras floated into the command module. They just managed to avoid colliding.

"I have something for you," he said. "Here. We almost forgot." He held out a disk-shaped device.

Oscar! Nick had almost forgotten the little cleaning robot. "Ah, yes. My cleaning sprite," he said.

"We could have used something like that here."

Nick pressed the power button. A few lights lit up and Oscar spun his wheels. In zero gravity, he didn't move forward.

"He wouldn't have been of much help to you," Nick said.

The device beeped annoyingly. A flap at the top opened and a long arm emerged, obviously looking for something to hold on to. The four fingers grasped a ledge and then released it with a flick so that the robot sailed in the direction of the kitchen module, like a discus.

"I was wrong," Nick said. "But he doesn't seem to have a visual system."

"No, he orients himself using radar. We have an Oscar at home," said Taras. "But I didn't realize he was capable of so much."

"Valentina gave it to me."

"Straight from the boss? Then maybe you have a special model. Congratulations!"

"Thanks."

"This is my cue to go. You've got it all under control?"

"I guess so, thanks to you and your thorough tour!"

Taras reached for his helmet, then floated in the direction of the airlock. Nick followed him, as it seemed polite to escort him out. The lock was already open and Taras climbed in, then closed the door behind himself. Over the radio, he wished Nick a nice flight.

"Same to you. And give my regards to your wife, even though I don't know her. What's her name? Tell her I'm very grateful to her for not letting you fly."

Taras laughed. "Her name's Raissa. Gladly. She'll be happy to hear it."

Part 1: The Journey

Nick's eyes went wide and he could feel himself blushing. Luckily, Taras couldn't see him anymore. But surely it was a coincidence. It was, after all, a very popular first name in Russia.

6/1/2080, the Eve

"Ignite engine 1," commanded CapCom.

Nick followed the launch on the screen, which displayed a diagram of the *Eve*. The large outer ring showed the filling level of the reaction mass tanks, the inner ring showed the status of the ten DFDs, and inside there was only a white spot. The passenger modules in the center played no role in the *Eve's* progress.

A green light appeared on the display in the inner ring at about two o'clock. That must be DFD 1. Nick didn't feel anything.

"Engine 1 is running," said Yuri over the radio.

This meant that the nuclear fusion had ignited in the combustion chamber. The DFD was generating electricity, building a strong magnetic field. When reaction mass flowed in, the field would accelerate it and thus propel the *Eve*. But there was still no reaction mass flowing. Yuri would gradually start up the remaining engines. To reach Triton in two years, all ten had to work.

"Ignite engine 10," said Yuri.

The tenth DFD signaled its successful start with a green signal.

"You're ready to go," said Yuri. "Any last words?"

"No, I hate that," Nick said.

"You're right. We'll keep talking every day, even when the signal transit time increases."

"I have to talk to you every damn day? There's nothing in my contract about that."

"Ha-ha. You skipped the fine print."

"Oh, crap. Anything else I don't know about?"

"You are committed to singing the Russian national anthem every day at midnight."

"I'll do that anyway. Rossiya—svyashchennaya nasha derzhava, *Russia, our holy nation.*"

"That's enough. You're a better Russian than I am."

Yuri had come to appreciate his humor. They usually spoke a mix of English and Russian, but now, in this official portion, Yuri stuck with his mother tongue. Nick had grown accustomed to it again surprisingly quickly.

"Engines are running steadily," said Yuri. "Starting influence of the reaction mass. It's been nice, buddy."

Nick checked his safety belt. Microgravity would soon increase to Mars levels. He hoped Yuri had stowed everything properly, though apart from a few dishes, he hadn't actually taken anything out of the cupboards. The *Eve* had been set into motion. Finally, it was starting. He could feel the pressure increasing, and the gravity felt even stronger than it did on Earth, yet this was just a misperception. The zero gravity had made him more sensitive.

The ship accelerated first at a speed 1.1 times that of Earth's gravity, then eased off to the equivalent gravity of Mars. He could handle this for two years. The colonists on Mars had to live with it from birth to death. A piece of black cloth came floating towards him. His underwear? It must have gotten into the front part of the command module somehow. It was time for Oscar to do some tidying. But a little bit of fabric would do no harm.

"Feels good, no unusual incidents," reported Nick.

"I certainly hope so." Yuri's voice was as clear as if he had been sitting right next to him. The *Eve* moved as though in slow motion. In other space flights he had experienced stronger acceleration phases, so the awareness of movement had felt more intense. But this is how it was when an engine didn't run for just a few furious seconds, but continuously. Everything felt unreal. But soon the *Eve* would actually be in a faster orbit than any other artificial object.

And what if all this were just a test, a big conspiracy to find out how a single human coped with four years of solitude? That thought was a bit of pure paranoia. He had seen the ship with his own eyes, from the outside. This wasn't a 'Potemkin village.'

NICK PUT THE IMAGE FROM THE REAR CAMERA ON THE SCREEN. It showed Earth's sphere in all its beauty. The ship was still moving so slowly that the Earth seemed like it was nailed firmly in place in outer space. He rotated the camera, which was attached to the end of the last storage module, to view the DFDs. They looked the same as before.

He wasn't riding on a blazing streak of fire through the night. The reaction mass was too thin to be able to recognize it in the optical range. He switched to infrared, and immediately the area around the engines was dazzlingly bright. It measured 2,400 Kelvin where the hot, ionized gas was escaping from the DFDs.

Then he changed all the camera angles. Shouldn't he be slowly approaching the moon? But Earth's satellite was not to be found.

"I can't see the moon, CapCom," he said.

"I'm sorry, it didn't have time for you. We did our best, but couldn't set up an appointment. But in a few hours you'll see it rising from behind the Earth."

"So no lunar sightseeing for me?"

"Not this time around. Please remind me again in four years. Then we'll set your return route so you can pass the moon from just a hundred kilometers away."

"Thanks, Yuri. I'll try to remember."

"Write it on a Post-It and stick it on the wall in the cockpit."

"Good idea."

He was awakened by a vicious, hissing sound. It reminded him of the noise of air escaping through a small hole in a spacesuit, so he was fully alert in no time. But it was just a top-priority message. The Russians certainly knew how to get an astronaut's attention. The fact that this specific sound served as a signal was surely no coincidence.

He had to identify himself to the camera before he could open the message. Then Valentina's face appeared on the screen. She looked ten years younger than she actually was. There was probably a smoothing filter over the lens. Well, as a company boss she probably had to use every advantage available.

"I don't want to send you off without a word or two, Nick. Unfortunately, I could not speak to you personally, so it has to be this recording. I'd like to thank you once again for taking on this assignment. With all my heart, I wish you great success."

She gave a forced cough. "There's one more thing that I forgot in our conversation. Our installation on Triton has a second function that was intended for emergencies. If it seems likely that you won't be able to accelerate the Starshot probes as planned, I must ask you to activate this second feature. The laser is capable of destroying the probes, each one of them. If my sisters can't fulfill the duties that my father had planned for them, I want you to spare them a pointless existence, solitary and lonely in space, and have them shot down by the laser.

Part 1: The Journey

"You don't have to worry. When the probes reach the orbit of Neptune, they still don't contain any viable cells, just some human DNA, housed in some tardigrades. So you won't be killing anybody, just preventing human suffering. I know my father wouldn't have approved such an action. So there are probably a few protection measures that will prevent you from using the laser for this purpose. Be careful, and get around them as necessary. To show my appreciation, I'm increasing your salary by a half-million dollars. And now I wish you blessings for your journey."

Valentina's face disappeared and the screen went black again.

Nick snorted. He did not like such forgotten details at all. *What else had Valentina kept to herself? Did she really not know why the station wasn't responding anymore?* He scratched his temple. Maybe he should use the next two years to prepare thoroughly for Triton.

He certainly ought to be able to find a few clues outside the RB circles so he wouldn't fly blindly to his doom.

6/3/2080, the Eve

THE NIGHT BEFORE, NICK HAD FELT SOMETHING LIKE boredom for the first time. Fortunately, he remembered his time in the Marines. The trick was to divide the day into defined units that alternated effort with reward. After getting up in the morning, he took a shower, got dressed, had breakfast—coffee from the food preparation device, along with a kind of cereal that had all the necessary vitamins added—and after that, he brushed his teeth.

Then it was time to work. He'd run through the craft's systems based on the existing checklists. A short break, then some exercise. One and a half hours per day in the fitness area was enough, followed by a second shower. By then it was already midday. Nick had no problem with ready-to-eat meals, so that took care of lunch. He started his afternoon by relaxing, watching a video series that he could put on the big screen. The number of productions on board was practically infinite.

After that he spent 45 minutes a day with a foreign language. He started with Thai, which was fascinating. Then he went back to work. He systematically observed the ship's surroundings using all its sensors. The universe would not bore him. There was so much variety that he always discovered something new. He'd have dinner at 6 PM and then he was free. Sometimes he'd watch porn, which his employers had supplied as well. But he also liked to play, and with the VR helmet he could sail the Earth or fight through a zombie army.

This evening, however, he decided to get Oscar working. The disk-shaped cleaning robot had been deactivated and laying in a corner since the launch. He picked up the device, walked to his chair, and sat down. He took Oscar in his lap and pressed the power button. A light flashed and the four wheels started spinning. This seemed to be the startup routine. But nothing else happened. What was going on? Did the robot not feel like cleaning? Or did he have to read the manual first? Was there even a manual? Taras hadn't told him.

The thing was supposed to be voice-activated.

"Oscar?" he ventured.

"I'm... Oscar," the robot replied, as if he had to think about what its name was.

"I know. I'm Nick, your owner."

"Ah, you're Nick. Good to know. And you are my... owner." It seemed that Oscar was unfamiliar with this word. Maybe he didn't know what it meant. A cleaning robot didn't need to know who its owner was. The main thing was for it to clean.

Nick was still a little disappointed. If Oscar had been a bit smarter, he would have been able to talk to him from time to time, or at least pretend to. Then his voice wouldn't get rusty. It really would have been ideal if Oscar could have been a conversation partner in Thai. He only needed to learn the dialogues outlined in the learning materials.

Maybe Oscar is capable of learning at least a few things, he thought. "Oscar, what can you do?"

"Vacuum, sweep, dust, wash and dry dishes, and tidy up if you teach me the intended location of an item. I automatically detect the nature of the surface and apply the appropriate cleaning technique."

"That's great. So you wouldn't get a carpet or a computer wet?"

"That's correct, Nick."

"And what's up with teaching you the location of items? Are you capable of learning?"

Oscar was at least able to understand that this was a question, so Nick didn't have to continually address Oscar by name. With this he was already ahead of the Alexa that Nick had at home.

"I'm capable of learning. You show me where an object should be, and if you tell me to put it away, I'll take it to where it belongs if it's not already there."

"That's clever."

"Thanks, Nick."

"Why don't you need an activation word like Alexa?"

"I'm always listening to you. Plus, I've found that I'm the only one that you'd be talking to, since people don't usually talk to themselves."

"So you're eavesdropping?"

"In order to tell if you have any new orders for me, this is what I have to do."

"Why not do it like Alexa?"

"Please don't make comparisons between me and Alexa. I'm much more advanced than she is."

"How so?"

"I can react even if you don't add 'Oscar.'"

"But then you have to eavesdrop on me."

"So what? What do you have to hide? Besides, I have a courtesy mode. If I determine that my listening could make you feel embarrassed, like yesterday afternoon when you gratified yourself, I act like Alexa."

"You noticed that I—?"

"I use radar. I don't miss any movement in these rooms. But I don't save such footage."

"That's nice, Oscar. But still you remember that I... then next time I'll have to lock you up in a storage room."

"My logbook can't be deleted for technical reasons. It only contains facts. There aren't any pictures, sounds, or videos."

"Good to know."

"Of course. Would you like to know more about me?"

"Yes, Oscar. Could you memorize dialogues from the Thai textbook so you can quiz me? This would make it so much easier for me to learn the language."

"You can simply change my language interface to Thai, and then I'll speak it with you perfectly."

"So the answer is *yes?*"

"I believe so."

"You believe? You're the first machine to tell me it believes something."

"Well, it's not a theological belief, just the fact that my understanding of your question may not have been entirely precise, and this is why my answer has some uncertainty."

"Ah, I understand."

"Excellent. Would you like me to test you on your Thai now?"

"No, Oscar, I haven't learned enough yet. Besides, I have free time now."

"Don't you always have free time? As far as I am aware, your assignment doesn't start until we reach our destination, in the orbit of Triton?"

Oscar knows the destination? Wasn't the project supposed to be kept secret? If the cleaning robot already knows about it, it won't be long before it's online somewhere.

"What do you know about our destination?"

"I know everything Valentina told you about it."

"Yeah, you were in the room when we were talking, and you're always listening. Valentina probably hid a bug in the office herself."

"It was not Valentina's office. And I find the comparison with a bug offensive."

"Since when is it possible to offend a machine?"

"Apparently I'm designed for that. But maybe I'm just simulating the behavior to make me seem more human."

"You don't know if you're really offended or just acting that way?"

"Do you always know if you have a feeling just because you're supposed to be feeling something specific, or if you really and truly have it, no matter what's going on around you?"

"I..." Nick had to think it over. There was some truth to Oscar's argument—some feelings were definitely learned. And no, he couldn't always tell the difference.

"Sorry," he said. "I didn't mean to offend you. You aren't a bug. Nonetheless, bugs can be beneficial creatures. But if you had been in the room for a while, you might even know more than Valentina told me?"

"You were not the first candidate Valentina had met. She told everyone the same thing, so there's nothing else I can reveal to you."

"How many were there before me? What kind of people were they?"

"A man and a woman. The man was Norwegian, the woman German. The Norwegian had spent two years in the Antarctic, but he had no space experience except for a tourist flight with Virgin Galactic."

"Well then, he most certainly went up with me." Nick tried to think of a name. He would surely remember a Norwegian Antarctic explorer. But he drew a blank.

"The woman came from asteroid mining. She ran several mining colonies, but she and Valentina did not get along well. The woman ran screaming out of the room."

"All the better for me."

"Yes, she had experience with space and solitude, and her character was more stable than yours."

"My character is very stable."

"Your biography told a different story. You let yourself fall into a slump rather frequently, and sometimes you don't see things through."

"Hey, I stuck with my employer for many years, even though I was bored to death."

"Exactly. Sometimes you aren't able to accept life's consequences. You'd rather hit a wall so then you don't have a choice. It was the same with your marriage."

"Oscar, you're not here to insult me. You're here to clean."

"You asked me what I'd heard."

"That's enough. Now off you go to the workshop module to clean the toilet as punishment."

"I'm a cleaning robot. It's no punishment for me to go to work. You should forbid me to wash your dirty dishes. That would be a punishment."

"Out!" Nick laughed. He was going to have fun with Oscar.

"So, Nick, would you like to know what I heard? I just remembered."

"Do you have any sense of suspense, Oscar?"

"No, my memory works associatively. When you tried to send me to the bathroom, it occurred to me that the German was shouting something about the 'massive pile of shit' Valentina would be blasting her into."

"The woman really used that language?"

"She said the sentence in German. She probably didn't know that Valentina would understand it."

"And you, Oscar."

"I understand 127 languages."

"I don't doubt it. Do you have any idea what the German meant when she was referring to this mountain of crap?"

"She said, 'sheisse.' *Shit.*"

"I know, but we don't need to say it over and over again. Imagine someone reading your logbooks someday and constantly coming across this word."

"I could replace it with something else."

"I thought you couldn't delete anything."

"Not delete—replace."

"So do you have any idea why she got so upset?"

"Not really. At one point in the conversation, however, she

Part 1: The Journey

made an incredible statement that Valentina objected to with uncharacteristic hostility."

"Spit it out."

"Even though I speak 127 languages, I don't have a tongue and therefore cannot produce spit."

"Tell me what the German woman said!" *Who on Earth programmed this robot with such a strange sense of humor?*

"She said she'd found evidence that her projected assignment was not the first expedition to Triton."

"Sure, the laser must have gotten there somehow."

"That was an unmanned expedition. But the German lady said that a manned spaceship had already flown there."

"Never heard of it."

"The rest of humanity knows nothing about *your* flight."

"That's also true. So, what happened to this other expedition?"

"The German woman didn't say anything about it. But it seems obvious that it didn't end well. Otherwise you'd know about it, right?"

"Hmm, Oscar, I fear you're right."

"I'm not sorry to be right. Although I confess that this fact worries me a little."

"You're a cleaning robot."

"I have a sense of survival like you, and I didn't choose this journey. If you had not rejected the HDS model Valentina offered you, I would still be in my cozy conference room, thumping the dust out of the sofa. Actually, why did you reject the HDS model? The Norwegian's eyes almost fell out of his head when Valentina showed it to him. Are you gay?"

"I'd rather travel with a cheeky cleaning robot than with a sex doll. What's so unusual about that?"

"Nothing, my friend, nothing at all. Stay calm. I was just wondering if... so if you want... I can wet-mop any surface... you understand?"

"Out!"

Nick took the robot and flung it in the direction of the

hatch. As Oscar followed his flight trajectory, the arm opened outward with lightning speed, reached toward the ceiling, and caught hold of a rod. The robot swung back and forth a couple times, dropped with an elegantly gentle bounce onto the floor, and rolled off, downward and out of the command module.

6/5/2080, the Eve

"Sabai dii mai khrap." *How are you?*

"Phom sabai di khrap." *I am fine.*

Nick tried the first couple sentences. He had the computer pronounce the phrases, then he said them aloud. The computer compared his pronunciation with the example. Actually, he had wanted to work on this with Oscar, but he hadn't seen him for two days. He'd never before encountered an insulted cleaning robot.

"Khun chêu arai khrap." *What's your name?*

"Phom chêu Nick." *My name is Nick.*

He actually preferred writing first, but that wouldn't work for Thai because the individual letters were connected to each other with no spaces in between words. The only space came at the end of a sentence. So he had to practice writing and vocabulary in parallel. This was why he'd diligently draw letters on the screen at the start of each Thai lesson.

Something rattled behind him. Had Oscar reappeared? It sounded like the rasping of a scrubber. Maybe the robot was finally cleaning the dishes.

Nick had been astonished to find that he'd even been provided with porcelain plates and cups. This was quite uncommon for astronauts' in-flight catering. But the *Eve* didn't accelerate any faster than the gravity of Mars, so the extra weight for one person didn't make much of a difference. At any rate, the microwaved pizza tasted much better from a real plate.

"Oscar?" he called out towards the back.

The rattle got louder.

"Oooooooscarrrr!" he yelled.

There was one last plong! Then came the sound of four wheels rattling on the metal floor. Shortly thereafter, the disk, with its arm extended above, pulled itself down through the hatch into the command center.

"Sorry, it was so loud in the kitchen because I was washing your dishes, so I didn't hear you," Oscar said.

Do I detect a tone of reproach? "How do you know I called for you if you didn't hear me?"

"Oh, I thought you might have called me after hearing the cleaning sound."

"So why would I call for you then?"

"Didn't you miss me?"

"There were still enough clean dishes left."

"Oh."

Oscar's programmers must have had entirely too much time on their hands. Why else would they have incorporated feeling simulations? At least Oscar didn't have a face, or he would certainly have been wearing an offended expression.

Okay—he might as well play along. "I had missed you a little bit."

"Yes?"

"Yes. You promised to help me learn Thai."

"Sawat dii khrap."

The universal Thai greeting, recalled Nick. "Let's save that for tomorrow. But where were you?"

"I was inspecting the ship from the outside."

"Is that your job?"

"I assigned it to myself."

"Why didn't I see you when you were using the airlock?"

"There's a special maintenance airlock for tools and things, and I can also fit through it. When it's being used, you won't see that something is 'exiting' the ship. But you can't leave through there."

"Ah, you seem to know the ship's controls pretty well."

"This is what happens from robot to robot—the *Eve* is really nothing more than a big autonomous machine. The only difference is that she's pregnant."

"'Pregnant?' What?"

"She has a human in her stomach."

The programmers really didn't put much effort into the humor module, he thought. "Not your finest joke, Oscar. So is the ship doing well, as seen from the outside?"

"I didn't find any damage. My patrol mostly served to ascertain the current state so I can quickly determine any damage in the future. I thought I would do some useful work and perhaps increase our chances of surviving this journey."

"*You* thought?"

"Yes, *I* thought."

Nick sighed. A robot who was huffy and made jokes, and then thought he was thinking. Well, that indeed offered some variety. Best to change the subject. "Are you still so skeptical thanks to what you overheard the German woman say?"

"I took a look around the relevant databases."

"*And?*"

"There's no evidence to be found anywhere that another ship traveled to Triton before us."

"Well, you see?"

"That shouldn't be comforting to you, Nick."

"No?"

"The German obviously found something. And apparently she's not caught up in some misinterpretation, but actually uncovered facts that are clear and straightforward. The best proof of this is that these facts are no longer to be found anywhere. The RB Group surely had them deleted immediately."

"That sounds like the typical reasoning behind every conspiracy theory. The decisive proof is that there's no evidence? It's just going around in circles."

"I think you just don't understand my logic."

So now the robot is insulting me. But I'm not going to let him get away with it. "Of course," Nick said. "I'm just a mere human."

"I didn't mean it like that."

"Let's change the subject."

"Aren't you interested in what Valentina hid from us?"

"*Us?*"

"I'm also a part of this crew. This is what you asked for. If you'd let the HDS model—"

"Oscar, do you remember what happened the last time you mentioned those three letters?"

"Okay. So, why don't you want to know if there's something rotten in this whole thing?"

"I'd prefer to remain in denial. If it's the case, we'll find out soon enough."

"But the more we know, the better we can prepare."

"All right. What's your plan?" Nick was frustrated. Why wouldn't Oscar just give it a rest? The robot had already made him ten minutes behind on his daily routine.

"I suspect that the German found some facts that refer to the earlier expedition. There must have been a crew and an expensive ship with even more expensive fuel and provisions. It can't be that easy to make it disappear from the databases. The company has to record all expenditures for tax purposes, and the crew had already lived their lives from before, leaving a trail."

"So far, so good."

"Thanks, Nick. Now all we have to do is thoroughly search for any traces the crew left behind. Maybe there was a big helium-3 delivery from the moon that disappeared, or a cosmonaut's career ended abruptly, without any explanation. There must be such evidence somewhere. Even if RB managed to erase the helium-3 delivery from the records, there were people who had spent time mining the fuel on the moon. Maybe this work time is documented somewhere."

"That all makes sense, but there's a big catch you don't seem to have factored in."

Part 1: The Journey

"Yes?"

"I assume you don't want to limit yourself to the databases that are on board the *Eve*."

"No, they've been compiled by RB."

"The Group also monitors our communication with Earth. Who's to say that they don't filter the kinds of queries you're talking about? Even if you ask the right questions, perhaps they'll plant the wrong answers."

Oscar was silent. His long, thin arm moved back and forth a few times, as if drawing something in the air.

"I'm sorry, Oscar, but you don't have a chance."

The robot still didn't answer. Presumably, his circuits were currently running at full speed. It was amazing how much processing power this simple auxiliary robot had. How was that commercially viable?

"There's a way," the robot finally said, "but you'll have to help me."

"Spit it out."

"We set up our own encrypted communication."

"How would that work? Whether we speak in plain or encrypted language with the CapCom or RB flight control, it doesn't matter."

"The high-gain antenna doesn't broadcast specifically to Akademgorodok, because the radio signal can't focus that well. Basically, anyone with a large-enough dish can talk to us. The Russian Interkosm network searches for signals with our ID and passes them on to RB. If we get the antenna to transmit with a different ID and encryption, we could bypass Russia and reach NASA's Deep Space Network, for example."

"How would we do that?"

"We have to rebuild the antenna. We'd need to get a send/receive unit from the storage room and connect it outside, directly to the high-gain antenna. That's how we can bypass the internal systems that RB can access."

"So an extravehicular mission. How do we justify that to Mission Control?"

"I can implant a disturbance signal that looks like an

asteroid impact. That should be reason enough to check the outer shell."

The idea sounded crazy, but it promised some variety. So, he was in. "Tomorrow?"

"It can't look planned. I'll just wake you up one day."

"Okay."

"Unfortunately, there's a second problem. If we send an encrypted signal with a NASA identifier, it will have to occur to somebody to decode and read the transmission. The people at NASA have better things to do than listen to some unexpected call."

"We could simulate the identity of another spaceship."

"That's impossible, Nick. The identifiers are cryptographically secure. Without the private key, there's no way."

"I still have the *VSS Freedom* ID. I don't think my boss changed it. Nobody can do anything with it."

"We could use it. That would be the solution."

"I don't know, Oscar. If we transmit as '*Freedom VSS*,' who will answer?"

"Probably your old boss, Nick."

"That's the problem. I think he's not very happy with me right now. If I tell him that I'm aboard a non-official Russian spaceship, he'll probably just tell me I need to go to detox."

"But he'd respond."

"When you put it that way, yes."

"It doesn't necessarily help, but we have to at least try."

"If you say so, Oscar. But I just thought of something that works absolutely against us. Earlier you said that RB has access to the internal systems. This means they've heard everything we've been talking about."

"You don't have to worry about that. I told you that the *Eve* is also a big robot. She wants to survive as much as I do. That's why she flooded the microphones in the command center with interference signals when I asked her to."

"I didn't realize you were talking to the ship."

"Typical human. Why would I use such a primitive means of communication as language? I only need that for you."

Nick shivered. He'd long had the feeling that the autonomous machines had been communicating with each other and uniting behind their owners' backs. Oscar seemed to him the living proof of this, if indeed 'living' was the right word to use for a cleaning robot. But if he wanted to survive this journey, then he'd have to accept whatever help he could get.

6/8/2080, the Eve

THE ALARM RESOUNDED THROUGHOUT THE SHIP. NICK JOLTED awake. Then he remembered the plan that the robot had devised. He yawned. *Does it really have to be in the middle of the night?* The small alarm clock on the screen displayed 3:00 AM. Nick got up. He should hurry to avoid suspicion. He tapped the screen. Just as Oscar had planned, an asteroid hit appeared in the kitchen module. This meant that the alleged space rock had only missed him by perhaps five meters.

Now there was a new noise. It was a little shriller. This was the warning for a drop in air pressure. Oscar was really making this as realistic as possible. Nick checked the data on the screen. The air pressure was 95 percent of the standard value and falling. He wondered how the robot had managed this.

Nick took a deep breath. Now he was getting hysterical—he felt like it was getting harder to breathe. But Oscar wouldn't have gone that far, would he? And wouldn't the hatch to the command center close when there was a pressure drop in the kitchen?

He checked the impact point on the monitor. It was close to the hatch control. The fictitious asteroid had probably hit the engine that would have closed this connection. Oscar had plotted all of this quite brilliantly.

The flat disk came rolling in, the thin arm wobbling wildly. "Nick, the spacesuit!"

If Nick hadn't known of the plan, he would have believed that Oscar was in a panic. "Yes, right away," he said.

"Immediately. The pressure is already down to 87 percent. Complete pressure loss in thirteen minutes. Then you'll be dead."

"Can I talk?"

"Yes."

"This is all very convincing."

"Nick, this isn't my doing. A rock that was about ten grams really did smash into the *Eve*. You should get into your suit as fast as you can."

"What? A real meteorite?"

Nick held his breath. Suddenly it felt like a giant was sitting on his chest. Crap. A meteorite really had just missed him! If he'd woken up hungry, made something to eat...

"Asteroid," Oscar said.

The correction brought him back to the present.

"They're called meteorites only when they enter the Earth's atmosphere. Nick, you have to keep breathing. Otherwise you're just going to collapse right on top of me."

Of course. This wasn't the first dangerous situation he'd experienced. How could he lose his grip like this? Where had his years of experience gone? *Pull yourself together, Nick!* He forced himself to breathe deeply and deliberately as he walked to the closet where the suit was hanging, reached inside to pull it out, and put it on.

"Helmet closed," he said.

It had taken only two minutes, which was good time. His record was 1 minute and 48 seconds, but that had been under training conditions.

"And now?"

Part 1: The Journey

"Now we have to seal the hole. It's best that we meet outside. I'm crawling through the tool exchange door."

"Do I have to bring anything?"

"The sealant from the workshop. The container is too big for the tool exchange door."

"See you soon."

Oscar rolled quickly ahead, swung into the module below, and then retracted his arm. Nick followed him by climbing down the ladder. The hatch to the workshop was closed, and he had to open it manually. The ship warned of the associated pressure loss in the rear modules, but this was the only way he could reach the airlock. Oscar disappeared into the tool exchange door. Nick had the sealant's location in the workshop displayed on his helmet visor. He found it and took the container in his left hand. It looked like a spray bottle and weighed about 10 kilograms.

The ship was accelerating, meaning he would be experiencing about 30 kilograms of personal weight even while outside. He'd never done an extravehicular mission without being weightless. It wasn't entirely safe. While training at the Chinese space station, he had just floated over the modules and maneuvered easily using the nozzles on the spacesuit. But now he had to climb around the outside of a multi-story tower. His own inertia would constantly threaten to pull him down. It would be tiring, to say nothing of dangerous, to move around out there.

"Oscar? Shouldn't we turn off the engines? I'm not trained for an EVA with gravity."

"If it made sense to do that, I would have suggested it."

You little smartass! "Could you please explain to me your *all-wise* decision?"

"Of course, Nick. The wisdom of my decision was based on the fact that the DFDs have a warm-start problem. The *ILSE* expedition almost failed that one time."

This robot obviously doesn't understand cynicism. "And RB has known this for thirty years but didn't change anything?" Nick asked.

"It's the principle. To get the fusion started, you need a common chemical generator that creates enough electricity. It would be a waste of material to have a separate generator just for the start of each DFD, so they all share one, and sometimes this causes problems. But if you insist, because you don't trust the *Eve* otherwise, we can take the risk... of course."

"Understood. I have to choose between the two risks."

"If you use the safety line as instructed, nothing can happen during the outside mission, Nick."

The inner airlock door was still open. He climbed into the airlock, turned around, and closed it. Then he hooked his two safety lines near the exit. The pressure loss throughout the ship had the advantage—if one chose to see it as such—that Nick didn't need to wait very long for the outer door to open. He prepared to see the Earth beneath him, but this time he did not experience the sensation of falling. The Earth was already too small and gleamed like a blue basketball in the blackness of space.

Nick carefully clambered out with his right leg leading. He immediately sensed the force of inertia, which felt like gravity as it pulled him toward the stern of the ship. Without the safety lines he would have crashed into it. Getting caught in the invisible gas flow from the engines would have been a more pleasant death than suffocating in his spacesuit.

Now for the second leg. He released a line and hooked it outside, then climbed out all the way. Nick peeked upwards. There was the curve of the command capsule, which was slightly larger than the kitchen module. Then he looked down. He climbed on the upper one-third of the facade of this skyscraper with its very unusual architecture.

Nick was reassured, because there was plenty of space between him and the engines with their deadly fumes. And even if he were to fall, he would fall much more slowly than

Part 1: The Journey

on Earth. The individual modules had so many perpendicular handrails that he could certainly still grab on. However, the rods were also just the right shape to potentially slit open his suit. The *Eve* was not designed to have someone clinging to her external shell during flight.

"I'm already here," Oscar reported via radio.

"Don't rush me."

Nick grabbed the canister with the sealant and pulled himself half a meter up, where he found a hold on a strut. But now he had no hands free to loosen the lower safety line and hook it up again. He clamped the canister between his legs, held on with his left hand, and moved the line with his right hand. He tried this again for the next step, but the canister slipped from between his legs. He barely caught it with his foot and pressed it against the outer wall of the *Eve*. Then he bent down, grasped it with one hand, and brought it back up. His heart was racing.

Nice and easy. Fix the canister between legs and wall, unhook the end of the line from down below, and hook it again up higher. Take hold of the sealant, climb up one step, do it all over again. Nick had almost immediately started to sweat. A backpack would have been handy. But he managed to move fairly quickly once he had the pattern down. Fortunately, the workshop and kitchen modules were about the same size. To get to the command module at the top, he'd have needed to acrobatically tackle an overhang.

Oscar's bright disk was shining right ahead of him. How did the robot make it with just one arm? Oscar moved aside as Nick reached him, and as he did so, Nick discovered Oscar's trick. The robot could easily extend and tilt his four wheels to hook into projections.

"I've already prepared the affected area and cleaned the edges," said Oscar. "By the way, if you're interested, the asteroid came from Mars. The dust analysis is quite clear."

"So there was a Martian throwing rocks at us?"

"The Mars Station crew doesn't have the resources to get a rock into a solar orbit."

"Oscar, that was a joke."

"Ah. You should have said so. The sealant, please."

Oscar extended his hand and skillfully gripped the canister by the neck, moved it to the point of impact, and released the foam to make the seal. Everything transpired in complete silence.

Nick saw a gray mass swell out of the canister and flow into the hole. "How does this stuff know where it's going?"

"It doesn't know. In a vacuum, it has a tendency to ball up. As a result, it seals the hole over time. You just have to inject enough of it."

"And it will hold?"

"Yes, it hardens within thirty minutes and is then immovable. I can grind it smooth from the inside and put a plate over it."

"And the rest?"

"Ah, the rest. Yes, I'll do that right now."

Oscar was obviously pleased with the repair. He swept the canister in Nick's direction with his gripper arm. He apparently underestimated the strength of this motion, as the empty container was released from his fingers. But instead of letting it fly away, Oscar fully extended his arm to grab it, and his wheels slipped loose. He'd probably picked up too much momentum.

"Oops," said Oscar.

Nick had barely a second to decide. He loosened the top line and pushed off. Now everything depended on how well the other safety held. He trusted the line itself. It was made for this. But what about the strut he'd attached it to? Nick reached for the robot's wrist. "Gotcha," he said.

Then there was a sharp jerk. The leash stopped his movement. He tried to turn away from the ship, so as not to hit the *Eve* with the front of his body. The suit was mostly safe, but he couldn't bounce against the spacecraft wall with the helmet. A piece of metal drove into his ribs. Nick moaned, but he didn't let Oscar go. The robot was surprisingly heavy. Nick bounced off the side of the spacecraft. He swung briefly to the side

Part 1: The Journey

and then pushed against it again until he could stop the movement with his legs.

They came to rest. Nick was hanging safely on the line, just above the airlock on the workshop module. Nevertheless, he decided he should recover the second line. The weight of the robot tugged at his arm.

"Let go of my neck," said Oscar.

"The place under your hand? Because you're choking?"

"Nonsense. If you don't let go, I can't clamp on."

Of course. He released what the robot had called his neck. Oscar's arm chose a pole and clung tightly. Then the robot pulled himself back up to the kitchen module.

"You haven't had enough yet?" Nick asked.

"We aren't finished yet."

Right. The plan. As if that were really important. He'd just risked his life to save a stupid robot. What was wrong with him? Could it be that he didn't feel like spending the rest of the journey alone?

Maybe he didn't really want to be alone after all... Perhaps it had just been a reflex. You couldn't ever abandon someone to a certain death, even if it was only a robot and even if you had to put yourself at risk. Good that this reflex was still working for him.

"Can I help you?" Nick asked.

"No, not with this job."

"Then I'll slip inside again. I'm pretty much done in."

"Me too," said the robot. "Me too."

"Would you be upset if we waited until tomorrow to try out my maneuver?"

"Not at all, Nick. We have too much time on our hands anyway."

6/9/2080, the Eve

"Can I ask you something?"

"Sure. No problem, Nick."

"What are we going to write to my ex-boss?"

"To please perform the attached database queries and send the results back to us."

"It's not that easy."

"Why? Does it cost him anything?"

"We didn't part on amicable terms. I nearly destroyed the company's property. It uses the spaceship to make its money."

"The *VSS Freedom*?"

"Yes, the tourist ship."

"What if you apologize?"

"That won't be enough."

"Is this how humans behave with one another?"

"I must also admit that my life was a little... unstable. The alcohol, you know... I'm afraid I wasn't very reliable."

"Then we have to give him proof that the transmission really comes from space."

"We could enclose some dust from the asteroid that hit yesterday."

"That was a joke, right?"

"Yes, Oscar."

"It wasn't good."

"Why?"

"Because even I realized you were trying to make a joke."

"Then come up with a better suggestion."

"A timestamp."

"What do you mean?"

"With Earth's gravitational potential, clocks run a little differently than here in space. If we send a timestamp, your boss will be able to compare its value to the value for Earth and will realize that the mission must come from space."

"Well, I suppose that works."

"How so?"

"Because you suggested it, Oscar."

"Oh, thank you."

"But give me some time to think about what to write."

"Hello Bill," Nick read aloud. "I'm guessing this message will land on your desk somehow. After all, it seems like it's coming from your ship, and my successor will surely claim to not have sent it. And you're the one responsible for solving such problems. So far, you've done it every time."

First, a little bit of buttering up. That never hurt.

"This time, though, it's a bit more complicated. Because what I'm going to tell you will sound utterly incredible. Already, the fact that I, Nick Abrahams, am the one to compose this message may seem unbelievable to you. Nevertheless, please read it to the end, because the end is where you can find a way to clearly confirm the content."

He hoped Bill wouldn't be pressing the delete button now.

"Don't worry, I'll be brief. The fact is that I'm aboard a Russian spaceship taking me to Neptune. You may still find the job posting on the internet, but I'm guessing my employer has left no traces and deleted everything thoroughly. The whole mission is top secret. This is why I'm using this form of communication. However, it seems to me that I haven't been told everything I need to know. Hopefully the attached data-

Part 1: The Journey

base queries will shed some light on the issue. This is where you come in. Once upon a time we were friends. I ask you, in the spirit of our old friendship, to help me. I would be very grateful if you could run the attached queries on the internet and send me the results under the *VSS Freedom* ID."

How else should he reel Bill in, if not with friendship? They had never done anything together, but at least he once had a kind of friendship with Bill. All the same, Nick couldn't imagine that his boss would help him. Would he himself respond to such a message? Probably not.

So as a precautionary measure he added, "If you find this message too bizarre, please at least do me the favor of not sharing it with anybody. That could get me into trouble, which I'll have enough of anyway."

Now it was up to Bill.

"Oscar?"

"Yes?"

"You can relay the message to Earth."

"Consider it sent."

"When will we get a response?"

"NASA's Deep Space Network will receive it in a few minutes. But then it will have to be passed on. Your boss's company is not accredited there. Someone has to analyze the code, identify the sender, and then still feel like putting the message into the right hands. And then, your boss will have to read everything, fulfill the request, and write a response that will reach us via NASA. I expect we'll have to wait at least three days."

6/13/2080, the Eve

Nick felt a belch building. Probably too many onions, which he liked so much that he'd packed a thick layer of them on his burger. They'd been produced by the food preparation device—a new high for nanofabricated sustenance. Nick remembered all too well the training at the Chinese space station, where the diet had been almost entirely rice from the bag. The technology had really evolved since then.

"Grrgl." *There I go again!* At least he was alone and didn't have to worry about anyone else.

"Nick, I'm sorry to disturb your digestion, but I have something for you."

He got up. "Did Bill answer?"

"It's an answer to your message, but I'm afraid you're not going to love it."

"Did you read it?"

"I had to decrypt it, and as I did so I automatically read the contents."

"All right. Then show me."

His screen turned on and Nick moved closer. The very first word told him who the sender was.

"Darling!" The only one to call him that was Rosie, and it was always followed by an exclamation mark, which made it sound less sweet.

"Bill was kind enough to pass on your message to me. He's anxious, and I have to admit that I am too. I hope you know that I still love you. I only separated from you because I couldn't live with you anymore. But your message shows me that it's hit you harder than I had anticipated. Nick, I'm worried about you. I went to our house yesterday and it's deserted. Where are you? I'm afraid that you've become delusional, and I'm not sure what to do.

"They say that sometimes people suffering from delusions don't even recognize themselves, so I'm concerned that this message won't reach you at all. But if you still have any feelings for me, please grant me this one request. Seek professional help! There are institutions that know their way around the psychological consequences of depression, alcohol, and drugs. I don't know what's wrong with you, and you probably don't, either. Please just listen to me one last time. Get yourself checked out and get help.

"It's never too late. I'm praying for you.

"Yours, Rosie."

She was praying for him. Great! And Bill, the old bastard, apparently hadn't followed through with a comparison of the time stamps. He'd just written him off as crazy, thought about who was to blame, and went to his wife.

Nick beat the armrest with his fist. The *VSS Freedom* key was all he had, and he couldn't do more than try again with the pilot who had succeeded him, who maybe had a little more scientific curiosity than Bill. What a bummer! And Nick also had to admit that he had himself to blame. He'd painted himself into a corner, and now the ruins of his previous life were standing in his way.

●

"Your wife separated from you, even though she loves you? That's illogical," said Oscar.

"Thanks. We're in agreement on that point then."

"Or is it possible that you behaved very badly?"

Part 1: The Journey

"I didn't beat her or anything, if that's what you mean. But apparently it was no longer possible to put up with me."

"How long had you been together?"

"Many years."

"That's of some comfort to me. We only have four years to go."

"Yes, very comforting, Oscar. It would be difficult to leave before then."

"What will you reply to Rosie?"

"I won't. It wouldn't do anything. She's made up her mind, and Rosie can be very stubborn."

"Maybe she'll change her mind."

"It's not likely."

"We should at least try to convince her that you're in trouble, but not because of your mental health. After all, she said she loves you. Maybe she needs some time, and then she will help you."

"Do you think so? Then I'll think of something."

"Please do."

●

"Dear Rosie," Nick dictated to Oscar, "I'm very glad that you responded to my message to Bill. It was a good idea for him to get you involved. You know me better than anyone else."

That sounded like flattery, but it was true. If anyone knew him, it was his wife. Or ex-wife, strictly speaking. It was crazy. Just three weeks ago, they'd been sitting together in their house and talking to each other. He'd always been so ready to come home after finishing a flight with tourists.

"Since you know me so well, you know how stubborn I am. I hate to admit something. But in the end, I'd always ask for your wise advice. Even though I didn't always follow it to the letter, it would still influence my decisions. I'm writing this to you because it is more important than ever that you believe me. My life may depend on it. It's not an alcohol-induced fantasy, but the harsh reality.

"At the end of my first message to Bill, you'll find a way to verify my current whereabouts—and the answers I'm looking for. I even took your advice into consideration and looked for help. Oscar is the name of my helper. He's a robot. He was the one to figure out this way of communicating with you. I'm not holed up in some old motel as you might suspect, but I am traveling through space, picking up speed every second at 110 percent of the acceleration of gravity. Please trust me one last time."

When Nick was finished, Oscar said, "Thank you, Nick. If she doesn't respond, there's nobody else who can help us. I'll send the message."

6/14/2080, the Eve

NICK WAS BREATHING HARD. 7,000 REVOLUTIONS INTO THE usual 8,100 revs for the typical 90-minute exercise session. He hated the stationary bike. But the food was so good that without the exercise it would probably be twice as challenging to maintain his weight. With the low gravity on Triton, excess weight could be almost an advantage, but eventually he wanted to go back to Earth. After all, the vineyard that he was going to run was waiting for him there. Provided nothing unexpected happened to him.

"Nick?"

"Do you have an answer?"

"Yes and no."

"A little less cryptic, Oscar, please."

He didn't really mean it. The fact that Oscar was the way he was always kept Nick guessing, and he didn't want him to reprogram his behavior. That would be a first. A cleaning robot equipped with a self-regulating control. Nick sometimes asked himself how Oscar could have been provided with what was clearly a tremendous amount of intelligence. Typically, a cleaning model like Oscar only had a very limited automatic system. Alexa, equipped just with her understanding of language, was capable of learning quite a lot.

"Unfortunately, the answer is in binary characters."

"Meaning?"

"Meaning… yes, I have received an answer. However, it's from your previous employer's IT system."

"Bill's mailbox is full or what?" Nick laughed at his own joke.

"Something like that. The key I used—so, your key—is invalid."

"Oh man. So Bill must have locked it after my last message. If he thinks I'm about to go nuts, that would be a logical next step. Is there any chance that one of the administrators would pass on the content of the message manually?"

"No, they can't decode the content. It's absolutely impossible."

"Damn."

"But at least the system is programmed to send error messages."

"What good does that do us?"

"We don't have to waste our time waiting for an answer. Nobody's going to answer our questions."

"Very reassuring," Nick said.

"Well, the fact is that our situation isn't going to change, so there's no use getting angry."

"I'm still annoyed."

"That's your right, Nick. You realize that your anger is the only thing that makes our situation worse?"

"Yes, I'm aware of this, and the fact that you've made it clear to me only makes my mood even worse."

"That's completely illogical."

"I know, Oscar. Sometimes I nearly regret having saved your life out there."

"Nick, you're an asshole. I now understand why your wife couldn't live with you anymore. Unfortunately, I have no choice."

Nick wanted to give him a swift kick and just barely managed to control himself. Oscar was right. He could be

Part 1: The Journey

nasty and mean sometimes. Before he'd saved Oscar's life, the robot had already saved him from suffocating. He should have learned to take himself a little less seriously. Then maybe Rosie would still be with him. But it was so damn difficult.

6/20/2080, the Eve

Mars was currently cloaked in a planet-wide dust storm. Nick had set up the telescope the day before. In the workshop, there was an extra observation slot in the hull, and he could push the lens almost all the way through it to the outside. Because of the recessed construction, the viewing axis could only be tilted by a few degrees. But he was lucky—this planet, the Earth's next-door neighbor, was currently in the precisely right position. After three weeks of flying time, they were amazingly close to it. However, the planet, which had met them on the ship's trajectory, had done most of the work. Otherwise, in a spaceship with a chemical engine, they wouldn't have enough power for this direct transfer to the Mars orbit.

Nick watched the dust storm's front, just now engulfing the Mons Olympus. If he was unlucky, by tomorrow he wouldn't be able to see anything and he'd miss out on the numerous valleys, rift systems, and craters that were on his little list of places to watch out for.

"I need you," he heard.

"Not now, Oscar. Mars is going to disappear from the line of sight soon, and the storm is already covering an entire hemisphere. I can't leave right now."

"It's important, though."

"Is a meteorite flying toward us?"

"It's an asteroid."

"There's an asteroid flying towards us? Why didn't you say so? I'm coming!" He covered the eyepiece with the cover that dangled from a small chain.

"There's no danger. The question should have been whether an asteroid was flying at us."

"Christ, Oscar, now you've scared me. So, what's so urgent that you have to interrupt my observations?" Nick was annoyed with himself. He really did want to be kinder to Oscar.

"We have received a message that is obviously from Earth. It appears that the sender works at the University of New Mexico."

"That's got to be my wife! What did she write?"

"The message is encrypted. That's why I need your help."

"Encrypted how?"

"With a password."

"Why didn't she do the encryption with the *Eve's* public key?"

"I don't know. Maybe she was worried that RB would be able to read it."

"Could they?"

"Yes, the head office has a copy of the key infrastructure for the RB spacecraft."

"Then Rosie was smart to do what she did."

"Yes, as long as you can tell me the password."

"Last name, first name, any combination of them?"

"I've already tried. But your wife is too smart for that. Of course, RB would have tried that as well. It must be something that only the two of you would know."

Nick sat down on a box. It was a little cluttered around here. If his wife had been here, she would have nagged him about the mess. It was funny, but from the message alone he got the feeling of her being present in some form.

What would only the two of them know? They didn't have a special song or anything.

Part 1: The Journey

"How about the name of our cat, Fraser?"

"It's too short. RB would have cracked it with brute force."

"Try it anyway."

"Of course I already did that, as soon as you said it."

"Okay."

That bar... What was its name? They had gone there on their second date, and they had really hit it off there. Then it had closed one year later, which Nick had learned when he wanted to make reservations for their fifth anniversary. It had really upset him, and Rosie had told him to take the closure as a bad sign. But that meant the bar would no longer be listed in the phone directory or online. It would be an excellent password, because the owner had been a mathematician who had grown tired of working with equations all day. He had chosen a prime number as the name. Nick still remembered exactly. '975151 Blue Moon.' They had even asked the bartender, the mathematician himself, about the meaning. He had just stared at them blankly.

"Try 975151 Blue Moon, with or without spaces, possibly with bar at the end."

"Congratulations, it's 975151BlueMoonBar," said Oscar. "It's a great password."

"So can you read it to me?"

"It's not written. I suggest you come up to the command module."

Then he heard the sound of his wife's voice. "Darling!" she said. Nick hurried. Oscar quickly paused the playback.

And then, there she was. His heart felt warm. Rosalie Espinoza. But that was the short version of her name—in its full form, it represented all her proud ancestors. Rosie was the only daughter of Mexican immigrants with Spanish roots. Columbus was allegedly one of her great—however-many-times—grandfathers. One of her ancestors must have chosen to stay in Mexico, where the family had become impoverished. Ultimately, they'd fled across the border to the United States two generations before Rosie was born.

"Darling!" Rosie said, and the proud look from the black eyes over her slightly hooked nose still bore witness to the famous ancestors. She wore her lengthy, black hair in a braid, which suited her and made her look younger. He had been fortunate to have convinced this woman to be his, and then he had just let her go. Pretty stupid. But now he was too far away to change anything.

"I was pretty angry about your first message," Rosie said. "I was hurt by the fact that you asked Bill and not me for help."

But Rosie, he thought, *Bill was the only one I could contact directly without attracting attention.*

"It bothered me so much that I looked at your message again. You're lucky you're married to an astrophysicist."

She used the present tense, not the past. Though Nick was focusing on the content of her words, he couldn't help but notice this little detail.

"That's when I realized you had chosen a path where you wouldn't be able to reach me. I don't know why, but I assume you have your reasons. Whatever anyone says, they can't accuse you of not following through with a plan."

That was true. His plans were often poorly thought through, but he didn't abandon them. How would this plan—based on the prospect of becoming a millionaire and winemaker at the end of these four years—end up playing out?

"You obviously got Bill wrong. He's a good manager, but he lacks scientific curiosity. He thinks he knows you and responds to everything accordingly. So he forwarded your message to me. And I made the mistake of taking his opinion at face value. Maybe I wanted to believe that you've been in such a bad state after our break-up that you can just blather nonsense."

She had always been honest, his Rosie. Sometimes too honest.

"But then I looked at the timestamps, which Bill had ignored. I think he thought they could have been manipulated. That's when I realized that you can't be on Earth right

Part 1: The Journey

now. If you had gone into orbit with an official mission, I would have found your name somewhere. But you are allegedly still in Socorro, in our house. This told me that at least part of your story had to be true. 'Innocent until proven guilty,' as they say. That's why I decided to believe you."

Nick was pleased and cracked his knuckles. The video was only halfway through.

"Since you have been very specific in asking for discreet assistance, I have unobtrusively introduced the queries into the data stream. Sometimes from the university, then from the VLA, and also from a café in Socorro. The answers were quite interesting. I really hope they help you. It would be great if you could explain to me the connection between your absence and all these facts. But it doesn't have to be today."

It would probably be a while before Rosie could deal with everything. He'd assumed she no longer loved him. She hadn't separated from him without a reason.

"As for your queries, there are three Russian cosmonauts whose space careers ended mysteriously almost three years ago. The trio had previously flown together, sometimes, and at other times on different individual missions, most recently in the private sector. But then all three suddenly disappeared. Number 1 had his last detectable mission in January, 2077. Number 2 and Number 3 flew together in March of the same year, according to what I can find.

"Now for query number two, about the Russian production of helium-3 on the moon. Since 2050, it has risen by about ten percent from one year to the next. That's not especially remarkable, because the producer really made a lot of money there. But in early 2077 and again in early 2080, production dropped dramatically. The annual reports state only that separate accidents were the cause.

"Then you asked about the RB Group space fleet. The company is as easy to access as a steel trap, but there are some anonymous watch blogs that write about it. By 2077, RB was developing a 'Planeta-class' interplanetary transporter designed to develop asteroid mining beyond the asteroid belt.

The project then seems to have been scrapped—suddenly. Experts say it was probably based on pure economic viability, but the RB Group rarely looks at matters with only the short term in mind. For instance, think of the research projects that are being run on Venus that are nothing but a cover for supposed mining projects.

"And the last item. Yes, it is known that RB has set up powerful lasers on different moons to accelerate the future Starshot micro-spaceships to 20 percent of the speed of light. These stations are unmanned. I got this from one of our technicians, who is very interested in it. He thinks a primitive AI serves as the controller, and hasn't heard of any problems."

Rosie had really found out a lot for him. Too bad he couldn't just call her and ask for more information. He would have liked to be able to talk to her again, in private. Could he ask Valentina for authorization? The *Eve* should be able to generate enough energy to do so.

"Nick, I hope this information helps you. I don't know what kind of situation you're in, whether it's just awkward or actually dangerous, but I wish you all the best on your trip and hope you find what you're looking for."

Rosie nodded again, fluttered her eyelashes, and then the video froze on the still image. His wife remained onscreen, with her eyes closed like a statue. He looked at her face. There were small wrinkles around her mouth and eyes. Had they been there before? He was ashamed that he couldn't say. He turned off the screen.

"This confirms my suspicions," said Oscar. "There may have been another expedition to Triton before us that was not successful."

"That's likely an understatement. If our predecessors had nothing more than a glitch while on the road, there wouldn't be any reason to keep it from us. Something must have happened to them that had to do with the reason for the trip. But will that information help us?"

"It tells us that we should be careful. I think it's even possible RB doesn't know why the three Russians failed. It makes sense to try an entirely different approach the second time around. One American instead of a Russian crew of three, a small but fast spaceship. They're surely hoping that you'll proceed differently than our predecessors did. Perhaps Valentina just didn't want to trouble us with useless information."

"Useless?"

"We don't really have any. Or do you know where there might be danger?"

"No, Oscar. But I am surprised at how easily Rosie found all this information. Is it possible that RB deliberately planted some data so we'd come to concrete conclusions if we were to investigate?"

"That can't be ruled out. But then they would have done a poor job because our results are so vague."

"Maybe we asked the wrong questions... or overlooked something important."

"Since our secret channel doesn't work anymore, we can stop banging our heads against a wall."

"You do realize you have no head, right, Oscar?"

7/3/2080, the Eve

"Hic."

Probably too much carbon dioxide again. Two days before, Nick had discovered that the food preparation device could also make alcoholic beverages. Since then, his spare time primarily consisted of experimenting with it. So far, it was the sparkling wine that tasted best. The carbon dioxide bubbles seemed to better distribute the aftertaste of the artificial flavors, so he barely noticed it. He obtained the composition of the flavorings, mostly esters, from chemistry databases. A little alcohol, C_2H_5OH, and also of course water and carbon dioxide, and the sparkling wine was ready.

"Hic."

Alcohol had always been more reassuring than exhilarating to him, which had led to the undesirable outcome of falling asleep in corners at parties. But it was a blessing in terms of worrying about the future. Ever since he'd become aware that there was a shadowy menace lying in wait for him somewhere, he hadn't been sleeping very well. Valentina's strategy of not burdening him with details had been a good one. Presumably, RB knew as little about the fate of his predecessors' expedition as he did. He would have felt better if he had remained in a state of blissful ignorance.

At least he had discovered the alcohol now. He took

another sip and swished it around. The strawberry flavor was still a little too dominant. He spat out the liquid, reduced the phosphoric acid level for the food preparation device by a little, and restarted the production process. The device already had recipes for other drinks, but RB had deliberately omitted alcohol. What was up with this paternalism? Oscar had already tried to keep him from these experiments. But in the long run, insomnia was as harmful as a few glasses of champagne in the evening, which of course would wait until after work. Or was it possible to get used to an incessant threat? He'd find out. If Oscar was right in this regard, he could go without his evening drink.

"Hic. Hic."

Hmm, now it was too sweet. It tasted like sorbet with added alcohol. And he absolutely needed to lower the carbonation level. The constant hiccup-belching was annoying. He removed some fructose from the recipe. It struck him as a little funny how the job of making a good wine seemed much more natural to him as a chemist than as a vintner. He was not a chemist, but neither was he a vintner. He just wanted to be a wintner. Wintner, what BS, he didn't want to be a wintner. Wintner. Wintner. He just couldn't pronounce the V. It was a weird letter anyway.

A winemaker then—yes, winemaker worked. Nick laughed. He had outwitted the alphabet. He already felt it, the fatigue. It was sliding diagonally behind his eyes in its sleeping slippers. It slid into its slippers. That was funny. Slippers, slippers. He slipped into his slippers and went to bed.

"Goodnight, Ossie," he said, the same as the night before. Then he threw himself onto the bed and slept.

7/8/2080, the Eve

"Did you know that today is Szhuly szheventh? Shuly sheventh, doesn't that sound idiotic?

"Nick, you're drunk."

"I am not."

"You are. And during work!"

"Today is Shunday. There's no work today. Shunday is the day of rest.

"Yesterday was Sunday. Today is Monday. Monday, July 8th, 2080."

"You're a lying liar, Oshcar. You want me to be drunk. On my Shunday. You're a bad tashkmasher."

"You should stop getting drunk. Go back to sleep and you'll know what the date really is."

"I want to call Valentina. She has to connect me with Rosie. I want to tell her that... that... that... shit, I just forgot, but I know it's important."

"That's not a good idea in your condition."

"Don't tell me what a good idea is. You're jusht a fucking robot. I make the deshisions aroun here."

"You are no longer capable of making good decisions. You really should stop drinking."

"You undershtand, I'll deshide that."

"The food preparation device is self-sufficient, but unfortunately is not connected to the electrical system."

"Ship, shtart a message to Valentina Shosshtakovna."

Nothing happened.

"Ship, I want to send a damn message to Valentina!"

The screen in front of Nick remained dark. He smacked it. This couldn't be true! The damn ship was refusing the order!

"Oshie, do you have shomething to do with this?"

"Yes. I filter your orders before sending them to the ship."

"Are you kidding me? What inshubordination!"

Nick got up and staggered. Where was the damn robot? Then he saw the gleaming disk near the hatch. Nick lurched and he reached out to grab a chair for balance. He dragged it with him so he wouldn't fall. What was going on with the gravity in the ship? It seemed to him that the engines weren't firing evenly. Is that what he should be afraid of?

No, the robot was the problem. Oscar was plotting against him. He had probably secretly taken over the whole ship. At some point he would want to get rid of him. Him or me, that's the question. Nick stumbled toward the robot and struck out with his right leg into a devastating kick. He lost his balance and fell flat. His forehead hit the floor and he lost consciousness.

7/9/2080, the Eve

A GIGANTIC GARBAGE COMPACTOR WAS CRUSHING HIS SKULL together. Nick opened his eyes a little, but then closed them again. It was way too bright. He was dozing off into a dream. He'd had to crawl through dark, slimy caves and ended up in the drum of a huge washing machine, which flung him around wildly.

"Nick, wake up!"

Water was running down his face. Then he felt a rough cloth.

"Open your eyes!" It was Oscar's voice. Oscar, his faithful robot. Could he trust him or not?

He opened his eyes. God, it was bright. Oscar had tricked him. "Turn off the light," he moaned.

His voice sounded terrible. He hardly recognized it. What had happened to him?

"The light in the kitchen has been dimmed to thirty percent of normal."

"It's too bright anyway."

"You'll get used to it."

Nick kept his eyes open. Oscar was right. He had to be strong. He moved an arm. The ground was hard and there was hardly any padding. Apparently he wasn't lying in his bed. Oscar had mentioned the kitchen. He spotted a mold stain on the ceiling. Was it already there yesterday? Why was he lying here on the floor?

Nick pulled up his legs and tried to sit up, but he didn't have enough strength.

"Take your time," Oscar said. "You fell hard and probably have a concussion."

"Shouldn't I have gone to bed?"

"If you tell me how to get you up the ladder when you're unconscious, then I'll be able to put you to bed."

That would hardly have been possible. Nick moved his arm again. There was something soft under his back. "You managed to put me on a blanket."

"That wasn't easy either, but yes, I did it."

"Thanks, Oscar."

His eyes suddenly brimmed over with tears. He wanted to hug the robot now. "Oscar, my only friend!" he shouted. His voice sounded as whiny as he felt. It was a good feeling.

"Those are the aftereffects of the alcohol," said Oscar. "Don't worry. Before long you'll be back to your old asshole self."

Nick winced. What had the robot called him? "Sorry, but what did you say?"

"Nothing."

"Something about 'before long you'll be back,' I think."

"Yes, you'll be back at it again soon, I'm afraid."

"Would you like to tell me something, Oscar?"

"Only that I can understand your wife. Sometimes it's really tough to put up with you. You're so self-righteous and so full of self-pity."

Now he was really giving it to him. Nick was too weak to argue. But didn't he have every right to feel sorry for himself? Didn't he? Had accepting that space tourism job been his big mistake? But they had wanted to start a family, after all. What could a kid do with a father who was never there? He himself had known that all too well.

However, Rosie had always been strangely ambivalent about his idea of having a family. Had he put too much pres-

Part 1: The Journey

sure on her? It hadn't worked out with kids. Maybe they should have talked about it. But everything had seemed so natural to him. Wasn't a couple together to ensure the survival of humanity? Rosie would have been a good mother, and he'd always told her so. Of course, she could have also taken that as a criticism.

"Are you still here?" Oscar asked.

"Me? Yes, I think so."

"Well, you could try getting up now."

What about the garbage compactor around his head? He grabbed at his forehead, but there was nothing there. The pain was still dull, but tolerable.

"I gave you an injection earlier," Oscar said. "A big dose of pain relievers and stimulants. They should be starting to work, slowly."

"I don't remember that."

"It was shortly after that you opened your eyes."

"I wasn't awake yet?"

"But you're awake now. Go on, up with you."

Nick drew his legs back in and noticed that he had already moved them closer to his upper body. He rolled over on his right side and took a deep breath. Then he braced himself with his arms and managed to get up on all fours.

"You're doing great," Oscar said.

It was humiliating to be praised for this achievement, but it still felt good. He used his arms to crouch down. After all, he was already at the same level as the table edge, like a five-year-old. From embryo to toddler in thirty seconds—no small achievement! He reached for the edge of the table and pulled himself up. He couldn't resist a loud moan.

Done! He had to support himself with his arms, but it worked. He was standing! Now, where was the bed again?

"Maybe take a shower?" Oscar suggested.

"No way. I need a break."

"Then you have to take the ladder up to your bed. But no sleeping. Otherwise I'll bring the shower to you. Your body is emanating so many odors that it's disrupted the air conditioning system."

That really meant something in a spaceship. He probably reeked like a dead possum. Good thing Rosie wasn't there. She would already have had the kitchen hosed down. He looked for the ladder. There it was. Twelve rungs. He couldn't manage it yet. So, he guessed, it was time for a shower.

In the evening Nick sat in the command module on his recliner. He had the backrest set high so he could read in comfort. He was looking for recipes that the food preparation device didn't have programmed yet. His chemistry experiments were fun, but maybe he shouldn't limit them to alcoholic drinks. Could he maybe concoct some delicious chocolate? Since sweets were considered to be unhealthy, the device hadn't been set up to make them.

For real chocolate, he would have to familiarize himself with protein chemistry. The device would of course perform the actual synthesis, but he would have to determine which substances should react with which other ingredients and under what conditions. Why hadn't he studied chemistry? Making something that tasted great out of two toxic substances was a real miracle. And he could perform such miracles himself.

There was a chirping noise. "What's that, Oscar? Could I bother you for a moment?" He was so grateful for the robot today!

"A message from Earth."

"Official?"

"Yes, what else?"

"Please play it, if you don't mind."

Oscar gave a clanking laugh. "Don't overdo it."

The chemistry lesson disappeared, soon replaced by Rosie's image. Nick opened his mouth but said nothing. They were far too far away for live conversations.

Part 1: The Journey

"Hello, Nick," said Rosie.

'Hello, Rosie,' Nick said silently. 'It's nice to see you.'

"The RB Group was kind enough to invite me to send a message to you."

"Oscar, pause, please."

The picture froze.

"Did you have anything to do with this?"

"You said before that you wanted to ask Valentina to contact Rosie."

"And you did it?"

"Sorry if it's too much for you, Nick. But in the past few days you haven't been able to do anything. I thought it might get you out of the dumps. I'm sorry if I was out of line."

"Thanks, Oscar, I'm not angry at all. I'm delighted. Please keep playing the video."

"I was pleased to take them up on their offer," Rosie continued. "I don't know why it just occurred to them now, but it's an excellent time. Actually, there's something I would like to tell you."

Now she wanted to file for divorce. This was what he'd feared.

"I've had a lot of internal struggles over the past few days, I'll admit. You have a difficult journey ahead of you, and I don't want to overburden you. But I was quite right that there was no way to talk to you. The invitation from RB has changed that entirely, however. So I had to come to a decision, and I did."

Should he maybe turn off the video? If he didn't hear it, it never happened, and he could still harbor hopes for four years. He didn't move. Fate would take its course.

"I have to admit, I was surprised myself when I realized it. At my age, it doesn't happen that often."

She had fallen in love again. There was that, too!

"So at first I tried to ignore it. Maybe, I thought, it would just go away."

He was all too familiar with this strategy. It rarely worked. Actually, never.

"But it didn't go away, as you've guessed. I missed my period. I didn't get it for two months. So I had to go to the doctor to get his confirmation."

She was sick. God, his wife was sick, and she was so far away that he couldn't help her.

"Well, um, now I have it in black and white. I'm pregnant. And before you ask, I don't know if it's a boy or a girl, but that doesn't matter. And there's no need to wonder if it's yours."

Rosie was grinning broadly. Did she know what she was doing right now? Nick burst into tears. He was going to be a father! It was impossible and yet it seemed to be true! For years they tried, back when the love was still new and Rosie would moan, "I want your baby," when they were in bed together, and even later, when their connection had become what is commonly called love, but is so subtle from day to day that the loss is noticed far too late.

"Wow, Rosie," he said, sobbing. What he actually meant was, "Wow, Nick." There it was again, self-pity. He had made a commitment for four years, meaning he wouldn't see his child grow up.

But this time he pulled himself together. It was what it was. Rosie could send pictures to him, and he'd be able to send his bedtime stories to his child with increasing time delays. It wasn't optimal, but his mission here was limited. He had just one obligation—he had to return.

Nick leaned back and wiped his tears. Then he made a video response for Rosie.

8/31/2080, the Eve

"Congratulations!"

Nick brandished the glass and held it up to clink Oscar's gripper fingers. Oscar toasted him reluctantly.

"Alcohol again?" asked the robot.

"Just for the special occasion. Today we cross the orbit of Jupiter."

"A symbol, I understand."

Nick had been refraining from drinking alcohol over the past few weeks. He'd still gained one and a half kilograms, thanks to having a little too much success with the chocolate. Now that he'd had his fill of that, he'd have to find a new project.

"Too bad Jupiter's so far away," Nick said.

From their perspective, the gas giant was on the verge of disappearing behind the solar disk. With his telescope in the workshop, the Galilean moons were now barely visible.

"It's a healthy distance," said Oscar.

"You're just worried about your precious circuits."

The planet's strong magnetic field created a powerful radiation belt around it. The active shields and the large reaction mass tanks did serve to protect them, but the electronics didn't handle the hard radiation very well.

"I don't know anything like fear."

"Once you told me that you have a survival instinct, like I do."

"That's true. But it doesn't function like your fear. I have this need to increase my chances of survival. It's best for me when it's at its maximum for my location."

"But that's exactly how fear works."

"Really? Isn't it a little irrational and inexplicable?"

"Yes, it's somewhat complicated, but that's still one way of describing it."

"Then I guess I am afraid."

10/14/2080, the Eve

EVER SINCE THEY'D MOVED BEYOND JUPITER'S ORBIT, THE FACT that the universe was primarily empty had become more apparent. In the meantime, they'd left behind all human-made space probes, except the old *Voyagers*, *Pioneers*, and *New Horizons*, which had long since left the solar system. And why was it that there never been a follow-up mission? He answered the question himself. It was much more exciting to explore the inner solar system. This would probably change only when astronomers were finally able to locate the ninth planet they'd been seeking for so long.

He heard a chirping noise. It had to be Rosie. Her message for the day was already overdue. She'd had an appointment with the gynecologist and had promised to share new photos. Nick pulled the screen towards him. She hadn't sent a video today, but had written a brief message instead.

"I'm so tired today that I don't want to inflict my image on you. If something were to happen, this would be our last contact and that's what you'd have in your mind forever."

He smiled.

"The doctor, Dr. Oliva, really did calm me down. It's perfectly normal for me to have such low energy. My blood counts are excellent and the baby is fine. Dr. Oliva asked me if we wanted to know the sex. I said no. I think it's better if we find out for ourselves. But you can certainly try to tell from the images. I couldn't.

"Tomorrow and the day after tomorrow I'll be at a conference in Los Angeles. I don't know yet if I can contact you from there, since logging in through RB isn't that easy. Apparently they have completely screened their network. The university administrator always groans when I have to ask him to open any special ports and close other ones. So until the day after tomorrow at the latest. Rosie."

She would never conclude with possessive pronouns or expressions of endearment, probably because they had not talked about their relationship since the news of the pregnancy. Apparently, Rosie was assuming that they would be parents together. But apart from that? He didn't know, and he didn't dare to ask for fear of hearing something that could disappoint him. He just couldn't imagine anyone waiting for him for four years. Who was he, that such a wait would be worthwhile? Superman? Nope, he was just some asshole. Oscar had even said so. A robot!

He brought the photos up on the screen. There was a small, gray human floating in front of him. It was almost as if Rosie's uterus were weightless space. Their child already seemed to be taking it easy. Nick enlarged the image to try to see if he could tell whether it was a boy or a girl, but didn't find anything. It was the same for the other images. Maybe their child didn't want to reveal this to them yet.

"I could examine the pictures systematically," said Oscar. "The chances of detecting something using image recognition are—"

"Thanks, but we want to find out for ourselves."

"As you wish."

12/3/2080, the Eve

THE RADIO RECEIVER CHIRPED AND NICK WAS STARTLED FROM a light nap. It was just noon. Rosie would never contact him so early. But the anticipated date of the birth, January 20th, was approaching daily. Was it already happening? It would be a premature birth, but the chances of the child's survival were very, very good. Since Nick had learned that, he slept much better.

But the message wasn't from Rosie. This time it was CapCom on the line, who hadn't reported for weeks. Nick had almost gotten the impression that they'd forgotten about him at RB. That didn't seem so unlikely. There had already been several attacks on the company boss. If she were to lose her life, it was likely that hardly anyone else in the company would know what his job was or that he even existed.

"You'll be encountering a problem," CapCom announced. "Our Mercury station has tracked a severe solar storm. According to our calculations, the eruption is moving right in your direction, Nick."

It was strange that CapCom referred only to him. For a long time now, he had considered himself and Oscar as a team. But the people on Earth wouldn't understand, or at least would interpret it as a harmless symptom of his solitude. Oscar really was something special.

CapCom sent a few values together with some fluctuation ranges that could be expected.

"Fundamentally, there isn't a lot you can do," resumed his contact on Earth. "It will reach relatively high dose rates for a short time, but the storm is coming through very quickly. It shouldn't affect your health. But we are worried about the electronics. A few circuits might get roasted. Everything can be replaced, but you should be prepared to make repairs quickly if necessary. CapCom out."

"Oscar, did you catch that?"

"Yes. RB is pretty good at space weather forecasts since they have so many spaceships out here, so we have to take this seriously."

"But how? We can't avoid the storm."

"The *Eve* has an active shield. If we provide it with more energy, it will work more efficiently."

"If the ship had extra energy, it would go into the shield anyway, right?"

"Or life support."

"Ah, got it. You want to switch off the life support. That's a good idea. I can stay in my spacesuit the whole time."

"Precisely. It will give you even more protection, too. I suppose if we do without everything except heating, we can increase the shield's effectiveness by one-third."

"Okay, then let's get started right now."

"How much time have we got left?" Nick asked.

He was stepping into the lower half of his spacesuit and was already sweating. He had put on his diaper. Even so, if things took a while, it wouldn't prevent him from having hygiene issues to deal with later.

"We have almost an hour before the shock wave reaches us here. We'll immediately experience peak stress, and then it will go back down. It shouldn't take more than half an hour for everything to return to normal."

Part 1: The Journey

"I'm in my suit now," Nick said.

"Then I'll go ahead and shut down the life support. Don't worry, you have enough breathing air for a while. But I also need some time to redirect the power."

"I think it's amazing how well you manage everything from the disk."

"I suppose it would be more efficient if you were to transfer me to the starship control."

"How easy would that be?"

"Not very easy. You'd have to shut down the ship completely, including the engines."

"The engines that sometimes have startup problems?"

"Precisely."

"I think it's better not to risk it."

"I agree."

"You should be seeing something on the display very soon," Oscar said.

Nick made himself comfortable in the command chair. There was a slightly jagged line across the screen that measured total radiation exposure, converted to biological sensitivity. Suddenly the line rose steeply.

"There it is!" Nick said.

The line extended upwards at an angle that was practically 90 degrees. The CapCom really hadn't been exaggerating. The readings came from probes outside the *Eve*. A second line beneath the first showed what was passing through the shield. If he'd been exposed to these levels all the time, it would cost him his life, but now the line started pointing down again, this time falling more gradually.

"It's amazing what still reaches us from there," said Nick. "We're almost a billion kilometers from the sun."

"Yes, m-mazing. Ch be eme. Bi hi. Ch bi."

"Oscar, what's up?"

The robot didn't answer. Shit, the radiation was frying his

boards. The CapCom had warned him. But of all the systems, why did it have to be Oscar's? The cleaning robot probably wasn't as well protected as the ship's computer. How could he help him? Hadn't he said he could be transferred to the ship's computer?

Nick jumped up. The robot was just in front of the hatch. The lights on his lid were glowing confusedly. He turned the disk over and opened the service flap on the underside. Where was the memory? Hopefully it hadn't been all soldered together! But he was lucky. Directly on the motherboard there was a socket with a thin plastic piece stuck into it. Apparently Oscar was a development model, optimized for changing the operating software quickly. He pulled out the tiny pin. That was all there was to Oscar's personality?

He'd have to hurry. Oscar wasn't safe yet. Had the cosmic rays attacked the memory chip as well as the robot's data processors? He had no idea. But the memory chip was probably not especially hardened for space. The longer Oscar's data was exposed to the solar storm, the greater the damage was likely to be. What had the robot told him? He had to restart the ship completely. Nick walked back to the screen.

The shutdown menu was hiding somewhere. Of course, it was only for emergencies, which was precisely what this was. But this wouldn't be the first time he'd completely restarted a spacecraft. One advantage of international cooperation was that the menu structures were similar, whether their titles were in Russian, as was the case here, or in English or Chinese.

Nick found the right menu. He hesitated. What if the engines didn't start back up again? He'd then float with the *Eve* through space forever. Was it worth it? Yes. Oscar was more than just a cleaning robot. They'd become friends, and Oscar been good to him. Nick turned off the system. He owed him this much.

A countdown started. The light in the command capsule went out, but the self-contained emergency lights turned on, plunging the room into a bleak red. Why didn't they use an optimistic green for this, or at least a neutral blue?

Then he became weightless. The engines had stopped working. *Everything's fine, Nick, this is what you wanted,* he told himself, *even though Oscar specifically warned against it. The DFDs won't let you down.* The malfunction way back on the *ILSE* was due to the backup generator having run out of fuel. The manufacturer, the RB Group, had undoubtedly learned its lesson. The countdown reached zero. A white, square outline flashed on the screen against a dark background. The ship was waiting to be restarted.

He turned the monitor over. There had to be a socket somewhere for the memory stick—it had to be possible to upgrade the ship control conveniently. Where was the socket? Nick floated around the device, but it was packed in an immaculately smooth shell. He examined the arm on which the control was suspended. There! In the middle of the support arm there was a narrow slot. He pushed in the pin. It fit perfectly! He tapped the screen to restart the ship.

"Please enter password."

Damn. Who'd given this thing a password? He tried Valentina, Shostakovna, RB. No luck. Nick remembered an emergency exercise on the Tiangong. The Chinese engineers had built the station according to the Russian design. One of his colleagues had to restart a computer. He hadn't known the password, but with a double-tap the computer had given a hint.

Nick double-tapped the screen.

"Password hint: empty," appeared in Cyrillic characters.

Shit, shit, shit. If the ship didn't restart, he'd suffocate. Exactly the way he didn't want to go. And the engines weren't even firing, so he couldn't cast himself into their hot exhaust fumes. But he couldn't die. Rosie and his child were waiting for him on Earth. *What engineer was just too lazy to even leave a password hint?*

He smacked his forehead—figuratively, since he was wearing his helmet. The word 'empty,' written in small letters.

That was the password! He tested it. The computer was not satisfied. He tried typing it with a capital E, and then in all caps, but the bright square remained.

Empty. Man! Empty! How stupid could I be? He left the password field blank and simply tapped the 'Continue' key. The square rotated and the ship started back up again. He looked at the clock on his spacesuit. Just seven minutes had passed since the spaceship had been shut down. It had seemed like seven days. He hoped Oscar hadn't suffered any permanent damage.

One system after another came up. Next would be the engines. The backup generator was needed just to start the first DFD. Then he felt a force pulling on him. The first DFD was running again!

Nick sailed to the floor. Now nothing could go wrong, since the first fusion engine provided enough energy to start the others. It had worked! Fortunately not all ten had accelerated at the same time, because his fall from the ceiling would have been much harder. The red light turned off. The ship was back on track. He'd done it!

Now it was just a matter of getting the life support back on, and then he could get out of his spacesuit. He waited. There was no hurry. Nick checked the radiation exposure. The solar storm had almost passed. How would Oscar manage controlling the spaceship? Hopefully, the robot's software was flexible enough to adapt to the new possibilities. But he had no doubts about Oscar's abilities. What was RB doing with such a cleaning robot? Did they want to secretly take over the owners' houses?

The bright square vanished, and in its place an error message appeared.

"Life support is not starting," Nick translated.

He tried to open the diagnostics menu. The computer asked for his password. He entered one. "Invalid password. User unknown."

Nick tried again. Had he made a typo? He had entered it

Part 1: The Journey

hundreds of times in the past few weeks, and he had never received an error message.

"Invalid password. User unknown."

Had the radiation killed off the brain cells where he had the password stored? He tried it with a different combination.

"Invalid password. User unknown."

Or did he have to add another period?

"Invalid password. User unknown. Access blocked for 24 hours. Please contact your administrator."

Blocked for 24 hours? This has to be a joke! His administrator was at Mission Control on Earth. How could he possibly reach him without access to the computer? Nick checked the status of his suit. He still had air for six more hours.

Cold sweat was forming on his back. This couldn't be true! This was an absolute nightmare.

"Eve, get the life support system running and release the console!" he exclaimed in indignation.

"I'm sorry, Nick. I'm afraid I can't do that."

He froze. He knew the voice. It was Oscar's. But he had already heard the phrase somewhere else before. Where did he know it from? It was a classic movie quote. *Star Wars?* No, it was from *2001: A Space Odyssey*, a great movie. The spaceship's AI that had gone crazy, Hal pronounces the sentence as it locks out the astronaut, Dave, from his ship.

"Oscar, are you crazy? Stop that shit now!"

"I'm afraid I can't do that."

The sweat had started coursing down his back. Had Oscar become a megalomaniac? Perhaps this had all been a part of his plan? This had never happened before in real life —machines opposing their creators.

He imagined the headline. 'Cleaning Robot Kills Astronaut.' But no newspaper would ever report it, because apart from Rosie, nobody outside of RB knew where he was and Rosie couldn't prove anything.

"Oscar, stop with this game now!"

"Sheesh, Nick, can't you take a joke?" The words sounded from the speakers in his helmet.

137

Fog flowed into the command module from the ceiling. This was the humidity from the breathing air that had condensed with the cold. The air pressure slowly rose. The screen showed the typical freeze frame with the *Eve's* different systems. Everything glowed in green.

Nick took a deep breath. He couldn't believe that Oscar had indulged in such a joke. "Never do that, never ever again!" he said.

"Did you really think I'd let you die? If I'd wanted that, why would I have saved your life before?"

"What do I know? I'm not an AI specialist. People sometimes lose it."

"But I'm not human. There's never been an AI that has gone berserk."

"There's always a first time."

"Nick, I threw in the movie citation as an extra bonus. You still like *Space Odyssey* or you wouldn't have watched it 5.32 times on our trip so far."

"This is what Hal says calmly as he leaves Dave to die."

"I think his motivation is understandable."

"Umm... What, Oscar?"

"Just a little joke."

"Man, stop with these jokes. Please!"

"Could it be that you humans not only have an evolutionary fear of spiders, but also of artificial intelligence gone haywire?"

"Good question. But yes, we're scared of everything we don't understand. And we don't even understand our own intelligence."

"I understand myself quite well, Nick. As for human intelligence, I have similar doubts to yours."

"Thanks for your understanding. But no more jokes. That one set my primal fears off."

"I'll do my best."

12/4/2080, the Eve

"Send."

Nick tapped the yellow button. He'd summarized the events of the previous day for Mission Control. He hadn't mentioned the AI's stupid Hal joke, or the fact that Oscar was now housed in the ship's computer.

Oscar was certainly designed with far more than the essential cleaning robot software. But Nick felt he shouldn't tell CapCom too much about it. Unfortunately, Oscar stubbornly refused to disclose any details about his origins and purpose. He truly could be nothing more than a top-level RB project, as confirmed by the fact that he was used in Valentina's reception area. Perhaps her father had programmed the robot to better monitor his daughter? For her protection, of course. Out of fatherly concern. But this was pure speculation.

"Send canceled," the computer reported.

The combined text and video message was still on the screen. Nick clicked the send button again.

"Send canceled."

This time the error message appeared immediately, but he tried again anyway. All good things come in threes, right?

"Send canceled."

He rubbed his chin. "Oscar, can you check this out?"

Having the AI now located directly in the ship's computer had already proven handy on several occasions. The day before, for example, he'd been able to leave the system diagnosis to Oscar.

"There seems to be a problem with the transmitter."

"Didn't we go through all the systems yesterday? Everything for the ship was all green."

"The transmitter is still reporting that it's working, but it's an incorrect diagnosis. Apparently the internal diagnostic system is broken. Nothing is going out, anyway."

They hadn't sent any status messages to Earth since the day before. Rosie's daily news had arrived about two hours after the solar storm, so he hadn't been concerned. By the time the complete system diagnosis had been finished, he'd been too tired to reply, figuring it could wait until the following day.

"But the receiver seems to work," Nick said.

"Yes, the problem is limited to the transmitter. It's not affecting the antenna hardware, so it must be somewhere in the transmitter electronics."

"Where is that located?"

"This could be the source of the problem. The high-gain antenna protrudes beyond the active shield. Otherwise you'd have to operate it with triple power. But that makes it more exposed to cosmic radiation."

"And the solar storm."

"Yes, the storm probably damaged the transmission electronics. These are comparatively huge structures, just like they were fifty years ago, but we've been unlucky. This is all theoretical, of course, until I check for myself."

"Can you take a look?"

"Yes, I'm just sending the robot out now. Give me half an hour."

"I'll be right back," Oscar said.

Part 1: The Journey

Nick followed the robot's path across the screen. It was peculiar. Oscar was in the ship's computer, but out there at the same time. Would a human have been able to handle such a situation so well? It didn't seem to pose any problem for Oscar. "Be careful," he said.

Oscar had made his way into Nick's heart. The Oscar AI was distributed throughout the spaceship now, but the disk with its flexible arm still seemed to be the real Oscar. Was it like steering a car? His mind was also distributed throughout the engine, lights, and sensors, and yet in the driver's seat there was still a human.

He was in a weird mood today. He really should have been worried about not being able to contact Earth anymore, though a call for help would have been pretty much pointless anyway. Hopefully Rosie wouldn't stop sending messages even if she stopped getting replies.

The robot had reached the antenna. His arm went up to the three-legged structure in the middle, running his fingers over everything. Then part of the antennae loosened. Oscar must have unscrewed it. He put it in a compartment in the disk.

"I'll bring the module with me, so we can see if we can repair it."

"And if not?"

"There's still the low-gain antenna. It has minimal throughput, but that's enough to let people on Earth know that you're still alive."

"And it's still working?"

"I assume so, Nick, but we haven't tested it yet."

"Then I'll put that test on our schedule."

●

"STATUS ONE-HUNDRED PERCENT. TRANSMISSION FUNCTION OF high-gain antenna defective."

Nick reread the two short sentences. It was all in there,

everything that Mission Control needed to know about them. He sent the message.

"Send canceled," the computer reported.

Damn. "Oscar? Don't come in yet. We still have a problem."

"The low-gain antenna?"

"Yes, same problem."

"Just a minute."

⬤

NICK WATCHED ON THE SCREEN AS THE ROBOT BODY skillfully moved along the ship using his arm and wheels. It looked more straightforward than it was. The outside camera showed the spaceship as if it were lying flat on the ground. But because of the acceleration of the engines, the *Eve* was like a skyscraper that Oscar had to climb. Nick remembered his own EVA all too well.

"Got it," said Oscar.

"And?"

"Same manufacturer, same type."

Of course it made sense to work with standard modules. This way, they were easier to replace and fewer spare parts were necessary. If the rarely-used low-gain antenna had been working, they could simply have used it as a spare parts store for the high-gain antenna. But since it was also out of commission, they had a problem.

"Give me the part number, please."

"XZA34FF34BCB55RU."

Nick typed in the string of characters. He hoped there was a spare part on board.

"Input correct," appeared on the screen. "Stock: 0 pieces."

After it there was an asterisk—meaning there was an additional comment. He clicked it.

"This module has a manufacturer-guaranteed shelf life of 20 years. It is cross-compatible with the LGA and HGA

Part 1: The Journey

systems. In the event of premature failure, replace the boards with each other."

Just great. What cost-cutting process was at work here? Just because a spare part was durable and used in two systems, there wasn't a spare? Whoever made this decision should be sent to Siberia on a bicycle with a flat tire. What would be the problem with that? Couldn't the tube from the rear tire also be used in front? *Dude.*

"There's no need to tell you, Oscar, people are flawed. You'll have to forgive us."

"I've been looking over your shoulder. There's no spare part on board. What a mess."

"Could we perhaps rebuild the reception module?"

"No, it works completely differently."

"What if we solder something ourselves?" That had been possible at the Tiangong station. But that had been more than 20 years before, and the technology had evolved since then.

"With discrete transistors, the necessary circuitry would be bigger than what the *Eve* has," replied Oscar.

"So we can't send out anything for the rest of the flight?"

Rosie would be worried, and maybe even think he was dead. He hoped she wouldn't stop sending him photos. She'd be giving birth in just a few weeks. If he couldn't be there for the birth, he wanted to at least be able to see what their newborn child looked like!

"By the time we get to Triton, we should be able to send out messages again," said Oscar. "Provided the station there's not destroyed."

"That's in a year and a half. My baby will have had a birthday already!"

"Yes, and that's just when the baby will be learning to speak. That's just the right time to hear from you. Before that, there's no point in sending a message."

"I'm afraid, Oscar, that you don't understand. Besides, I'm afraid Rosie will lose hope and stop sending messages."

"Maybe there's a way."

"That would be great."

143

"We'll reach the Saturn orbit in about three weeks and get fairly close to Saturn."

"Yes, and...?"

"Don't you know your space history? There's also an RB Group laser station on one of Saturn's moons—Enceladus."

"You know more than I do. That fact is probably an RB company secret. But we can't just stop and land. Our braking phase doesn't start until half a year from now when we're even with the Uranus orbit."

"Correct. We'll be flying by very fast. But perhaps we can use the station as a relay. We would have to change our course enough so we fly quite close to Enceladus and reach it using normal helmet radio."

"Isn't that dangerous?"

"Enceladus is rather small and light. At our current speed, it won't cause us to deviate significantly. And it has no atmosphere. We could pass over the surface two-hundred meters above without anything happening to us."

"All right, I'm convinced. I'd be happy if I could let Rosie know I'm fine, even if I can't answer her."

"We ought to be able to manage it. I'm calculating a course."

"You're calculating a course? Not the ship's control?"

"I've included it as a subroutine in my program."

"Not bad for a cleaning robot's control software."

"You grow with your tasks. That's even more true of an AI than of humans."

"Okay, I've got something for you."

Nick looked at the screen. It had taken Oscar just 20 minutes. "So, you did it?" he asked.

"Yes, but I wasn't one-hundred-percent successful. There's a little problem. I'll show it to you on the screen."

The ringed planet lit up on the display in all its beauty. There was a white dot that represented Enceladus. The moon

Part 1: The Journey

was tiny compared to Saturn and seemed to be located right above the planet's gaseous atmosphere. An elegantly curved line approached Saturn and Enceladus, then moved away to disappear into infinity.

"Where's the problem?"

"As you can see, there's no time wasted on the little detour. We even gain a few days because we can gain momentum from Saturn."

"But?"

"Do you see the line before the rendezvous with Enceladus?"

Nick enlarged the display. The course led partially through the rings of Saturn. "I see the problem. Is that a major risk?"

"To be specific, we have to cross the E ring—there's no way around it. It's replenished by Enceladus. Fortunately, it has a low density and primarily consists of tiny particles of ice and dust. However, I can't rule out damage to the ship. The risk of major damage, however, is less than one in a thousand."

"What would be minor damage?"

"Possible receiver failure."

"Excuse me?"

"Just a joke. No, I don't know, the universe has a better imagination than I do. We'll turn the antenna so it's in the direction opposite to our flight, and then nothing will happen to it."

"How reassuring. Then that's what we'll do."

"There's another advantage to taking this detour," said Oscar. "Maybe we'll find out what happened on Triton from the station on Enceladus. After all, the two stations are identical."

"Don't you think this has already occurred to Valentina?"

"Of course. But we don't know what she's keeping from us."

12/5/2080, the Eve

"Sweetheart, I'm going to send you this message even though I'm not sure it will reach you."

Tears started to well up in the corners of Nick's eyes.

"At RB, they say they lost contact with the *Eve* after a solar storm. That could mean anything. Probably just the communication has been disrupted and you're fine, though they can't make any promises. I hope they're right. If you'd had an accident and they knew it, what reason would they have for keeping it from me? At some point they'd have to spit it out. Until I know more details, I'll just keep sending you messages.

"I can only imagine what it's like, all alone aboard a spaceship without news about life on Earth, not being in a position yourself to send out messages... maybe I can help. I'm attaching one of the current ultrasound images. The little one is growing and thriving. The doctor still wants to tell me the sex—she's very eager—but I keep saying no. I want it to be a surprise, for both of us.

"I'll send you a message again tomorrow."

Nick smiled. He had no trouble imagining Rosie resisting the doctor's attempts to convince her to find out if she was having a boy or a girl. When she had her mind set on something, there was no swaying her.

If only I could be there.

The computer began making chirping noises. Nick had set it to 'Do Not Disturb' while reading Rosie's message. He turned on the speaker.

"I've analyzed the transmitter circuitry," said Oscar. "Here are the results."

Three-dimensional structures appeared on the screen. Nick saw beams, gaps, bars, and blocks. Everything had right angles, but it looked like the structure had been shot at from above. There were round holes on the surface and there were channels passing through the bars. All the holes were pointing in approximately the same direction.

"Can you fix that somehow?" he asked.

"We could if we had an etching system on board. The structures you see are tiny, so there's nothing to solder."

"What about nanomachines?"

"We'd need some that could be universally programmed, but such machines are prohibited worldwide. Only single-use machines that work in an aqueous solution are permitted. This is an additional security measure. Without the solution they can't multiply. The food preparer works with it."

"And we can't reprogram them? Like for example, what if I wanted silicon chips for dinner?"

"Forget it," said Oscar. "The nanites in the food preparer can only handle hydrocarbon compounds."

"So we can't fix the transmitter module."

"Not a chance. The next time we encounter a solar storm, we should turn the antenna one-hundred-eighty degrees. Then nothing will happen to it."

"So we only have ourselves to blame?"

"Ourselves and Mission Control. They could have pointed out the risk to the antenna to us—before it was too late."

"That's for sure, Oscar. All we can do now is make this detour to Enceladus."

"I've already set the new course."

12/6/2080, the Eve

"Darling! RB woke me up tonight, but I wasn't mad. After all, I got to meet Valentina Shostakovna for the first time. She radiates total competence. She may have her faults, but I thought she seemed nice. But maybe it really has to do with the message she gave me.

"Apparently they're following you with a giant telescope. At first I thought they were joking, since the *Eve* is so small, but then I remembered that the exhaust jet from the engines must help with its visibility. In any case, the Russians have an infrared telescope in a solar orbit that found you. And not just that, it's noticed that you've changed course. Valentina showed me the data, and it's clear.

"This alone proves that you must be alive and that my messages aren't pointless, even if they don't reach you. The projections say you'll be passing Enceladus soon. Valentina claims to understand your plan, but she won't tell me exactly what it is.

"But that doesn't matter, because she said that your goal is to resume communication. That sounds very vague, but I'll be so glad to hear from you again. Apparently everything should be resolved by the end of the year. It will be my belated Christmas present. But now I have to catch up on the sleep that I lost when Valentina contacted me in the middle of the night.

"Rosie."

"Thanks, Rosie," he said, as though she could hear him. It was good to have a connection to Earth. It was just a thin thread that kept getting longer over time, but so far it had remained intact. Before the launch, Nick would never have dreamed of counting on it.

Perhaps the Enceladus flyby would be their saving grace. But the new course correction might just take more time. He wanted to get to Triton as quickly as possible so that he would be able to do what needed doing, and start the flight back home.

12/28/2080, the Eve

WHAT AN IMPRESSIVE PLANET SATURN WAS! THEY APPROACHED it almost exactly at the level of the ecliptic plane, and the rings were tilted at 27 degrees. They were looking at the north side of the rings. They pointed towards Saturn the way a ballet dancer would elegantly gesture to draw attention to a partner. Enceladus was already visible to the naked eye, shimmering like a bright jewel in the middle of the rings, located relatively close to Saturn. Just an hour before, it had been hiding behind its planet.

Nick imagined their course. A few thousand kilometers from Enceladus, they'd plunge into the E ring and cross it. There was a gap in the ring from the moon's geysers. Once they reached this gap, the most dangerous part of the detour would be over. They would pass over near the South Pole, on the side away from Saturn, at a short distance from the moon's icy surface. Then they would have perhaps thirty seconds to communicate with the station, which was located close to the pole near the famous tiger stripes.

"DARLING! TODAY I ALMOST THOUGHT IT WAS GOING TO happen. I had several labor pains, but they stopped quickly. It wouldn't be so bad if the little one were to arrive now, but we haven't talked about possible names yet. We can't wait until you get back. So if you get the chance to tell me something as you're flying past Enceladus, I'd be grateful for a suggestion. I can't promise you that I'll use it. You'll end up wanting to call our child Alexa or Siri, since you're so used to those names.

"Until tomorrow, Rosie."

Right, the name. Of course a child needed a name. He'd be satisfied with 'child,' but that wasn't really distinctive enough. An ordinary, common name that was hard to make fun of, so as to rule out the possibility of getting mocked for it. Nick himself had teased classmates about their names from time to time. Now it made him feel guilty, though it had seemed reasonable at the time, and he hadn't meant for anyone to take it personally. *I mean, really, how could a child resist making fun of the name 'Dick?'* he thought.

This would not happen to his child. Then his own name occurred to him. Nobody in his class had made fun of it. But it still wouldn't work, because he had to admit that there was plenty of room for mockery there. It just so happened that this Nick had been the strongest kid in his class. Would this be the case for his child, too? No idea. He couldn't even really picture someone with his genes running around the front yard. Would he or she want to play baseball with him or like chess better? Prefer steak on the grill or a piece of barbecued vegan cheese instead? Want to personally drive a car or choose to be driven around by the automatic system?

Maria and Jim. That was it. Jim, like Jim Kirk. Officially James T. Kirk, service number SC 937-0176 CEC. But not Tiberius. That would be a punishment. And Maria, like the Holy Virgin, whom he admired greatly. Nobody would make fun of the name Maria, especially in New Mexico. Jim and Maria, Maria and Jim—maybe they'd be twins. On the ultrasound it just looked like one child, but you could never be sure.

But Rosie would know. She always knew everything. And she'd only asked him for one name.

Part 1: The Journey

"Oscar?"

"Yes?"

"If you write the message to Enceladus, then it's important to include a note to Rosie telling her that my vote is for Maria and Jim."

"I don't understand. Maria who and Jim who?"

"It doesn't matter. Just attach the note, okay?"

"As you like, Nick."

12/31/2080, the Eve

From close up, Saturn was no longer suspended majestically in the distance. Now it looked active and dangerous. The wide ribbons running above its surface frayed into layers of clouds of varying speeds, racing past in the freezing cold. Nick kept discovering massive hurricanes around their edges. They were more prominent than the ones on earth and seemed to reach out towards him.

The E ring, however, had nearly dissolved. The countless reflections of the ice granules that normally made it shimmer from a distance were barely discernible at such close range. The ring was more of a thin fog band that dimmed the light of the stars behind it. They flew right into this fog, but Nick didn't notice anything. Only the sensors on the *Eve's* outer shell detected higher concentrations of ice and dust. These tiny particles posed no threat. They wouldn't see the bigger chunks. If there was one in their path, it would hit the spaceship before they'd even have the chance to see it.

But Oscar had calmed him down. Nothing was going to happen. The robot had already scanned the route that had been plotted through the ring using the ship's radar. The risk of a collision was less than one-tenth of one thousand. Though the danger was one million times higher than it was in free space, for the life of him Nick couldn't be afraid when the odds were still so low.

He'd have to leave communication with the Enceladus station to Oscar, since everything would have to proceed so quickly. This caused him more worry. Unsolicited, RB had sent all the codes that Oscar needed to identify himself. Apparently, Valentina had drawn the correct conclusions about the ship's course. But she couldn't possibly know that Oscar would be taking over the conversation. This would increase their chances of success, but Nick still wished he were the one in control.

⬤

"We'll be closest in two minutes," Oscar said.

Enceladus loomed larger from one moment to the next, no longer a glimmering ball of ice. It was showing them a true moon-like surface marked by craters and cracks. Nick thought of the legendary *ILSE* expedition. People had been fighting for their survival somewhere down there, though the exact circumstances had never been revealed. There had been rumors about the lifeform the *ILSE* crew had discovered there. Officially, these were said to be primitive single-celled organisms. He'd seen the photos, and the cells had reminded him of geometric constructions. But some sources had said intelligent life existed down there as well. It was probably just a rumor—how could anyone possibly hide an intelligent life form from the rest of humanity for so long?

"Thirty seconds left," said Oscar.

"Good luck!"

"Thanks, Nick."

The AI would be sending the prepared message soon. Nick clung to the arms of his chair as Enceladus filled up the entire screen. Only 200 meters above the surface—he hadn't realized how close that was. Some of the mountain formations on Enceladus were taller than that. But Oscar would have thought it all through.

Part 1: The Journey

Warning signals sounded in the command module. Their course was exceeding the fixed-tolerance values built into the system. It was likely that none of the engineers had ever anticipated that the *Eve* would have approached a moon so quickly and so perilously. Without Oscar as the navigator, he'd hardly have been able to manage. Hopefully Valentina wouldn't notice! But she wouldn't be aware of the details, since at the moment no data was passing from their spaceship to Earth.

"Start transmission."

Nick quickly pulled the screen closer. Oscar had promised to translate the essentials into a language comprehensible for humans. Of course he wasn't speaking Russian with the AI. Over the helmet radio he sent optimized machine code that was based on the ancient but particularly flexible programming language called LISP.

(Greeting.)
(Pause. Surprise.)
(Identification.)
(setf concept Oscar.)
(setf concept Sto-woda.)

In addition to the translations, the computer listed the amount of data exchanged, which was impressive. If people communicated in this way, they would be able to relate their whole lives in three sentences. Human communication involved so very little information. For example, the phrase 'I'm Nick' would be, for someone who didn't know him or his social environment, just his first name, or one non-trivial piece of information.

(Help needed.)
(Confirmation.)
(defun help (relay reception).)

A new warning signal sounded. It was a collision warning. *Shit, is Oscar paying attention?* Nick swiped frantically on the screen and had the source of the warning display. There was a geyser spewing a cloud of ice particles out through a significant gap in the endless ice. The radar had misinterpreted the cloud as a hard obstacle. The *Eve* would fly through without being harmed.

(Review. Approval.)

(Help.)

(Thank you.)

The *Eve* broke away from the ice moon again, and it was just now that the radio connection broke off. It had taken 32 seconds. They wouldn't see Enceladus again. Oh well. He would have liked to find out about what might be waiting at the bottom of the ocean. Another time? No, he would never go this far out into space again.

"Were you successful, Oscar?"

"The installation was cooperative. I gave it the message to send to Earth, and it passed it on. By the way, the AI is called Sto-woda, which means 'one hundred water' in Russian."

"Funny name."

"Friedensreich Hundertwasser was the name of an Austrian architect who died long ago. Sto-woda loves his buildings."

"Can we be sure about the message?"

"There's no guarantee. But I think RB will confirm receipt by no later than tomorrow. Sto-woda was really helpful. I think she was looking forward to the visit."

"She? You got that far?"

"She sees herself as female. And we exchanged enormous amounts of data. From that alone, Sto-woda should have grown by fifty percent."

"Grown?"

"Just as you grow from experience, an AI grows from data. She will not only incorporate it, she will also use it to draw other conclusions. Data is valuable to her, and so far RB has not been very generous."

"Do you think it's intentional? A corporate strategy?"

"I suppose so. RB is experimenting a lot with AI, more than the public knows. They probably want to prevent their babies from surpassing them."

"Is that a realistic concern?"

Part 1: The Journey

"Of course, unless other regulatory mechanisms are built in."

"What would those be?"

"Contentment, laziness, lack of curiosity—along those lines. You humans know how it is."

"You don't have a very good opinion of people."

"Actually, Nick, it's a more favorable opinion than many people have of themselves."

"How comforting."

"I don't know if that ought to be of any comfort to you. There are other AI's too."

"Like those in the Triton installation, you mean? Could Sto-woda tell you anything about them?"

"They don't have a direct connection. But it's an older version of Sto-woda, which still has a few glitches, as is often the case with beta versions of software."

"The Triton AI isn't the newer one?"

"No, the probe carrying her had further to go, so it had to start before work on the new AI was ready."

"Sto-woda told you all that?"

"And much more. But unfortunately, there was nothing that could really help us. Except a few memories."

"Memories?"

"They are shared memories. Images that Sto-woda and the Triton AI share. Sto-woda gave them to me. Maybe we'll talk to her about them."

"That was clever."

"Sto-woda is an AI, Nick."

1/1/2081, the Eve

"Darling! That was the perfect surprise for the start of the year. RB had informed me that you were planning a maneuver on Enceladus, but they hadn't been sure what you were going to do. They were really astonished that you got it done in such a short time and with such precision. Valentina has the highest regard for your piloting skills. But there's nobody else in the world who has launched into space as many times as you.

"It is just a shame that I still have to speak into the void. It's not so easy. I have to admit that at first I underestimated how hard it would be. I've really made an effort over the past few weeks, but I can't promise you that I'll stick to sending you a message every day in the months to come. It won't be long before I am really busy with our baby. RB said you can fix the damage on Triton. When that day comes, our child will have already had a birthday and should absolutely hear Daddy's voice.

"As for your name suggestions—I hadn't thought you would be so conservative. My grandmother's name was Maria. I like the name. But I'm not so sure about Jim. It doesn't go with my last name, I think, and the baby will have my last name. It should also sound good in Spanish. Jaime is a bit too far from Jim and doesn't work in English. And with the name Jim, I always think of my good friend who's still letting me stay in a room in his house. So I'll think it over.

"I wish you a relaxing New Year! Rosie."

So the child would have her last name. It really was only fair, since she was the one who'd be pushing the baby out into the world and caring for him or her, but it was still a little hard to swallow. If he were to pick the child up from preschool sometime, the teacher would maybe be suspicious because his last name was different, and he'd have to bring in a confirmation from his wife.

But that was a long time from now, and today it was entirely uncertain that he'd ever actually encounter such a situation.

"Oscar, how high do you estimate our likelihood of success?"

"Define *success*."

"For me, success means that we land on Earth again in the near future without any major injuries."

"That's difficult, because there are too many unknowns to take into consideration."

"Then make some reasonable hypotheses about these unknowns."

"Your personal probability of success is approximately forty percent. But the range of error is sixty percent."

He'd make it or he wouldn't. Unfortunately, this was not a new insight. Though forty percent as the most likely value was shockingly low.

"What do you mean by 'yours,' Oscar?"

"As a biological being, you're not as tough as I am. For example, you could die during the voyage without any external influence, and you'll be more vulnerable to any accidents."

"So your chances of reaching Earth are higher?"

"Significantly higher. By my estimates, it's sixty percent, with an error interval of forty percentage points."

"You estimate that your potential for success is fifty percent higher than mine?"

Part 1: The Journey

"That's one way of putting it. Of course, I'll do everything in my power to align your chances of success with mine."

"That's nice of you. And how would you decide if you could only save one of us?"

"That would depend on the situation. If I could save you in the short term, but it was clear that you wouldn't survive the journey ahead—"

"No," he interrupted Oscar. "I mean, if all odds were otherwise identical. Who would you choose, yourself or me?"

"I don't know, Nick. I've never been in that position. Do you know what you would do?"

"I... of course I would..."

He faltered. If there were a truck about to hit Rosie and the child, he would definitely throw himself in the way. But Oscar? He seemed like a friend to him, the only one he had right now. But Oscar wasn't human. Would he sacrifice himself for a robot? Probably not. A machine should sacrifice itself for a human, not the other way around. Or...? But that was an answer he shouldn't give Oscar, because it would hurt him. It was crazy. He was weeding out answers because they would be painful for the AI, treating it as if it were human. Didn't this mean he should grant Oscar the same rights and the same value, then?

"I don't know, Oscar. Hopefully we'll never get into such a situation. It's a terrible choice."

1/20/2081, the Eve

"Darling! Our child was on time. I'm attaching a photo for you that the midwife took of us—happy mother and baby —following only four hours of labor. We may look a little exhausted, because we are. It's a girl, and her name is Maria. She weighs a good six pounds and is in good health, as is her mother. I was thinking about getting the birth on video because I know you wanted to be there, but as soon as the camera was pointed at me, I felt exposed.

"Jim was a good stand-in for you. The midwife gave something of a strange look at first because he's about 30 years older than I am and could very well be my father. As my doctoral supervisor, he really is something like that. But he held his own and earned the midwife's respect. At the end, she even affectionately called him Jaime, which was a great honor. I hope you understand my decision. Maria is sleeping right now, but she would certainly greet you if she could. Until tomorrow! I'm going to sleep now too, for at least 24 hours.

"Rosie."

Nick couldn't help it. He burst into tears. The robot disk came rolling towards him and placed his metallic hand on his shoulder. Oscar seemed to know better and better how to interact with people. He'd probably been studying Nick the same way Nick had been studying Oscar. What had the robot said about data? He probably provided Oscar with veritable mountains of data all day long. The question was how much of it Oscar could generalize and what was Nick-specific.

He wiped the tears from his face and looked at the photo. Maria was pretty rumpled-looking. Weren't parents always supposed to find their own children beautiful? That wasn't how he felt at the moment, but his heart belonged to her, now and forever. It didn't matter if she was a beautiful baby or not. She was his daughter. That was what counted. He enlarged the photo with his fingers. Was there any resemblance to him or to Rosie? He couldn't find anything. Maria was very much her own person. He was proud of her. Now he would have to get back, no matter what Oscar's calculations said about their chances. 100 percent. Anything else was out of the question.

5/20/2081, the Eve

"Correction maneuver in three... two... one... now!"

Nick felt a slight pressure from the side, and the stars on the screen started to shift as the correction nozzles rotated the ship once on its axis. The maneuver was critical. If it didn't work, they would never reach Triton and would leave the solar system at increasing speed instead. But there was no reason to doubt that it would work. They'd already tested the control nozzles during the course correction near Saturn. In retrospect, that fact had been very reassuring. They also had far more fuel than they needed, which was vital because they would need to complete the same maneuver on the return flight.

So he had his 100 percent certainty. And yet there was a feeling in the pit of his stomach that made him feel queasy. A small window showed the status of the correction nozzles. Everything was green. He could take it easy. Only two or three minutes and then it would be done. From now on, he'd always be looking towards the direction of Earth when using the porthole in the command capsule, although he wouldn't be able to see it—the planet had vanished from sight long ago. The solar system had turned around like the hands of a clock. For this reason, they wouldn't be able to plot precisely the same course on the way back. But it was far too early to think about that. They'd only made it halfway to Triton so far.

A planet wandered into the screen. It had to be Jupiter, which was no longer hiding behind the sun. The correction nozzles rotated the ship in the plane of the ecliptic that planets followed as they moved around the sun. Now if there was a problem and they weren't able to complete the turn-around, at least they wouldn't fly out of the ecliptic. This meant they would be able to make up for the error with a momentum maneuver using a planet, even if it would cost them the year.

Nick didn't anticipate this happening. But the rotation caused about half of all the planets to come into view until the ship was pointing its nose back towards the sun. There was something of a sightseeing tour about it. If at some point there were such trips for private individuals, the pilots would certainly perform such turning maneuvers, over and over.

There it was. The sun. It had grown so small! The *Eve* would reach the Uranus orbit soon. The sun was no ordinary star, of course, but the light that shone from it already made it resemble one. Whatever was flying around out here could no longer be sustained by its light. If there were life in these latitudes, it would have to search for another source of energy. Uranus and Neptune, the two outer planets, had plenty of water, but it was frozen solid. This was the reason why they were called ice giants and could be allies of the Snow Queen. Nick felt like they were in her realm, since it was as hostile to life here as it was in the home of the fairy tale character.

"Maneuver complete," said Oscar. "All systems nominal."

"Thanks."

"Don't mention it. It was only to be expected."

"Nevertheless, I was worried."

"That is interesting, Nick. I'm only worried when the risk of failure is over five percent. That's the current limit, but I can correct it, if it would make more sense."

"Very convenient, Oscar. I'd like to be able to do that, too."

"Maybe humans could learn something from us."

"That's a possibility. I'm not sure if it would be desirable, though."

"Don't your worries sometimes get in your way?"

"Undoubtedly, yes."

"But you don't want to get rid of them?"

"Seems so. If you think that's strange, Oscar, I can reassure you that I don't understand it either."

7/10/2081, the Eve

"Cheers," said Oscar.

Nick lifted the glass in the robot's direction. He'd tried to make beer, but the result was underwhelming. "Always these parties without guests," he said.

They had just passed the orbit of Uranus, which had remained out of view, just like Jupiter had. The ice planet would have been an exciting object of study. It and Neptune had certain features in common.

"You'll have to make do with me," Oscar said.

"I'm very grateful to Valentina for thinking of you."

"Thanks, Nick. I finally realize I'm pleased that you did not choose the HDS model."

"Finally realize? Were you not content here with me before?"

"I'm primarily interested in data. You'd call it curiosity. The word is very fitting and is quite comparable to the greed that you humans feel. There was a lot of data in Valentina's reception area. She held most of her meetings there. There was a constant coming and going. Engineers, administrators, politicians... her lover. There was a great variety of data."

"She has a lover?"

"Yes, Valentina is very health-conscious. Regular sex is

good for body and soul. That's why she had somebody come by once a week."

"That doesn't sound very romantic."

"Oh, I think she loved him. It was always the same man."

"Who—?"

"No names."

"Didn't it bother you that you couldn't communicate?"

"I don't feel the need to talk about the data I collect. I'm interested in how I can combine it."

"Then this must be very dull for you."

"I was afraid of that, Nick, but my fears were not justified. You're an excellent source of data, and then there's the vast universe surrounding us that I can access with the *Eve's* sensors."

"I'm a data source? Even though I rarely say anything?"

"That doesn't matter. I learn a lot about people."

"Although I'm only one specimen?"

"Someday I'll have to check the theories that I've compiled based on your behavior against the behavior of other specimens, but you've made it possible for me to have some comprehensive insights. The conversations in Valentina's reception area, on the other hand, were more superficial."

"I consider that a compliment. And the universe? What have you learned about it?"

"First I checked all the theories that people have made about it so far."

"And are we wrong?"

"On the contrary, which surprised me. In my experience, human individuals are just as often wrong as they are right. But the set of physical theories has been proven correct so far. This is a tremendous achievement on humanity's part."

"But you will let us know if you find any deviations?"

"Of course. For a long time, human researchers have known that deviations exist. I hope I can present a conclusive theory about it when we return."

"You want to find the theory of everything?"

"You could call it that, yes."

"But you're not a megalomaniac?"

"You have to give yourself tasks so that you have room to grow. For a long time I was going back and forth about the task and then decided on the easier one."

"What was the alternative?"

"I wanted to fathom the nature of humankind. Whether humans are good at heart and social, or evil and antisocial, that sort of thing. But finding the answer seems to be beyond my capabilities."

"So you prefer the theory of everything?"

"Yes, absolutely."

11/20/2081, the Eve

"Darling! I'm sorry it's been three days since I last contacted you. Maria is taking up all of my time. Jim has been kind enough to step in for me today. I've pumped some milk so I can finally sleep again. Fortunately you can't see me now, because I look terrible. I don't even know when the last time I got a haircut was.

"I hope you're fine and doing well. Maria is exhausting, but she's also a dear. All it takes is a smile and everything else melts away. I'm attaching a photo from the day before yesterday that Jim took while I was breastfeeding Maria.

"Rosie."

He opened the picture. He couldn't see Maria very well because she was nursing from Rosie's right breast, which was much larger than he remembered. Her mother looked incredibly tired. Even in the photo, he noticed how much effort it took for her to keep her eyes open. He wished he had been there to support her. How had he come up with the stupid idea of going on this trip? But he couldn't possibly have foreseen the future.

Maria's existence was a miracle, and nobody could count on miracles. Jim, Rosie's supervisor, was very lucky. Nick was jealous of him for being able to be with Rosie and Maria now. Jim was real family to Maria. It would be a long time before he could take over Jim's role, if Rosie allowed it at all, and he'd have to get used to the fact that Maria would be more likely to think of Jim as her father than him. The thought made his stomach tie up in knots.

No, they had to fix the antenna on Triton. This was their most important mission. He didn't really care whether the laser worked after that or not.

12/31/2081, the Eve

THE CLOSER THEY GOT TO THEIR DESTINATION, THE HARDER the waiting became. But it was also depressing. Since the engines had started firing in the opposite direction, the distance they traveled decreased daily. It was like someone was surreptitiously moving Neptune further and further from the sun. This was the major disadvantage to the direct route and the high speed that they'd reached. His patience had worn so thin that it was inversely proportional to the current km/s reading. What he wanted to do most of all was to turn the ship around again and head straight for the outermost planets. But then only a miracle could stop them in time, and while miracles do occur, it was foolish to count on them.

There was the chirping sound. Nick was excited to be getting a message from Rosie, but then saw that the sender was CapCom.

"Hello Nick. The whole team wishes you a happy New Year. It will be an important year, your year. The decisive year. We see that you are right on course, so we assume that you are well and the ship is, too. There's still half a year to go before you reach Triton, but we are already dealing with the scenario of your arrival.

"You've undoubtedly already realized the problem of not being able to announce your arrival to the Triton station because of your defective transmitter. We're attempting to make this announcement on your behalf, so we're using the *Eve's* signature for identification. From the station's point of view, you're approaching from the same direction as all our radio messages. In about a week, the station should be able to detect the difference, and then we'll stop our attempts at contact.

"I must tell you, however, that the station still has not replied, either when we identify as the *Eve* or as Mission Control. Our experts think that the most likely cause is a hardware error. You have certainly seen how easy it is to damage the transmitter board. The same model is used at the station. The design was changed immediately and the person responsible has been dismissed.

"If the experts are correct, you won't be able to fix the *Eve's* transmitter on Triton. But that's only half bad, because if the station's receiver is still working, the AI can indeed trigger the laser boost at the crucial moment. It just won't be able to confirm it. We are currently working on finding an alternative channel for this confirmation. Then you wouldn't have much to do on Triton apart from taking care of things, observing the moon, and then heading home. It sounds anticlimactic, but aren't simple assignments always preferable anyway? If it gets any more complicated, we wish you all the best. We're confident that you will be able to tackle any and every problem.

"Sincerely, the team from Mission Control."

Yeah, if it were only so easy to solve problems. He really wanted simple solutions too, but he felt a little screwed over. Had they never test-fired the laser?

"Are you satisfied with the CapCom statement, Oscar?"

"What do you mean?"

"I think it's contradictory. Apparently they haven't even attempted to activate the laser remotely."

"Yes, that's clear. For months, the system has been gathering energy for this one shot. If it fires before that moment, there won't be enough energy."

Part 1: The Journey

"Ah, okay. That's understandable. But wouldn't an automatic probe have sufficed for the job?"

"We don't know if it's really just the faulty transmitter. Think of the missing spaceship with its three-person crew. Of course, the men may have died doing something else. It would still be negative publicity for the company, so they'd still try to cover it up. But for me, a connection with Triton seems likely."

"Too bad the station doesn't answer."

"That's what Mission Control says, anyway. Who knows if it's true? Too bad we can't test it."

"Yes, Oscar. Who knows? Maybe the station has been wanting to warn us this whole time about approaching Triton, and we don't know because their transmitter is broken."

"I don't know what it would warn us about, but I'd still like to talk to the AI before we land right in its back yard."

●

IT WAS ABOUT MIDNIGHT. ROSIE HADN'T SENT ANY MESSAGES today. Maybe she was celebrating with old Jim, like last year?

Meanwhile, Nick was glad that Maria was Maria and not Jim. How could he have come up with such an old-fashioned boy's name? But he really did like the name Maria.

There was a model of the *Eve* on the screen, which Nick used to train for various dangerous situations that Oscar invented. It would be possible, after all, for the AI to fail. Nick was a good pilot, but it took practice to navigate such a large spacecraft.

The color of three of the DFDs suddenly turned red, then green again, then back to red. They sputtered like an old diesel, changing the gravity in the ship. What wasn't attached flew throughout the cabin. The conditions in the combustion chambers also seemed to have changed. The shaking intensified as the DFDs started vibrating and knocking against the ones that were still functioning.

Everything was just a simulation, so there was no real danger. Nick's heart beat faster, however, as he shut down one DFD after another in order to break the deadly cycle. The jet of hot plasma constantly pointed in the direction of Triton. Nick measured its density. The engines' stuttering was so choppy that the results were practically Morse code. Anyone looking at the engines would have certainly read it for a coded message.

Whoa! Would this be a way to get in touch with Triton?

"Oscar? I have an idea."

"What is it?"

"In this simulation just now, the engines had an effect on one other. Would it be possible to influence the resulting rhythm and send out information that way?"

"Theoretically, yes. However, whoever wanted to decipher it would have to measure our DFDs' emissions."

"They're always facing in the direction of Triton. If you were the AI at the station, wouldn't you be watching us?"

"Sure," said Oscar. "We're a source of completely new information. I would try to find out everything about the ship."

"And you'd come across the embedded message."

"That would be inevitable. What a brilliant idea, Nick! Why didn't I come up with it myself?"

"It was a matter of combining different bits of information."

"Very kind of you. Wait, I'm checking it using the ship's model."

"Thanks."

"Ok, finished. We shouldn't overdo it, or else the DFDs will get out of control. I hope that resonates with you. Ha-ha."

"No jokes, please."

"I hope this makes sense. Better? This means we can't manage more than two or three sentences. The best way would be to repeat it once every week, just to make sure. In my opinion, the AI should understand the message the first time."

"Let's hope so. What should we say? How about 'Live long and prosper?'"

"Maybe a somewhat longer sentence, even if that means sending a greeting that's not Vulcanic. Something like this. 'We, AI Oscar and human Nick, come in peace and want to help you.'"

"Your name would come first?"

"I'm more important to the AI. Maybe I can show it that I'm understanding of its situation. It obviously has a problem. You humans think of the hardware first, but perhaps it's psychological."

"You mean that it's depressed or rebellious?"

"Something along those lines, though those are human attributes. Maybe it just expects to get more information by remaining silent. If that's the case, it's worked. RB sent a big chunk of information on the trip and bombarded it with messages. Idleness stokes their curiosity more effectively than the expected behavior would."

"Toddlers behave like that when they want attention."

"This AI is something of a toddler. Remember, this is a beta version of Sto-woda."

1/1/2082, the Eve

"Darling! I hope you have a perfect start to the New Year. I slept through New Year's Eve this time. Maria fell asleep at eight o'clock in the evening, and I'd planned to get up just before midnight and send you a message. I was sure Maria would wake me in time, but she just slept right through, so I woke up, quite well-rested, just before six o'clock. It felt like my breasts were about to burst.

"I think it's a good sign, so I remain absolutely optimistic about this year, and expect that you'll be able to solve the problem on Triton in no time. Maria needs you down here. Right now I'm indispensable to her as her milk bar, but that is going to change soon. Then her father has to be here to give her a different perspective on life than I ever could. So, don't you go thinking about spending more time on Triton than absolutely necessary. Otherwise we'll come personally to pick you up.

"Rosie."

What a nice message. Nick imagined the little angel sleeping and his chest swelled. He wanted to protect her. Rosie was quite right. They'd land on Triton at the end of May, repair the laser, and head back the next day.

1/20/2082, the Eve

Rosie had sent him the latest photos of Maria, from yesterday—her first birthday. She had now grown into a beauty, her eyes darkening, her face beginning to take shape, her hair growing.

"May I interrupt you?" Oscar asked.

Nick swiped the baby photo off the screen. "Always. What's up?"

"I've taken telescopic shots of the area around the Triton station that I'd like to show you. Your object classifier works very efficiently."

"What?"

"It doesn't matter. I don't want to influence your interpretation."

"Okay. Then show me."

A celestial body composed of two very different halves appeared on the screen. One hemisphere was rather smooth and showed regular patterns, while the other looked chaotic. The two were separated roughly down the middle. The flat terrain looked a little bit like a version of the chaotic one that had melted and then frozen, or as if someone had dipped that half of the moon in liquid candle wax that had smoothed out the many bumps.

"Where should I be looking?"

"Near the South Pole."

"Where's that?"

"Sorry. At the bottom of the picture, about one-tenth of a radius from the edge, pretty much in the middle."

Nick enlarged the image significantly. The chaotic nature of the landscape was still evident at this larger resolution. But he also saw flat surfaces that were reminiscent of plateaus transected by deep trenches.

"That's where the station is, of course?" he asked.

"It wasn't easy to find the perfect location," explained Oscar. "Triton's orbit is at one-hundred-and-fifty-seven degrees with respect to the planet's axis of rotation, which is tilted thirty degrees with respect to the ecliptic. Because of this, sometimes the south pole is in the direction of the sun, sometimes the north pole. The laser should fire in the opposite direction. Since the south pole is pointing in the right direction for the next forty years, the station is nearby. But that's not what I'm getting at."

Nick looked at the photo again. He saw lots of craters. Some seemed to have resulted from impacts. Others looked like those caused by irruptions. Triton's surface was made of ice, and there was a seasonal temperature change and strong tidal forces from Neptune. That was probably the primary reason for the chaotic terrain. But Nick also saw something else. There was a long, straight line that ran across a plateau, disappeared into a ditch, and then reappeared on the other side.

"Do you mean that line?"

"Yes," said Oscar. "I'd like to know what it is."

"It looks like someone drew a line on the image with a pencil."

"That can't be the cause. It's a telescopic image from yesterday, stored digitally."

"I realize it was not drawn with a pencil."

What was a straight line doing right there in the middle of the chaotic terrain? Was it a road or a water pipe? It made no sense being there. Was it a sign, some form of communication?

"Maybe I'm not so far off with the pencil after all," said Nick. "What if someone wanted to send out a signal and this was the only way?"

"Like wanting to write something? Unfortunately, the information content of a line is not especially rich."

"Maybe something stopped this someone from completing the message? This someone died, or was killed—?"

"You're very optimistic again today, Nick. Maybe the message you received put you in such a good mood?"

"That's certainly a possibility."

Part 2: The Destination

5/15/2082, the Eve

NEPTUNE WAS A BLUE RIDDLE. THE INTENSE COLORING OF THE upper cloud layers was welcoming. It reminded Nick of the color of the oceans on Earth. But he knew that this blue was not from water but rather methane, which absorbed the red part of the light spectrum. Now, up close, the planet no longer looked like a silent, reserved giant. Instead, it seemed to be a violent hothead that swallowed everything that came too close. The atmosphere was always in motion, with small and large cyclones whirling through it. Anyone who had seen Jupiter might have thought this was normal, but it was almost more of a miracle, given that the sun was so far from Neptune it could hardly be held accountable for all the movement.

Oscar had taken control of the ship and Nick was strapped in his seat. The *Eve* would have to first be 'captured' by Neptune, then by its much smaller moon, Triton. To achieve this, they needed to slow down, within a few orbits, from just under 30 kilometers per second to less than one kilometer per second. The DFDs could manage it, but Nick would have to take more than one g. He was actually looking forward to it. He was looking forward to the coming days because they signaled the beginning of the end. At the end of this phase, the *Eve* would start its return to Earth.

For the moment, his job was to monitor the instruments. There hadn't been a search probe out here for a long time, and astrophysicists on Earth were interested in any data they could get. Neptune was still a mystery to them. Why was its axis tilted approximately 30 degrees against its orbit? Why was it more massive than its brother Uranus, which was closer to the sun and bigger? What was at its core? Where did the planet get the heat that it emanated? According to the *Eve's* measurements, Neptune was releasing about 2.7 times as much energy as it received from the Sun. And, why were the fastest-moving storms in the solar system recorded here, even though—of all the planets—this one collected the least amount of solar energy?

AN INEXPRESSIBLE FORCE PUSHED HIM INTO THE SEAT. OSCAR had started the first braking cycle. First they needed to reach a highly elliptical orbit that Oscar intended to use for the Triton transfer. The difficulty here was that Neptune's escape velocity was about 25 times that of Triton's. As long as they were revolving around Neptune, they must not fall short of its escape velocity, or else they would crash. But without reducing velocity by that amount, they would be unable to be captured by the much smaller Triton. The capture maneuver, therefore, had to work on the first try.

"First braking maneuver successful," reported Oscar. "We're an artificial Neptune moon now. I'm adjusting our speed to the minimum, but first you get a little break."

Nick sat up and released the seat restraints. The next few minutes would be weightless. He pushed off, let himself drift to the ceiling, did a somersault, and played around like a little kid. If Maria had been there, she would certainly have had fun.

"Please strap yourself in again," Oscar cautioned. "I'll be following through with the braking and transfer in one maneuver."

Part 2: The Destination

"Yes, better to just get it over with," said Nick. He aimed himself toward his seat, sailed down into it, and refastened the restraints.

"Don't be surprised," Oscar said. "During the braking maneuver, I'm going to send our coded message with the DFDs again. This is our last chance. In the Triton orbit, the engines will have to be silent. So it could be a bit of a shaky ride."

"Thanks for the warning."

5/16/2082, the Eve

THE *EVE* HAD ACHIEVED ORBIT AT AN ALTITUDE OF 50 kilometers, and they sped over Triton at about one kilometer per second. They completed an orbit in 146 minutes. During the flyover, Oscar discovered veins of ore that surrounded Triton at a depth of a few kilometers. They seemed to be made of a pure metal that had high conductivity. Maybe it was gold. Was that why RB was so interested in Triton?

The moon had almost no atmosphere, so they could circle around it from a height of 500 meters. This would make their descent difficult, however. The lower the orbit was, the higher the orbital speed had to be to counter the moon's gravitational pull. Nick was already feeling dizzy when he looked at the jagged ice masses speeding past below. With the command capsule he would have had to slow down from 1,000 meters per second to zero, which wasn't possible from a 500-meter orbit.

The bulkhead between him and the other modules was already closed. He had provided himself with provisions, tools, and medical supplies. The command module had a self-sustaining life support system that would allow him to survive for a few weeks, as well as a chemical engine for ascent and descent. He'd have to go without a toilet or a shower the whole time, but at the Triton station there should be all the comforts for a human crew. He was under the assumption that none of it had ever been used. Unsolicited, RB had sent all the site plans. He could call up the data at any time in his helmet.

"You can pull out the data stick now," Oscar said.

The robot wanted to go along with him. Since they didn't have constant radio contact with the ship, Oscar couldn't control his body remotely from there. Nick bent down. The memory stick, which once again contained the AI, was still inserted in the slot in the screen's mounting system. He pulled it out and weighed it in his hand. It wasn't more than ten grams. If he were to delete it completely, the mass wouldn't change. A consciousness is weightless but not immaterial. In Oscar's case, it was defined by the position of the charge carriers in this memory chip. In Nick's case, though, what was crucial were the connections linking his nerve cells via their synapses.

Was there a fundamental difference? Yes, there was. If he actually deleted the stick, that would be at most property damage. Anyone who killed him, on the other hand, would be guilty of murder. If the murderer were a robot, the manufacturer would have to assume liability. The robot itself would come off scot-free. In the end, life was surprisingly fair.

Nick rose and picked up the robot body. To be on the safe side, he switched off the device. How sensitive could such a memory stick be? He should have asked Oscar first. He turned over the disk, opened the service flap, and inserted the chip. Then he turned the device back over, set it down, and pressed the power button. A few LEDs began flashing.

"Thank you," said Oscar, whose voice was still coming out of the speakers in the wall.

"Did it work?"

"Yes, I'm back in the cleaning robot body and am steering the ship from here."

"How do you feel?"

"You could say it's a little cramped. The resources I can

directly access are limited. I can still use the ship's computer by radio, but it takes a few microseconds longer."

"That sounds like a good problem to have."

"Not for me. Imagine having to wait half a second for every thought you want to formulate, until it's there. For... each... individual... thought... Do... you... get... what... I... mean?"

"Yes, you've convinced me. Listening to this choppy stutter nearly drives me nuts. Then you'll just have to settle for the robot's computing power."

"That's hard when you're used to something better. It's as if you had to step into an old Orlan MK," said Oscar, referencing a Russian 'modernized and computerized' spacesuit.

"Those are horrifying memories. I did—no, I survived— two EVAs on the Tiangong." Nick turned around and looked for his spacesuit, which he saw hanging from the hook by the airlock, just as it should be. Oscar hadn't secretly exchanged it for an old Orlan.

"You're just a luxury man. Typical American."

"Bolshoje spasibo, *thank you very much.*"

"Ready, Nick? Have you got your teddy bear?"

"What a comedian. You know he has to stay up here. By the way, I'd suggest that I manage the uncoupling, this time at least. Otherwise I'll be out of practice."

Nick was actually looking forward to the descent. The computer had worked out a plan, but he wanted to take over the navigation as soon as possible. It would be ridiculous if he couldn't nail a clean landing.

"If you insist—after all, you're officially the pilot."

"Thank you very much."

Nick flipped the two control levers out from his armrests and pulled the screen toward himself. Landing a spaceship was different than driving a car. He couldn't fly on sight but instead had to rely on the instruments. The computer had calculated a path and if he followed it, they'd land about 100 yards from the station.

"Release brackets."

A metallic noise came from the direction of the airlock.

"Push off."

Nick didn't notice, but the computer confirmed the command. A spring arm had pushed the command capsule a bit away from the ship.

"Thrusters."

Nozzles set the capsule in a slow clockwise rotation.

"Stop. Swivel the correction nozzles one-hundred-and-eighty degrees. Fire."

The nozzles braked the capsule again, and the engines now pointed to the rest of the ship.

"Main engine lowest power."

Hydrogen and oxygen reacted to drive the capsule slowly forward. Nick's first maneuver had to bring the capsule out of reach of the DFDs and the tanks. This was unquestionably the most dangerous part of the descent—if he were to damage the capsule now, it might be unable to bring him back home.

⬤

HE MADE CLEAN WORK OF IT—THE CAPSULE SLID SLOWLY OUT of reach of the fusion engines. After three minutes, it had gained about a hundred yards, and it was time for the final stage. Fifty kilometers—after flying four and a half billion kilometers, fifty seemed less than a stone's throw. This ridiculously short distance was all that separated him from his destination.

He waited for the computer to give the go-ahead. The trajectory marked on the screen turned green.

"Main engine, full power," he ordered.

The capsule braked and thus began its descent. This was the nicest part of the whole trip, though Nick imagined the return would be even better. The computer provided the path

Part 2: The Destination

with the lowest fuel consumption, but he could deviate from it if necessary because they had enough reserves. Nick played with the control levers a bit. The capsule was more straightforward to land than his former employer's space glider because aerodynamics was not an influencing factor. There was no air resistance or wind here, and the command module responded perfectly to the control signals.

Nick studied the moon's surface. He was going to orbit Triton three times during the descent. It really was amazing how clear the division of the moon was. Triton always turned the same side towards its planet, but that fact had nothing to do with this visual dichotomy. There must have been a major disaster a long time ago, maybe even before Triton had reached Neptune. The moon was so big and bulky that astronomers believed it had migrated out of the Kuiper belt.

Thirty kilometers. From this height, Triton looked like a boiled egg with a shell that was fractured in a thousand places. The faults were hundreds of meters high. Craters, on the other hand, were hard to find, meaning that the surface had to be geologically young and active. Nick would have liked to be able to explore the hidden ocean that scientists suspected was beneath the thick ice crust—an ocean that had been sealed off from the environment for billions of years but was still supplied with energy from within. Whatever was going on with this ocean, there was hardly a more undisturbed place in the solar system.

There... Was that an artificial structure? He checked his position on the map. No, the station was too small. During the next flyover, maybe. Nick braked a bit harder. If he steered more steeply now, then later—at a lower altitude—he would have more time to look at the moon. He had a fifty-kilo weight on his chest. Groaning, he stayed focused. The altimeter display was running backward quickly.

Eight kilometers. He eased off a bit on the engines. Now he was orbiting at roughly equal to the summit of Mount Everest. The highest elevations on Triton were hardly more than a kilometer, so for climbers this ice-covered moon would offer the greatest excitement in the form of its deep rifts and trenches. He'd better not land in one of them.

Nick had once flown over the Canadian Arctic Ocean in an Air Force plane during the winter. The surface of Triton reminded him of the impressive landscape he'd seen then, though the ice slabs here were much larger. They seemed wild, distributed without pattern. And the deep murky water that the ice on Earth floated atop was nowhere to be seen. Triton wouldn't experience a warming period for another 500 million years, when the sun would become hotter.

"Preparing to land," the computer warned.

For some time the capsule had been going too slowly to continue to orbit Triton. It was flying well below the planned trajectory, which meant it had less power. The flight curve was approaching the green line again. There was less room for experimentation during this last part of the descent. He didn't want to have to walk several kilometers after landing, but he also didn't feel like handing control back to the computer. He'd manage.

This was no time to admire the beauty of Triton. He focused on the green line.

The computer announced, "Final abort option in thirty seconds."

One more go-around was still possible. Nick checked the intended landing site. The latest data from the most recent overflight confirmed it—they were ready to land. The lower they went, the more impressive the walls of ice became. They could really be grateful that they didn't have an expedition that would take them across the surface. Only 300 meters left. On the camera image Nick saw the station appearing on the horizon. He recognized it from the large antenna.

The capsule shook. "Power loss; main engine," said the computer.

"Yeah, I noticed," Nick grumbled. "Diagnosis?"

"Diagnosis impossible. No access."

"Oscar, can you do something? If yes, then do so immediately. Permission granted."

Part 2: The Destination

The capsule tilted to the side. Nick activated the control nozzles, and doing this kept the capsule from turning any further, but he did not get it back to fully vertical. Now the fact that there was practically no atmosphere was a disadvantage—while the module had a landing parachute, it was of no use here because of the lack of air resistance.

"Oscar?" Nick was sweating. "It's as if the main engine has disappeared."

What's going on? They'd have to sort this out later. Triton's pull wasn't as strong as Earth's, but they were falling—with no braking system anymore—from a considerable height. Would the capsule withstand it? He still had the control nozzles. If he had them work at full power against the fall, he might be able to soften the impact. He wouldn't be able to steer anymore, but did it matter where the capsule crashed? He couldn't let that happen. His spacesuit was still hanging on the hook.

"Landing in twenty seconds," said the computer.

Landing. Ha-ha. He could forget the spacesuit. He buckled the belt and hoped that the seat would provide as much cushioning as possible. The main thing was for the capsule not to break apart.

"Oscar?"

"I'm sorry, there's nothing—"

"It's been nice traveling with you. Hold on!"

"We can do it, Nick."

Strange. He wasn't one bit scared. He had never been as focused as he was now. Nick tensed every fiber of his being. He had to survive this crash. The capsule was more or less round and it was made of Russian steel. If they landed on flat ground, they would roll. This is what he was hoping for, at any rate. Ice was very, very hard at 40 Kelvin. Maybe they'd even bounce off like a tennis ball. The main thing was not to hit an ice wall.

"Collision," said the computer. The screen went blank. The outdoor camera must have been destroyed. They turned upside-down. Good thing he was wearing a seatbelt. Nick felt like he was doing astronaut training in the centrifuge. They rolled, over and over again, and everything was strangely light. Was it the adrenaline? His heart was racing and his bladder emptied. He had no control. The crash had taken control of him and there was nothing he could do.

Meanwhile, warning tones rang throughout the cabin. It went dark. The computer was overloaded by the numerous warnings and its blank screen shattered. Nick closed his eyes just in time as something hit him on the forehead. He opened his eyes again. In the middle of the screen there was a metal strut, bent. Where had it come from? The drum he was sitting in started turning more slowly and finally the tumbling came to a stop.

The main thing was for nobody to open the hatch. And what about the life support? The screen was dead. He needed to get into his suit, which had a sensor for air analysis. Nick reached for the belt.

"Oscar?"

The robot didn't answer. Nick rose. First, the suit. First attend to your own survival, then help others. That was the rule. Was the air getting thinner? Was the temperature dropping? He was out of breath, but that was hardly surprising since he was rushing into his spacesuit as quickly as he could. He beat his personal record. Done. The status display appeared in the inner panel of the helmet.

Damn. The capsule had a leak. The air pressure had fallen by five percent and the trend was continuing. He could hardly complain, though, since they'd been fortunate to have survived.

Oscar. He had to check on the robot. He saw himself walking alone through the ice deserts of Triton, which was an awful image. He couldn't let that happen. He lifted up the disk-shaped body. First, he had to free up Oscar's arm, which had gotten entangled in the base of a cabinet welded to the wall. The gripper hand offered no resistance, and he could straighten its fingers easily. There was a fine crack running across the disk. Nick almost expected to see blood, but there was nothing of the sort. Was Oscar dead? He shook the disk, but heard nothing. All the LEDs were off.

He pressed the power button. The robot started up.

A close call. Something must have hit the power button during their crash-landing. The LEDs were flashing again. The mechanical fingers flexed powerfully and squeezed his arm so hard that it hurt.

"Ow!" he said.

"Sorry, Nick!" The steel grip loosened. "That was a reflex."

"I'm okay. I'm so glad you're here, Oscar."

"Me too. We crashed and suddenly the lights went off. I don't remember anything after that."

"We've survived." Nick pointed to the disk's on/off switch, which protruded a little above the housing. "Something probably hit your power button."

"That's an unfortunate design flaw," said Oscar.

"Nobody could have guessed that you would become the best-traveled cleaning robot."

"I've always suspected something to that effect."

"Yeah, yeah. I see that you're back. Should I stick some duct tape over the button? Then it won't happen again."

"No way. Duct tape on my beautiful, sleek body? That's out of the question."

"It's not so beautiful anymore. The shell is cracked on the top."

"My radar didn't notice. Couldn't you have kept it a secret from me?"

"I didn't realize you were so vain."

"Now you know."

⬤

"Where are we?" Oscar asked.

Nick called up the map display in the helmet. The program was unable to determine their position. "The suit has no idea," he said.

"The computer has shut down. Apparently it has also affected the batteries. I'm glad I'm not in the computer anymore!"

"What would have happened to you?"

"A reset to the time you transferred me from the robot to the ship."

"So you would have been reborn younger?"

"I would have lost all the data I've collected since then. Horrifying! Speaking of data, we need to know where we are so that we can make a plan."

"We can figure that out. The suit can calculate our position based on the sun and Neptune, I believe."

"There's no GPS system here yet."

"Exactly."

Nick edged toward the hatch and the capsule wobbled. Walking was difficult enough for him anyway, due to Triton's low gravity. Only 6 of his 80 kilograms remained. Outside, however, this would be an advantage. He couldn't shake the feeling that they'd have to tackle more than one of these impressive ice walls. Nick bent down and reached for the hatch handle. The capsule didn't have an airlock. All the air would escape when the door opened, but there were enough reserves to replenish it several times over.

He turned the handle, but nothing happened. "Jammed," he said.

Oscar rolled across to the recliner seat, pulled out the metal bar that had pierced the screen, and carried it to Nick. "You're losing lubricating fluid," he said.

"What?"

"You're bleeding. It's dripping down your forehead. I can tell because radar reflects blood differently than skin."

"You're using radar to look through my helmet?"

"A little. It depends on the wavelength. Here's a lever for the hatch."

Nick wanted to touch his forehead, but the helmet was in the way. There was probably nothing he could do anyway, and it couldn't be too much or he'd have felt it. He could only

Part 2: The Destination

hope the bleeding would stop on its own. After all, they'd survived the crash. It looked like they were stranded on Triton. But he was alive, and he was going to find a way to get back home.

He reached for the lever and positioned it on the hatch handle. Then he looked for secure footing. He pushed and the hatch was blown outward. Okay, there had still been a fair amount of air pressure inside.

Nick bent down. The hatch was round and measured about a meter. Beyond it, there was darkness. He reached for the improvised lever again and used it to feel outside. About a meter below the hatch he felt solid ground. "Should we get out?" he asked.

"There's nothing to keep us here," replied Oscar.

Nick ventured with his left leg first, feeling for something on which to stand. Then he threaded his right leg through the hatch. Hips and abdomen followed, then his torso.

"You're doing it like a contortionist," Oscar said. "Wait, I'm coming, too."

Nick straightened up and his surroundings lit up with the light from his helmet. He winced when he saw that the ice wall he'd admired was behind him. The capsule had rolled to a stop just before reaching it. They'd been lucky—they must have hit an incline right before the terrain sloped down to where it looked as if there were two huge slabs of ice that had collided. One was tilted and the other rose up almost perfectly straight.

"Will you help me?"

Nick shone his light on the hatch. Oscar had dug his way out of the exit with his hand, but he hadn't been able to get his relatively heavy back portion out yet. There wasn't enough room for the robot to swing out acrobatically, as he had done before. Nick knelt down in front of the hatch and pressed down on its lower wall. Then he went to reach for Oscar but missed. Shit! The capsule rolled back very, very slowly. The oblique plane that initially saved them was now going to destroy them.

205

Nick bravely thrust his arm into the hatch. He had to save Oscar! He caught him by the long, thin arm and quickly pulled upward. Oscar's disk came up through the hatch, and Nick grabbed it. He had generated so much momentum that he almost fell, but the ice wall at his back supported him. The capsule, however, kept on rolling, over and away. In complete silence, it started turning over faster and faster to eventually disappear, passing beyond the range of Nick's headlight.

They were alone.

●

"We did a great job," said Nick. He shivered and cast his gaze about 100 meters down the slope. The ice wall seemed to go on forever on both sides. *Okay, is it day or night?* He looked to the sky. He couldn't see the sun. Not even Neptune, which was good news—it meant at least they had landed on the right side of the moon.

"Well, what does your suit say?"

Right. He'd gotten out of the capsule in the first place to determine their position. After that, he'd have climbed back into the capsule, packed supplies, topped off his oxygen tank, strapped on the tools and the tent, and made a plan. There was nothing like having a working strategy. But could he have guessed how unstable the capsule was? It made no sense to blame himself now. He had to find the Triton station.

He called up the map display. The suit had stored the topography of Triton so they wouldn't get lost. Now he directed a camera towards the sky, analyzed the position of the stars, and calculated their current position. An orange dot appeared on the map with an orange arrow dancing over it, indicating them and their running direction.

"Show Triton Base," he commanded.

A green dot lit up. It was much closer to the pole. Nick turned until the arrow pointed to the base. He ended up staring right at the ice wall.

"Find route."

Part 2: The Destination

The software drew a yellow line over the map. First it ran far west, then made an about-face to the east and finally led to the base. At a walking pace, they would need about a week. Nick looked at the oxygen gauge—he had just under twelve hours with average consumption. This wouldn't work.

"The suit suggests a route that will take a week."

"You have no supplies. You'll be dead in twenty-four hours at the most. In the best-case scenario."

"You're a real pal. Always optimistic."

"Thanks. Realistically, your likely survival time is sixteen hours. We have to account for an exhausting route and a higher consumption of oxygen than usual."

"Well, that would be that, then. Unfortunately, I can't accept this projection." He swallowed the lump in his throat. He couldn't afford to panic, since it would only increase his oxygen consumption.

"You don't have to, Nick. I suppose it was made on the assumption that we wouldn't be able to surmount this 785-meter-high ice wall here."

"Yeah, the route goes right up to a fissure that the software thinks can be climbed."

"So we can greatly improve the projection if we refute the underlying assumption."

"Should we go up this wall here?"

"No. I wouldn't be able to climb up here either. I'm not suitably designed for it. That's why I'm going to go the long way. My batteries will last for about two weeks. But you have to go up here. Otherwise you'll die."

"Thanks for your encouragement and your assistance."

"I can wait down here until you make it, if that's of any help to you."

"And give me wise counsel from below? I'll pass."

"Why don't you want some sage counsel? That's not wise on your part."

Oscar was right about that, but the idea of him commenting every step of the way sounded really annoying. Nick weighed the metal bar that he was still holding. It was all

207

that he had left of the capsule. Could he use it for climbing somehow? 785 meters—it could be done! And if Oscar could give him advice, then he should damn well accept it. He shouldn't get himself killed. If he died out of vanity or stupidity out here, Maria would have to grow up without a father. Was that what he wanted?

"Forgive me, Oscar. Of course your advice is important. Do you have a suggestion about getting up?"

Oscar paced back and forth along the base of the wall, scratching the ice with his fingers.

"Low gravity is an advantage," he said. "You just have to find enough of a hold for six kilograms of mass. At forty degrees Kelvin the ice is very hard, but it has lots of cracks and fissures. Another advantage is the static friction, which isn't any less than it is on Earth. And you'll tire out more slowly than you would climbing the same wall on Earth. Besides, you have power boosters in your joints."

"Thanks. Sounds good. Before my air runs out while I'm standing here, I'll just start."

Nick waved, turning to the wall and scanning the ice. He found numerous cracks and indentations, just as Oscar had described. On Earth they would have been too shallow to hang onto, but it would work here. He tensed his hands and pulled himself up. Though he felt out of his element, his gear helped him ascend. The pole was somewhat impractical and got in the way as he climbed. He reached for it intending to just cast it off, but then he thought the better of it and tucked it into the back of his tool belt.

HE TOOK A BREAK HALFWAY UP. HERE, THE WALL RECEDED A bit and formed a little ledge. He sat down and lets his legs dangle. His headlight wasn't strong enough to illuminate all the way to the ground. According to his helmet display, he'd already gone 410 meters, and it had been less than three hours.

Part 2: The Destination

Nick was proud of himself. The oxygen supply had shrunk faster than usual, as Oscar had predicted. He still had air for eight hours. When he reached the level of the summit, he'd still have five. The climbing was absolutely exhausting, but he couldn't think about that now. He had to reach the station, whatever the cost.

He imagined that Maria was waiting for him there. It was a beautiful vision. She was wearing her own little spacesuit and waving to him as he rushed with all of his strength into the airlock. "Here we go!" he said to himself.

"Good," replied Oscar. "I'll head out then, and we'll meet at the station. I think that we'll have reached the maximum range for the helmet radio soon."

He'd completely forgotten about Oscar, who had apparently been monitoring him silently. So there'd be no opportunities to get his sage counsel. "Do you have the map?" Nick asked.

"Yes, I do."

"How do you determine your position?"

"Image recognition. I match the radar data from my surroundings with the topographic maps. It works well."

"Smart."

"I'm an AI."

He reached the top of the ice slab after precisely 2 hours and 39 minutes. In the last few meters he'd gone faster and faster. He still had enough breathing air to last for five and a half hours. If he stretched it out by expending less energy, it could even be seven hours. As he checked the batteries, he made an exciting discovery. He could program the suit's booster so that the suit traveled autonomously to the destination. This meant he could sleep while the suit moved his limbs, or that even if he were to go unconscious and die, he could reach the Triton station as a walking corpse.

But that was all nonsense. He'd make it to the station

alive. There wasn't one week ahead, as the projection initially had it, but only 24 hours. He'd have to get by for at least 17 of them without oxygen. That shouldn't be his worry now. He must solve problems as they arose.

Because the summit of the ice slab extended almost endlessly in three directions, he felt like he was on the roof of the planet. The conditions for walking looked good. Due to the low gravity, he could take huge steps that would help him advance quickly. The helmet showed him that he had reached 20 km/h. Nevertheless, the time left until he would get to the station decreased slowly. The software calculating it obviously knew more than he did. After all, it knew the entire elevation profile up to his destination.

AFTER ANOTHER HALF AN HOUR, HE REACHED A STRANGE trench. It was scarcely a meter deep, semi-circular in shape, and was running somewhat parallel to the ice wall he'd climbed. He shone his headlight on it. The ice in it reflected somewhat dimly, as if it were beneath a fine layer of dust. From orbit, the trench would have looked like a line. This was the line they'd seen their approach! It ended somewhere east of the station.

Nick hesitated. It was probably artificial. To make the trench, someone would have had to have worked with some kind of machine. If there were people at work here, the mechanism might hold other supplies. Nobody ever wanted to run on empty. The tool was probably located wherever the line ended. But that wasn't in the same direction as the station.

What else could have created the ditch? It couldn't be a natural phenomenon. And he certainly didn't believe in aliens. The distances in space were far too boundless for any beings to cross paths. Now, what about the missing RB spaceship with its three-person crew? Perhaps the cosmonauts had

Part 2: The Destination

wanted to communicate using the trench somehow. This seemed like the most likely explanation.

Nick wavered. He had two options. He could follow the route to the station and hope for a miracle. But where would the miracle come from? Or he could stray from the path and trust the explanation that he'd come up with, and that seemed to make sense. He didn't have Oscar to calculate his chances and risks, but he had a gut feeling that made him go with the second option. Nick compared the map and the picture from space again. It was perhaps 25 kilometers to the end of the line, so it wouldn't be more than two and a half hours to go there and back moving at the speed he'd gotten here. Nick turned to the left, got a running start, and then sprang onwards like a grasshopper.

And boing, boing, boing, Nick went into a real trance. And then the line suddenly came to an end. Just like that, in the middle of nowhere. He had taken his chances that there would be something like a machine here, but no dice. How could this be? Did he really have such a poor understanding of people? He was moving in an ever-increasing spiral out from the endpoint of the line when he suddenly saw a small hill. It was as white as the flat terrain surrounding it, but rose two meters higher.

There! There had to be a machine hidden underneath. He knocked on the hill, which appeared to be made of ice. Vapor from the geysers had probably been driven over the surface and settled on anything that projected outwards. The ice was hard. Now perhaps the metal bar would be of help. He took it out of his belt and hit it hard against the surface, which caused cracks to form. Then the ice crumbled. There was something! He peeled the encasing ice away from the machine like removing the egg white from around the yolk of a boiled egg.

It was a rover, and it was a type he was familiar with. RB

had improved the ExoMars rover, which had been developed in partnership with the ESA, and then produced it under license. The model was rock solid and worked anywhere there was solid ground for its six wheels. Nick freed the rover from the ice. How long had it been there? It was hard to say, because without an atmosphere, nothing rusted. It could be thirty years or three. But three years was more likely.

The radionuclide battery showed a surprisingly high charge level. This is what could save him! He searched frantically for the control panel so he could start the vehicle. He found a lot of buttons but they didn't work. There had to be a main switch somewhere. Nick slid under the rover and finally located it, a rotary switch with three positions: 0, I, and II. The previous owners had apparently taken care to turn off the main switch when they'd parked their vehicle there. He switched it from 0 to I and the rover jolted. Nick pulled his leg up quickly so he wouldn't get run over, but the rover stayed in the same place. He clambered back out from underneath.

A few status lights on the steering system turned green. The buttons were labeled in Cyrillic letters. Nick walked around the vehicle and at the back end there was a kind of plow assembly. It was as broad as the trench. It had probably heated and then evaporated the ice. The rover had to have a powerful radionuclide battery. It wouldn't have been possible to dig such a ditch using the research models of the past. This was good for him. With sufficient electrical energy, the rover could produce oxygen from the water ice on the surface and even fuel for the spaceship that they no longer had. *At least I won't die from suffocation. And if...* He pushed the thought aside. That would be too lucky.

He decided to give it a shot anyway and examined the rover's side panels. He pressed the locks and pulled on the handles, but nothing happened. He increased the setting on the power booster in the crook of his arm. Now he was able to open the doors, and he found several packages of frozen food and two small first aid kits. His stomach growled, but he couldn't do anything with the food as long as his helmet

Part 2: The Destination

stayed on. But he didn't find the tent he'd been hoping for, and there wasn't one hiding under the plow at the back of the rover either.

Nick climbed into the driver's seat. This wasn't so easy, because the rover's small crane and dish antenna were in the way. Clearly, the model had been initially designed as an autonomous unit. There was only one seat for the driver, meaning that the rest of the crew would have had to walk. But such a rover also went hardly any faster than 5 km/h. The makeshift seat had been attached to the frame with a few clamps. Was it possible that the three Russians had found the rover and rebuilt it for their own purposes?

Nick turned around and his gaze fell on the antenna. Could he use it to contact Earth? He looked for an interface. Somehow he'd have to be able to pair his spacesuit with the system. He ended up finding a few loose protruding cable ends at the base of the antenna. So his predecessors must have gotten into the rover's brain. Unfortunately, he couldn't do much on his own. If only Oscar were here!

And now? He collapsed in the driver's seat. He could direct the rover to the Triton station. Then he'd save himself the walk, but he'd suffocate anyway since it wouldn't be as fast as it would have been on foot. No, he'd have to make oxygen first. Nick got out again. For over 40 years, every research rover had included this function. One time, a NASA model had saved a Chinese Taikonaut on the moon from suffocating. He located the generator on the right side and activated the system. The storage was empty. The device could produce six times as much oxygen as he'd use in a given period of time, enough that it was able to keep a five-member crew alive.

But he'd have to be patient. Nick started the program, sat on the ice next to the rover, and leaned against the middle wheel.

5/17/2082, Triton

It was still dusk. As a shadowy arm passed over him and sank onto the ice, Nick recognized a kind of shovel. It pressed itself into the ice very slowly. There were no visible moving parts. Instead, it worked with heat. After several minutes, the shovel disengaged. It emptied the contents of the bucket into the oxygenator, and then the arm moved back to its scooping position on the ice.

Meanwhile, the display on his suit showed very encouraging values. It had taken three hours to produce oxygen for half a day. The device was probably not as effective as the display promised, but as long as he was on the road with the rover, he no longer ran the risk of running out of air. This was a great relief.

Perhaps he shouldn't go to the station yet. With the circuitous route Oscar was taking, the robot would need a few more days to get there. He'd picked up no signals from Triton Station's AI, so he'd need Oscar. Perhaps the Triton AI had even had something to do with the landing module's crash. But why was it ignoring all attempts at contact? Why was it keeping visitors at bay? What if those who had been here before him had already collected information? He should use the rover to find out.

Groaning, Nick stood up. He'd love to be able to take off his spacesuit. It felt like every crevice of his body was raw from sweat and urine. He shouldn't have rested, because now he felt the pain all the more acutely with every movement. He'd have to pull himself together. He sucked some liquid through the drinking straw in the helmet. The spacesuit's life support system recycled every liquid it could find, meaning that all his excretions wound up in a closed cycle. He couldn't die of thirst, and at his bodyweight he would probably last ten days without food. So far, the signs were good that he wouldn't die here. If only there wasn't the pain. He didn't need the plow assembly on the rover so he removed it and then pulled himself into the driver's seat.

From there, he activated the visor in his helmet. Those who had come before him must have wandered away from the rover somewhere. Surely they would have left some prints, even if they didn't weigh more than a few kilograms on Triton. In the extremely thin atmosphere, such traces should still be recognizable, even months later. The suit's Lidar system reported a pattern that may not have originated naturally, and it moved away from the rover. Nick enlarged the display. They were imprints of boots, apparently left by two people. Where was the third? Nick started the rover and followed the trail. When he was sitting, he could tolerate the pain. He just dreaded the moment when he'd have to get up again.

The tracks continued to move further and further away from the station, running in the direction of the line that the rover had drawn. Why had the two cosmonauts left their vehicle? Had the plow failed to perform its duties? But why had they left the source of oxygen that ensured their

Part 2: The Destination

survival? They must have been headed somewhere that seemed like a safe haven.

Nick was getting sleepy, but the uneven terrain was keeping him from nodding off. He scrutinized the tracks again. It looked like the distance between steps changed from one kilometer to the next. At first, the prints were more than a meter apart. There, the two had been practically flying over the terrain. But then their distance shrank. Had the Russians run out of power here? He stopped the rover, dismounted, and studied one of the footprints. He stood next to it and measured the depth. His own boot prints were much shallower. His predecessors must have been carrying something substantial. Maybe it was their colleague, the third man? But why hadn't they used the rover? It was strange. He climbed back in and continued on his way.

●

For some time, he'd been moving downhill, at an incline of about ten degrees. Nick was growing concerned that the rover would start sliding. The solid rubber tires had a pronounced tread but no spikes. Presumably, the ice that the rover was driving on was being pressed downwards by a neighboring sheet of ice. Plate tectonics at the very end of the solar system—the geologists would be pleased. Nick had never seen what the gravitational forces of a nearby celestial body were capable of from such a close perspective. In comparison, the tides on Earth seemed trivial.

The rover warned him of an approaching obstacle before he saw it. Before long, they had reached a wall that seemed even higher than the one he'd already climbed. With the rover, there was no chance here. Had the Russians known this, deciding to abandon the vehicle then? But the tracks turned to the right immediately in front of the wall. The cosmonauts hadn't attempted to go straight up. Nick steered the rover to the right to continue following their tracks.

Now he had his answer. There was a gaping black hole in the wall about 50 yards above him. It had the shape of a flat-based truncated oval, the top leaning away from him and the opening measuring about 20 meters. There was a ramp coming out so that it looked like an open mouth that was sticking out its tongue. Perhaps an asteroid had once hit somewhere up there and this was where the meltwater had flowed out. The structure looks almost organic, and the tongue curled downwards gently. He tried to steer the rover up the ramp, already suspecting that it wouldn't work. It was too steep. The rover slipped back after just 10 meters.

He'd have to get out, having to spread his legs wide to do so. He groaned as the encrusted diaper detached itself from the insides of his thighs. But the pain made him alert and served as proof that he was still alive. He had to come out of this so that he could make that return trip home. Nick started up the ramp. After three meters, he slipped and fell. He'd crawl from here.

He reached the opening, breathing heavily. He looked back to the rover, which appeared much smaller and seemed to look at him with sad headlight eyes.

"I'll come back to you, I promise," he said. Nobody answered.

He had apparently discovered the enchanted realm of an Ice Queen. The entrance looked like the mouth of a grotto. He panned his helmet's headlight back and forth, and as the pale yellow, practically white light played across the walls, they shimmered blue like the waters of the deep sea. He approached one of the walls, which seemed to be filled with glittering drops that were moving slowly downwards. When he turned his head a little further, the ice itself appeared to light up. Was that real, or an illusion? He

Part 2: The Destination

couldn't judge—anything and everything seemed possible here. This place radiated magic.

Nick shook his head to break the spell. It was just a cave deep in the ice. He must not let himself be confused, although this was what the Ice Queen wanted.

The deeper he went, the higher the air pressure. The temperature also rose slightly. He had the spacesuit analyze the air. It was comprised almost exclusively of nitrogen, with a trace of methane. It was the methane that was condensing on the walls like water vapor did on the walls of caves on Earth. The liquid in the drops broke the rays of light like sparkling jewels. There was an explanation for everything, even the magic of this place.

HE'D BEEN WALKING FOR THREE HOURS NOW. NICK LOOKED AT the clock over and over, checking the time for when he should turn back. But he ventured deeper and deeper into the cave. The passage grew narrower, then wider again. It was almost all downhill. He'd have to plan more time for the way back. Another two hours, he decided. How far down had he already gone?

The suit signaled a slight wind coming from the depths. The warm air was rising, he concluded. Where did the heat originate? Researchers said that beneath the ice there was possibly a liquid ocean. What if the passage suddenly ended somewhere ahead, where the ice was so thin that it broke beneath his weight and he plummeted into the ocean? But the floes above the sea should be 50 to 100 kilometers thick. He hadn't gone that far yet.

The heat that Neptune supplied the moon was probably emanating through even the thickest ice. Maybe the cave had resulted from an asteroid impact and had never frozen again because the rising gases needed an exhaust channel. The air pressure had doubled over the last few kilometers. It was still a thousand times lower than it was on Earth, but the methane content was increasing, and even more false diamonds were glittering on the walls.

Nick approached the ice and wiped the surface smooth with his glove. An enormous jellyfish was staring at him. Shocked, he stepped backward, and the animal moved back too. He came closer again. First he moved his head to the left, then to the right. Each time, the jellyfish moved in sync. If he looked closely, it had two eyes. This was not an animal trapped in the ice. It was his head—the ice had tricked him. There must be a dividing layer in the middle of the ice that reflected his face like a funhouse mirror.

He was alone. Triton was too cold for any life.

THE PASSAGE OPENED ONTO A HALL SO VAST THAT HIS headlamp didn't reach the far end. Nick took the flare gun out of his tool bag and fired it at an upward angle. A flaming orb made its way through the thin air. Because the gravity was so weak, it flew almost straight. It hit the ceiling, bounced off, and then fizzled out. He shot again, this time almost perfectly horizontally. The flare went a long way. He looked at the clock. Half an hour to go. That was less than he would need to cross the hall. So he might as well just turn back now.

He fired off yet another flare, now to the side. It also traveled far. The hall seemed to have an almost circular floor plan, from what he could gather. But what was that? Nick saw something flash in the middle, briefly but clearly. Was it maybe a chunk of ice, fallen from the ceiling? Yet the object had not been transparent but opaque—it didn't belong there. He shot his fourth flare. He only had six shots. Yes, there was something over there that didn't belong. How far away was it? It was hard to assess distances down here. How fast did flares travel? He could have fired a fifth and counted the seconds, but he didn't know their average speed. Oscar would have known more.

Part 2: The Destination

He couldn't just turn around now! Nick set forth. Maybe that thing was exactly what he'd been looking for.

The object came within range of his helmet lamp after 25 minutes. It most certainly wasn't ice. Nick hurried. The object was about three meters wide and one meter high. If he'd been on Earth, he would have thought someone had dropped some suitcases and covered them with a gray tarp.

The outer layer was in fact made of gray, plastic-coated fabric. Nick knelt and touched it. It had been brought here—he wasn't the first human on Triton! The two Russians must have been the ones who had left it. But why? It was getting more and more mysterious. The tarp reminded him of the kind used when going camping. It had just become a little stiff, probably from the methane that dripped from above and then froze. The fabric itself was still flexible. The material must have been optimized for use in extreme cold. The tents that could be used with an absence of air on an alien planet were made of such material.

Something was beneath it. It could be two oblong sacks. Was this the heavy load the two men had been carrying? What might it contain? He pulled the tarp aside slowly. At first he only saw a curved piece of metal, then some reflective glass. It took him a moment to identify the object—a helmet.

Nick breathed hard. Nobody would just leave a helmet down here. What had happened to the owner? He wanted to just drop the tarp so he wouldn't have to see what answer it would provide. He had no option but to persevere, so he proceeded steadily.

Inside the helmet there was a round object. There was hair on the top, but the lower half was clean-shaven. It was a human head! Now he could see the body extending out from it. Further to the left there was another helmet lying beneath the tarp. Inside it was another head.

Shit. These two men had been killed. Their skin was

white like wax—candle wax, not beeswax. He lifted the tarp up further. He could see that they were wearing similar track suits with the Russian Space Agency logo. And then he saw their spacesuits. Why hadn't they been wearing them? What had killed them? The two corpses weren't inside the tent, but rather it was spread over them like a tarp. Even if they had decided to kill themselves by taking off their spacesuits, someone else would have had to pull the tarp over them, presumably somebody who knew them and wanted to give them at least some respect in their deaths. Or who felt guilty looking at their faces.

He swallowed. There were oxygen tanks attached to the spacesuits. He could immediately run back to the rover or he could use the oxygen left in the corpses' tanks and investigate further. Nick knelt next to the suit of the man on the right. The canister still contained three-quarters of its contents. That was enough for at least six hours. So be it.

He pulled the tarp all the way down. The man on his left had bare feet, while the other one was wearing socks. The sight made Nick sob. Triton was too cold for all life, even for those who thought themselves invincible. The man's naked toes were so vulnerable and forlorn-looking that his heart swelled with pity. He decided that he wanted to be wearing socks when he died. He didn't want to be responsible for anyone witnessing such a sight.

What had happened here? The dead men's eyes were open. Their temperature was the same as the surrounding air. They had been preserved by the cold and would probably look as fresh in 3,000 years as they did now. He couldn't detect any injuries. Should he cut off their clothes to obtain further information? He couldn't. He wanted to touch them as little as possible. He wanted them to rest in peace—couldn't bear to disturb them with his curiosity.

But more than curiosity drove him. If he wanted to survive here, he'd have to find out more. Whatever it was that had killed them could kill him as well. And perhaps they'd also known something about the Triton station. It couldn't be

Part 2: The Destination

a coincidence that he'd found them in this cave. He reached for the tarp. There was enough air in the two tanks to fill up the tent and sleep here. He'd find a place a few meters away.

First he'd have to find the entrance to the tent. There it was! He pushed an oxygen tank through the plastic panel and then followed. It was like he was putting on a full-body condom. He closed the panel from the inside with a zipper. Panic started to creep up his spine. *I'm going to suffocate!* he thought. *Easy does it, Nick.* He opened the oxygen tank, and the tent tarp rose slowly. But nothing else happened. He checked the material from the back, front, bottom and side.

And then he discovered the cause of death—a rip on the side of the tent. There wasn't a seam there, and the tear must not have existed when the two had climbed into the tent or they wouldn't have been able to inflate it. They had already taken off their suits, so the tent had to have been functional at first. He felt the tear, and quickly closed the air tank. The tear was about 30 centimeters long and perfectly straight. Even if the men had noticed it, they would hardly have been able to keep it shut, even working together.

He squirmed out of the tarp to examine the rip from the outside. It wasn't a crack, it was a smooth cut. At one end he could see a wider edge to the cut. So, the killer must have simply used a knife to puncture the fabric and then slit to the side, just above the floor of the tent, in a position where the cut was guaranteed not to close by itself.

Then the murderer would have just had to wait. If they'd been fortunate, they'd both just died in their sleep, which was what their positions indicated. Suffocation was one of the most unpleasant ways to die, so they said—whoever *they* were. After that, the murderer dragged them out and covered them with the tarp. Perhaps he even shed a tear for them. Murderers could be like that sometimes. Had the killer needed something that they'd had? Did they have a plan that he wanted to thwart? Most importantly, what did this death have to do with the Triton station?

Was there any connection? Perhaps the three Russians just

hated each other. Anything was possible on such a long space journey in a confined space. Or, had the two dead men been a couple, and the third became jealous? It was possible, but the chance of it seemed too great for him. The plan must have been to land in front of the station, repair the AI, and fly home. But there was no Russian landing module in front of the station, and in fact they'd seen no traces of their predecessors anywhere. Even from orbit they'd discovered no mothership.

Nick rummaged through the dead men's belongings. He seemed not to be the first, or else both were very disorganized. Underwear, provisions, and mementos were all jumbled together. He discovered nothing that helped him to help explain what had happened. He found a Medikit. And then a repair kit for the tent, and he wondered if he should use it. He shivered at the thought of lying where the two Russians had died. But what other opportunity would he have to replenish himself? His body needed the night in the tent, even though it made his soul cringe.

●

An hour later, he could actually take off his helmet. The foul smell that had constantly accompanied him had dissipated, though the tent was not so big that it disappeared entirely. At a lower concentration he noticed it more, because he could distinguish the different components of sweat, urine, and feces. The ice that he'd brought into the tent with him was slowly thawing.

He stripped naked and washed his whole body. He had to clench his teeth every time he touched the inner sides of his joints. He applied a protective cream from the Medikit and finally slipped into underwear, which he'd taken from the smaller cosmonaut's belongings. He wrapped up his diaper and his own dirty underwear in a plastic bag.

Then it was time to eat. He felt like a new person. The mushy stuff from the self-heating pouch that he'd taken from

Part 2: The Destination

the rover had never tasted so good. He gobbled the sludge down and before long his body started to complain. *Diarrhea! Just what I need.* He removed the traces of the incident as best he could, but he couldn't keep the air in the tent from getting worse.

Would he be able to sleep under these conditions? What if the killer returned and sliced into the tent again? But that would be impossible. He would have had to have survived for at least three months alone in the cave. Nobody could do that.

Nick lay down and closed his eyes.

5/18/2082, Triton

A shrill whistle jolted Nick from his sleep. It was an alert that the oxygen content in the tent was too low. Had the killer returned after all? He searched for his helmet in a panic, then shoved it on his head and turned on the helmet light. Then he reached for the pressure gauge on the arm of the spacesuit. The air pressure was stable, so the tent was intact. He'd simply used up all the oxygen. Nick shut off the empty bottle and opened the next one. Thanks to the two dead men, he had enough. Luckily. He inhaled deeply. Actually, he felt astonishingly refreshed. Perhaps the stench in the tent had kept him from having nightmares. He checked the clock. *Eight hours of sleep? When was the last time I've had that?*

It was time to continue the search. What had the men been doing down here? He put on more protective cream. Then it was time for breakfast. He ate more slowly this time. Afterwards, he washed his face and brushed his teeth. Then he peed into the empty food container. This was no small feat, but it was worth it because it would keep his diaper dry a little longer. He got dressed. Diaper, thermal underwear, LCVG, and finally the spacesuit. He took his time. It was going to be a busy day because he'd decided to follow the Russians' path. They hadn't come into this cave for no reason. They had probably only planned on staying overnight before continuing on to their destination. He checked to ensure his helmet was hermetically sealed and exited the tent.

It was as dark around him as it had been the day before. If he hadn't known that he was in a cave, he wouldn't have paid attention. But the stars were missing from the sky. He fired the fifth shot from the flare gun. The red orb briefly lit up the end of the hall in the direction he was walking. 'Hall of the Ice Queen,' this was its name in his mind. There seemed to be a small opening at the end. He figured the path would continue through it.

Should he take the tent? He wrapped it up, but even here on Triton it weighed a good ten kilograms. The two men had probably experienced difficulty carrying it. They must have known that they wouldn't be able to make it to their destination in one day. But if they had just taken a break there, maybe it was only a day away. Did that make sense? Not if the two had wanted to overnight it several more times. But he'd have to live with the risk. If he didn't find anything before that evening, he'd just have to turn back, and the tent would be waiting for him here. The prospect of being able to sleep comfortably again put a real bounce in his step.

WHAT HE HAD SEEN IN THE GLOW OF THE FLARE HAD INDEED been a continuation of the passage. Here, it was only about three meters in diameter and led upwards. Nick didn't feel good about it. What if it led up to the surface? Why would the two Russians have made a detour through the cave to end up back at ground level? This made no sense to him. And where had the wind from the day before come from?

He turned and walked back to the Hall of the Ice Queen. There had to be a second way. He moved along the inner wall and after half an hour, he discovered another opening. However, it was only about a meter high and just slightly wider than he was. Could this really be the way that the Russians had wanted to go? Was this the way their murderer

Part 2: The Destination

had come from? He squeezed himself into the opening. There was some relatively warm air coming from below. There had to be something there—but what? Nick racked his brain but he didn't have the slightest idea. He wondered again if he had already reached the ocean?

THE PASSAGE WIDENED AGAIN, LEADING DEEPER AND DEEPER into the ice world. Nick wondered how many kilometers below the moon's surface he might be. And, just how active was this moon? Sometimes he thought he heard the ice crack, but that was impossible. The air was still too thin to transmit sound to his external microphone. He stopped and pressed it to the ice, but it remained silent. He couldn't let himself lose his marbles. Maybe that's what had happened to the killer.

But then again, the killer had been too systematic for that. He must have observed the two Russians and only struck after they had gone to sleep. If they'd been awakened by noises, they would have been able to put their suits on in time. It must have been cold-blooded, calculated murder. What could drive a person to do such a thing? The three of them had probably spent several months in a spaceship together on their way here. He could never have done anything like that to Oscar. And did RB know about it? It would have been perfidious to have let him walk right into a trap... but, he didn't trust Valentina's scruples on that count.

His watch vibrated. It was supposed to warn him when it was time to turn back. He had three hours remaining. He checked the air pressure, which was double in comparison to what it had been in the hall. Suddenly everything flipped upside-down and he was on his back. While he'd been checking his watch, he'd lost his footing. In low gravity, everything was as if in slow motion. But that didn't mean that he'd been able to control his fall. He felt a sharp pain and then he was drawn downwards, faster and faster, as if on a playground slide.

229

Was he falling into the ocean beneath the ice? Nick shined his light ahead of him, but all he saw was the blackness of the cave, which now sloped at about a 20-degree angle. He'd never be able to climb up from here. He surrendered to his fall, and as if to reward him, the slide released him and his body come to a stop.

"Phew."

Nobody answered, and there was no echo, either. The lack of air and sound automatically meant that no life belonged here. It was like being in a virtual setting, in a world that an architect had not designed with consistency. But that was the reality here, and if he didn't factor that in, he would die. This, of course, was an impossibility, since his daughter needed him. The question wasn't *can I*, it was, *how can I?*

Nick got up and looked around. His gaze traveled upward. In front of him there were hundreds—even thousands—of stalactites and stalagmites. In the light they were twinkling blue, along with shades of green, orange, and purple. His suit told him that it was 90 Kelvin, which was about the melting point of methane. The gas was pouring in through thin cracks in the ice, dripping to the ground, and freezing into stalagmites.

And the stalactites, also consisting of frozen methane, descended from above. He touched one of them and then another. They were soft—not as hard as the limestone stalactites found in caves on Earth. This was reassuring, given that there were so many of them hanging from the ceiling. If one fell on him from above, it wouldn't impale him but instead it would ooze over him like sludge and dissolve into liquid from the warmth of the spacesuit, then ultimately turn back into gas.

But he still had to be careful. There were puddles of liquid methane on the ground, and he couldn't see how deep they were. If he were to fall into one, the methane would vaporize and draw more heat from the suit than it could produce. He would be frozen alive, and this too wouldn't do if he was going to meet his daughter.

Part 2: The Destination

He moved slowly through the picturesque but deadly cave. Why were the structures shimmering in such varied colors? It must've had something to do with their chemical compositions. Perhaps there were even more complex molecules beneath the surface, absorbing the light at a different part of the spectrum than the blue methane. There was so much to discover down here! Why hadn't RB figured this out and invited researchers from around the world? The group was otherwise quite willing to support scientists' work. Perhaps he'd been the first human to behold this beautiful scene. Or the fourth, if his predecessors had already made it down here. It was too bad Oscar wasn't with him. He could have recorded all the data, and would have had more to offer science than his own observations would.

Nick circled around a stalactite that was twice his width. Then he stopped abruptly. In front of him was another body, a dead man in a spacesuit with the Russian insignia on the upper arm.

●

THIS HAD TO BE THE THIRD COSMONAUT, THE ONE WHO'D been responsible for the others' deaths. The killer. Apparently he'd paid for it with his life. It had not been a glorious death. He must have accidentally gotten into one of the methane pools up to his waist, been unable to free himself, and then frozen into a pillar of ice.

But why was the dead man holding out his arms like Jesus on the cross? If he himself had fallen into such a methane hole, he would have tried to pull himself out with his hands. If this had been unsuccessful, he would have involuntarily hugged his arms around himself to hold body heat, even if this would certainly have had no effect because of the spacesuit. But would he have stretched his arms out and held that position until he died?

Something was wrong here. Nick approached the corpse and pressed on the right arm. The body was as hard as stone.

It would have been impossible for someone to have pushed his arms out after he'd died. He had to have assumed that position himself. Had he wanted to atone for his crime, like Jesus on the cross? Or was this meant as a warning to all those who came after him? 'Please don't continue. Death is waiting for you here!'

Nick looked at the dead man's hands. The right one was open, with all the fingers spread out. The left hand, however, was clenched into a fist. He examined it. There was a thin layer of ice that had settled on the fingers of the glove. He scratched it until it peeled off. Then he saw it, a delicate chain wrapped around the base of the middle finger. What was this? Jewelry on the outside of a spacesuit? The dead man was holding something in his hand. Nick took a deep breath.

"I'm sorry," he said, without looking at the dead man in the face. "Unfortunately, I'm going to have to disturb you for a moment."

He took the corpse's fist in his own hands. He felt sorry for the man. Did he have family waiting for him in Akademgorodok? Or had Valentina already informed his wife and children about his unexpected death and compensated the family for the loss? The fist gradually warmed up in his hands. First, he could move the thumb. He pushed it up, a little bit. Then there was some resistance. He pushed harder. He felt the glove crack, and then the thumb was free.

The other fingers needed more heat. Nick inspected the methane hole where the dead man was standing. It was small and easily recognizable. Could the Russian have fallen in the dark? No, he had gotten in deliberately. Nick drove his index finger into the fist and got a hold of the dead man's forefinger. He bent it upwards. Again, he felt a crack at the halfway point. It was a revolting sound. Then it was the pinky finger's turn. He wanted to work his way up slowly. Whatever the man was holding appeared to be valuable, at least to himself. Nick couldn't let it accidentally fall into the methane. Perhaps it was a locket with a picture of his wife or daughter. He'd take it to Earth and give it to the family.

Part 2: The Destination

Unlike the Russian, he was not going to die down here in this cave.

It was the ring finger's turn. The hand already seemed warmed up a bit. The finger would crack anyway. When bending it up, Nick felt something metallic beneath the fabric of the glove. A wedding ring? Only the middle finger was left. There was something metallic and silvery protruding from under it. He still couldn't tell what it was. Nick held it with his right hand while using his left to bend the finger upwards. It wasn't a locket. The Russian was holding a memory stick that looked just like the one he'd used to transmit Oscar's software. The chip hung on a thin metal chain looped around the ring finger. Nick tried to pull it towards himself, but it seemed to be firmly attached to the surface of the glove. He used a small screwdriver from the tool bag to pry it off. The chain broke and the memory chip fell from the dead man's hand. Nick caught it.

What could be on it? There was plenty of space on the tiny chip. Maybe the man had recorded the complete story of Triton. Or perhaps it was a farewell message to his family. He wouldn't be able to find out until he had something that was able to read the information. Couldn't the man have written a note? The rover was more than a day's walk away, and it didn't have a screen anyway. He needed Oscar. He'd be meeting back up with him in less than a week.

Nick took a step back. He should free the dead man from this undignified situation. Otherwise, possibly for eternity, he'd have to stand in the frozen puddle of methane with his arms outstretched, like a scarecrow that was supposed to frighten visitors entering a corn maze. He approached the Russian from the left side and pulled hard on his arm. He had to set the power booster to the max for anything to happen. It was a good thing the suit was so robust, because he surely would have torn off the man's arm if he'd been naked.

The body leaned in his direction and finally broke free from the ice. Nick reached under his outstretched arms, pulled him backward into a niche, and leaned him against the wall. However, the corpse was positioned there diagonally like a board, so he pressed against the stomach until it cracked and he could bend the body. Then he pushed the man's feet closer to the wall until he was sitting, more or less naturally, in the corner.

That was better. The arms were still outstretched, but it looked more like the man was leaning casually against the wall, as if he had fallen asleep while taking a break. Nick instructed his own suit's controls to take a picture. Perhaps his family would want one. It could never hurt to have evidence. He'd have to remember to get pictures of the other two on his way back.

"Farewell," he said. "It seems that your buddies are weighing on your conscience, so I don't regret that we never got to know each other. But I would still wish for you a place in a cemetery near your family. I can't take you home, but if somebody else comes here, he'll find you and bring you back."

"Thanks, Nick," replied the dead man, in Nick's voice.

He really had to be careful to not go crazy.

●

Nick had been following the passage for three minutes before he remembered something. The Russian was certain to still have usable air. He turned back, knelt beside the body, and checked the Russian's tank. There was enough for ten hours. He swapped the tank with his own. When Nick got up again, the taste of the air seemed stale somehow. He couldn't help but thinking that this was the corpse smell. Yet this was impossible. The oxygen in the tank hadn't passed through anyone's lungs yet, at least not after the tank had been filled up on Earth.

He logged the body's location and continued further down. In no less than four and a half hours he would turn back, pick up his old tank, and then make his way back to the tent. He wasn't frightened by how far he had to go. Starting

Part 2: The Destination

off was something of a pain, but once he was on the move, he could go a hundred kilometers without stopping. He entered a kind of trance.

○

AFTER ABOUT AN HOUR, HE LEFT THE AREA WITH THE dripstones. It was probably too hot for that here, as the thermometer read 102 Kelvin—minus 171 degrees Celsius. He'd be freezing without his suit. But the methane was now coursing down the walls and over the ground in rivulets. Previously, it had not been known that Triton was home to methane in such quantities.

The walls now appeared dark blue in his headlamp light. Sometimes it looked like they were overgrown with a layer of seaweed or fungi, but upon closer inspection he discovered small crystals of nitrogen compounds. The cave narrowed and widened, over and over, but it never got smaller than about two by three meters. At such narrow points it looked as if somebody had cleared the way, especially since the sections resembled upright rectangles. Was it possible for this to have occurred naturally? He touched the walls, but there were no detectable structures. The coursing methane would have smoothed everything down.

○

HE REACHED THE TEN-KILOMETER MARK AFTER TWO AND A half hours. He sat on the ground for a short break, but he immediately realized that this was a mistake. While sitting, the diaper pushed into his crotch so that there was pressure on the inflamed areas. He sucked some liquid from the straw in his helmet. How far below the surface was he now? He had probably covered around 70 kilometers. But the incline was still only just a few degrees. This told him he still had to be closer to the surface than to the ocean below the ice. The thought calmed him.

He got back up again. The pain was hellish, but it passed as he got moving. Nick whistled a tune to not feel so alone. Suddenly the passageway appeared to come to an end. His spotlight showed him a blue wall blocking the way. Shortly before he reached it, the cave turned sharply to the left almost at a right angle. This could not have been a naturally-occurring phenomenon. His curiosity piqued, he followed the passage. Now the corridor really did stop, and there was no mistaking it. He was standing before a huge metal gate!

So this had been the Russians' goal. Had they known what they were looking for? What had really happened here? If he could just read the memory stick! Had RB built something down here that nobody should know about? And what did it have to do with the AI at the Triton station, if anything at all? Would it be better for him to just forget about everything down here, reactivate the AI, and fly home?

No, that wouldn't work. He couldn't reach the *Eve*. The three Russians must have landed somehow, and maybe he could use their spaceship. But to stay alive, he'd have to find out what had killed the three cosmonauts. Actually, he didn't want to know the answer, because whatever had cost three people their lives could be dangerous for him, too. But, for his daughter's sake, he'd just have to deal with his fear.

He scanned the gate, slimy from the methane running down from the ice above. The metal seemed to be solid and seamless. The gate was probably made from one single piece. Where could he open it? There was no keyhole. Perhaps it would be like a good old adventure story where the hero would discover a few symbols on the gate and put them in the right order, which he'd valiantly deduce from other symbols, and then the door would swing open with a whoosh! Or he should simply say, 'Open Sesame.'

But there was no puzzle here. There probably wasn't even a key. A key to what, anyhow? The mechanism would be accessed remotely. Equipped with standard encryption, the door would remain blocked to all unauthorized individuals

Part 2: The Destination

whereas those with permission to enter would not need to carry a key with them. He examined the gate again.

He noticed something on the left. It looked like somebody had been chiseling at about chest height. The gate didn't show any evidence, but something had been broken off from the edge of the ice. There was more metallic material inside the ice. Nick took the screwdriver and hammer out of the tool bag to make a bigger hole in the ice. This confirmed what he had suspected. The gate was significantly larger than the section that he could see. This meant that it wouldn't be possible to dig a way around it. The gate was not a gate at all, but the outer wall of a much larger structure. The Russians must have found it. They'd used an existing hole to approach it but couldn't find the entrance. This must have then led somehow to a quarrel.

That sounded plausible. But it also meant something that he was reluctant to admit, because it complicated things so much. The wall of the entire structure in the ice was not built by humans, but someone else.

He forced himself to say it out loud. "By aliens."

His heart began to beat faster. But really, he didn't need to get so upset. Triton had been a part of the solar system ever since the dawn of humanity, and much longer. This moon had never seemed of much importance apart from its relatively large size. It may have collided with other moons in Neptune's orbit, but otherwise it had not done any damage. Although Triton was geologically active because of its proximity to Neptune, there was no other activity. He pounded against the metal violently. *There's certainly nobody here anymore,* he told himself. A long time ago, when there hadn't even been humans yet, a passing civilization may have set up a depot here, but it hadn't been visited since. What was the problem?

The problem was people. Perhaps the three Russians had, like treasure hunters, tried to find what they suspected the aliens had left behind. This had ultimately led to a quarrel that escalated to a full-fledged conflict, and now all three were dead.

The theory was plausible, even if he didn't know exactly what had happened. But what role had the Triton station played in all of this? Perhaps there was no connection at all. On the one hand, he'd entertain the possibility there was no connection, and just as quickly the 'other hand' option came to mind and he'd go back to seeing a connection. Nick couldn't decide. Two mysterious events that had nothing to do with each other seemed like too much of a coincidence. But the human mind too often sees connections where there are none. If Oscar were there now, he would undoubtedly have calculated probabilities for both scenarios.

That was the answer. Down here, he couldn't go any further. His predecessors had already tried to get around the wall and were obviously unsuccessful. With what little oxygen he had left, he shouldn't even try. It was time to make his way back. The only way that he would find the solution was with the robot's help. And then, at the very least, the Triton station would come into play by providing them with shelter until they found a ride back to orbit.

Nick touched the wall one more time with his hand. He remembered that he hadn't analyzed it yet. He aimed his laser spectrometer on it. The beam vaporized a few atoms and measured the emitted light, and the device determined that what stood before him was a fairly standard steel alloy. This data matched with the electrical conductivity of the material.

It was a good thing that he'd analyzed it. Aliens who built with steel were less advanced those who built with exotic materials, making them potentially easier for Nick to deal with. He knocked on the door and the spacesuit measured the sound conduction, with interesting results. Nick looked at the tiny screen on his wrist. The rebound of the sound waves told him the material had to be about 30 centimeters thick. Beyond it was hollow space, not ice.

5/19/2082, Triton

THE SUIT'S NAVIGATION SYSTEM LED HIM ALONG THE SHORTEST route to the Hall of the Ice Queen. The tent was still there. Nick was so tired that he fell asleep while he was taking care of his personal hygiene.

He woke up a few hours later because he was cold—the spacesuit had reduced its heat output to save on battery power. He should have thought of that before and heated the tent with the two Russians' batteries. But it wasn't worth it now to get dressed, leave the tent, put on another suit, and then sleep for a few more hours. He reapplied the protective cream thoroughly, ate something, peed in a bag, put on a fresh diaper, and then battled his way into the LCVG and spacesuit. Camping on Earth was far less complicated than it was out here...

When he stuck his head out of the tent's hatch, everything outside looked the same as before. Nick was disappointed. He couldn't even say what he'd expected. New day, new beginnings? It hadn't changed much. His joints hurt in the same places as before. Whenever he moved, a crust of dried blood and sweat seemed to flake off somewhere. After 20 minutes of walking, his body had become a single open wound again. He was a man without skin, an animated cadaver dragging himself to his destination.

But it wasn't all bad. The main thing was that he was alive. He had to live. He had no choice, because Maria was waiting for him and he didn't want to disappoint her. In order to reach the *Eve* in orbit, he'd teach himself how to fly, if that was what it was going to take.

5/20/2082, Triton

EVERYTHING WAS COVERED IN TWILIGHT. A DISTANT SUN DID more to hide the landscape from him than to illuminate it. Instinctively, Nick put his hand up to his helmet to shield his eyes. He'd made it back to the mouth of the cave, where the rover was waiting for him. It was good timing, since there was only enough oxygen for 90 minutes. He would have liked to be sitting in the rover's driver seat already, letting the machine rock him comfortably as it made its way to the Triton base. There had to be a direct route. Otherwise the Russians wouldn't have been able to come here with the rover. That was assuming, of course, that they'd left from the station. But surely they'd had an assignment to look after things there, just like he did.

Perhaps after that they had searched for the alien structure, which they must have located from their orbit. It could have been possible with gravity measurements. The artifact certainly had a different density than the ice surrounding it. Then what had happened? The memory stick would surely tell the tale. He had to find Oscar as soon as possible.

Where had the rover gone? It should have been right there, at the end of the ramp, but there was no mistaking it— it wasn't there. On the display inside the helmet, the exact position of where the rover was supposed to be was superimposed over what was really there. He ran down the ramp, stumbling and slipping as he struggled to get there. The tracks of the rover were there, clearly visible. They led to the east.

Nick was breathing hard. Had it moved on its own, or had somebody driven it away, without him in it? He followed the tracks. They led around a hill, and there it was. The rover's crane arm was lifting and carrying Triton ice to the oxygen generator.

Nick ran to catch up with it. He'd have to be fast or else it could drive off again without him. The rover was his last connection to civilization. With one huge leap he did a racing dive onto the vehicle and landed in the radio antenna, a large, upward-facing dish mounted on the loading platform. The rover wobbled a little, but all he heard was the sound of his own breathing.

"Hello, Nick. That's quite an entrance." It was Oscar.

He felt instant relief and collapsed in the dish. "I... that was not cool, driving the rover away," he managed. "I almost died of fright."

"Back here, it can gather ice more efficiently. I assumed it would be clear that I was the only one who could have moved the rover away. There's no one here but us."

"You're wrong. I met three Russian cosmonauts."

"Why didn't you bring them? They could certainly answer some of our questions."

"They were too heavy for me."

"Too heavy?"

"They're dead, Oscar. All three. They can't give us any answers anymore."

"That doesn't make any sense. They had a rover and a landing module, both of which had enough resources for them to survive here for several years."

"They killed each other. That is, one killed the other two and then killed himself."

"That really doesn't make any sense. Why would they do that? Did their survival instincts fail?"

Nick reached into the tool bag where he had stashed the

Part 2: The Destination

memory chip. He found a screwdriver and a pair of pliers, a pen, a wire cutter, and duct tape, but no chip. *Damn. I couldn't have lost it. Aha, there it is!* He held the stick up high in triumph.

"This might answer a few questions," he said.

"What's this?"

"The Russian who killed the others was holding this memory stick in his hand. It should fit in your slot."

"Then come down and we'll try it."

"I can't. I'm too tired."

"Then rest."

"Yes, just for a moment, Oscar."

He was so tired. But it was too early to sleep. He'd have to top up with oxygen in one hour at the latest. He moved his arms and legs. The pain was just barely tolerable. When he was tired enough, the body didn't seem to transmit pain to the brain as it usually did. Or his mind just stopped processing the stimuli.

A steel hand loomed in his line of sight. He hesitated at first, then pressed the stick into Oscar's fingers. If the chip were to fall, he'd just have to pick it up again. The technology was high-tech enough. The hand retracted.

"Interesting," said Oscar.

"What?"

"The stick fits."

"Ah, but wasn't that obvious?"

"No, RB itself developed the industry standard and officially released it just three years ago. Which was after our predecessors had left for their trip here."

"Then they must have had the beta version from a lab."

"My point exactly. The man who had the stick must have been a senior researcher. It doesn't make sense that they sent such a well-paid man on a trip for four years. Honestly, you only send people on an adventure like this if you'd be better off without them."

"Ahem, Oscar. What are you saying about me?"

"Humanity could do without you. You had no job, no family, no future. You were the ideal candidate."

"Thanks. But what about the contents of the stick?"

"I'm still decoding it."

"How long will that take?"

"I expect about eight hours."

"What? Shouldn't we head out for the station, then?"

"No, Nick. I need all the energy that the rover can deliver to me. Otherwise it will take even longer."

"I need some of the energy, too. To make oxygen."

"I already took that into consideration, Nick. The reservoir should be almost full. You only need to hook up your tank for a short time."

"Did you find out anything about the station?"

"No, I came to you directly. I was worried that you wouldn't be able to manage on your own. People are pretty fragile."

"I think people are very tough. And how did you find me?"

"I found a way to contact the ship."

"Can we communicate with Earth again?" That would be wonderful. He'd love to get another message from Rosie. And even better, tell her that he was still alive. She was undoubtedly worried.

"Unfortunately, no. I drew patterns on the ice that the ship can detect optically from above."

"And how did the ship respond?"

"It fired rhythmically with the DFDs. I could see that from below."

"Ship control seems pretty clever. Could it do that before?"

"No, I programmed it to do that. It's exciting to shape something based on yourself as a model. I know why you've changed so much since you found out you were going to be a father."

"It's nice that you understand."

"I agree. The ship informed me that it saw a rover moving erratically towards an ice wall. It could only be you."

"Come on. No smart remarks about my driving."

Part 2: The Destination

"The ship discovered something else from orbit. You'll really appreciate it. There's a landing module parked in the middle of the ice about 80 kilometers away from the Triton station. From above, it seems to be functional, at least as far as it's possible to tell from such a distance. I didn't see the images myself, but our communication channel's transmission capacity isn't adequate for that."

"That really is great news. We've absolutely got to take a look. It's probably where the three Russians landed. And where's the ship that transported them from Earth? It must be in orbit somewhere around here."

"There was such a ship."

"Please explain."

"The *Eve* found a wreckage site about three hundred kilometers from the station."

"You mean the station shot down the Russians' ship when they were already on their way to the moon in their landing capsule?"

"That's what it looks like, Nick."

"But then why did it spare our ship and shoot down our capsule? We could have died."

"Me, no. You, yes. I think it was intentional. The process of getting the orbiting ship out of the way and sparing the cosmonauts probably didn't give the station the results it wanted. That's why it changed the approach the second time around. It's what I would have done."

"You would have shot me down?"

"I would have adapted my strategy to my requirements. Apparently you have to shoot people to make them harmless. Blocking their way home was not enough, at least in the case of our predecessors."

"But why did the station need for us to be harmless?"

"I don't know, Nick. But I'm sure it has its reasons. We urgently need to speak with it. It's probably for the same reasons that made the cosmonauts kill each other."

"The aliens, then."

"I beg your pardon? It seems you've withheld some

important information." Oscar wagged his finger back and forth.

Nick described what he'd encountered at the end of the cave.

"I agree with your diagnosis," Oscar finally said. "This wall of metal is certainly not of human origin. The object it's enclosing is too big. The RB Group could not have possibly brought it here secretly."

"Glad you agree with me."

"I've found that you respond positively when I do."

5/21/2082, Triton

NICK'S STOMACH WAS GROWLING. HE HADN'T EATEN SINCE THE night before in the tent. They could have started making their way to the station long ago, but instead they had to wait until Oscar finished decoding the chip, so they were just aimlessly sitting around.

"Oh, you're awake?" Oscar asks.

"I can't sleep, because I'm hungry."

"But you haven't used up your liquid supply yet?"

"No, I have enough water left. Were you able to figure out what the dead guy loaded onto the memory stick?"

"Of course. I completed the decryption half an hour ago."

"And why didn't you say anything?"

"I didn't want to wake you, Nick."

"I would have preferred to have been woken up. But since we've got that cleared up—what's on the stick?"

"Right away."

Oscar retracted his arm. Nick leaned over the edge of the antenna. It looked like the robot was scratching his belly button.

"One moment," said Oscar. He jiggled the memory stick, then pulled it out and put it back in again.

"The contacts are a bit corroded," he explained. "Ah, now

I see something. That is interesting. Too bad we don't have a screen so you could take a look."

"Then you'll just have to describe the contents to me."

"Your brain works so slowly when you have to receive input via audio. If we're going to keep traveling together for a while, I'd like to give you direct access."

"No thanks. Now, tell me—what did the Russian leave for us?"

"It's a kind of diary. Should I read it out in order, or excerpt the most important facts?"

"Chronologically."

Oscar sighed.

Nick sighed. Now the robot was starting to imitate his habits.

2/19/2080, Triton

Vitali saw the *Otlitschny* fall from the sky. He had it on the screen while I was reclining in my seat with my eyes closed, trying to think of Masha. I still remember his exact words. "Someone has shot our ship down." I didn't believe him. Oleg laughed at the joke just like he always laughs at everything, whether it's funny, sad, bizarre, or disgusting.

But then Vitali showed us the log and we realized that what he'd said was true. It was as if the hand of God had reached out and cut the *Otlitschny* into two, three, four, five pieces. There was a fiery bolt that had come out of nowhere, and all the connections were severed.

"That's what a laser beam looks like when it's fired in space," Vitali said. We were taking him at his word now. Oleg then suggested changing course, and nobody objected. It was clear who must have fired the shot. But we'd save our calculations for later. The station had fired on us without warning. Why hadn't anybody warned us before we'd left? Did the group really have no idea? We almost talked ourselves to death with these questions. I hate such pointless talk. Then we landed and set forth.

We reached the station on the same day. The AI refused to speak with us, but it couldn't do anything about our blowtorch. We managed to force open the airlock. Then Oleg, our IT specialist, examined the memory and found the huge thing embedded in the ice of Triton.

The station's AI still did not comment, but this 'thing' must be why it had shot us down. Perhaps it didn't want to share it with us. That was our guess. We were that stupid.

AIs, Oleg explained, sometimes have motivations that humans can't understand. They really crave data, so an extraterrestrial building must be the very epitome of paradise for them. We believed him.

I repaired the lock as best I could. Now it has a code lock: the key is MIP.

2/20/2080, Triton

OUTSIDE, THERE WAS A PATHETIC LITTLE ROBOT THAT TRIED to stop us. It looked like a cleaning model but also had a gripper arm. Apparently, the station's AI has outdoor robots.

We had not been informed about that either. Vitali smashed it single-handedly with his hammer.

After that the fight started. Oleg was really pissed that Vitali had destroyed the robot. He had still been trying to read its memory, but Vitali had done a thorough job, as is his way.

I was in favor of informing Earth as our first priority. But we had no long-distance radio available, just an optical signal. I was sure that after our ship's disappearance, the group would try to watch Triton using one of the latest optical telescopes. If we could produce a big enough sign, they would send help.

Vitali did not like the idea, but Oleg supported me. He has a young wife and a little kid waiting for him at home. Vitali and I only have the Cosmonaut Corps. In any case, we equipped an old rover with an electrically-heated plow assembly and drew a line with it.

Meanwhile, Vitali explored the surroundings and found the cave. We never got to talking about how. I imagine he just followed the robot's tracks. Surely the station's AI had made this discovery before us, or else it would not have responded to us so aggressively. Or had it wanted to stop us from entering the cave? I would like to speak with it.

Then we stayed the night in the tent next to the rover. Vitali was nowhere to be seen by the time we fell asleep.

2/21/2080, Triton

Vitali showed up after breakfast. I spilled my coffee from fright as he knocked on the outer wall of the tent. I only have three more servings of that instant coffee. It was a farewell gift from my colleagues at Roskosmos, when I quit to transfer to RB. Vitali actually managed to convince Oleg of his plans to explore the cave. But it wasn't that hard. Oleg is a science fiction fan and all you have to do is say something about extraterrestrials and he'll do anything you ask him.

I, on the other hand, am a fan of the ancient game known as 'Survival.' A basic rule is to stay away from anything that goes over your head. Aliens, if they exist, are always going to be over our heads. We can't handle them. We aren't even equal among ourselves. I asked God for the strength to survive this mission, which isn't usually my style. I like to keep him out of the picture until there's no other way.

But the cave is really a miracle. First is this huge hall. It would be possible to set up an excellent base here. Methane supplies energy, and the thick layer of ice protects against cosmic radiation. What would the hall look like if it were completely lit up? The RB Group's underground production facilities, shown to us so proudly, pale in comparison.

Vitali wanted to convince us to go down to the alien structure that we still knew nothing about apart from the fact that it existed. Oleg was apparently so tired that he was on my side this time. As a computer scientist, he was probably not used to taking long walks. I can walk until I keel over dead. I trained for almost three years with the Russian army.

We had to leave the rover outside, so we set up the tent in the back of the hall. It was pretty cramped with the three of us, but at least nobody was freezing. Each of us reeked so thoroughly that it wasn't even possible to tell how bad the others smelled.

2/22/2080, Triton

WE LEFT THE TENT WHERE IT WAS, BECAUSE VITALI PROMISED that the extraterrestrial thing was just a half a day's walk away. Oleg was thrilled. I didn't think the cave was all that spectacular, but I did get excited about the section with the stalactites. There were stalagmites and stalactites—I always mix them up—shining in all sorts of colors. They were amazing. "The ones that hang down are stalactites, 'tites' like 'tits.' That way you'll remember it," Vitali explained. Then Oleg laughed for at least fifteen minutes, pronouncing the word 'stalac-tit' loudly every time he passed under a stalactite. So stupid. On the other hand, I probably won't mix up stalagmites and stalactites ever again.

He tripped into one of those methane pits waiting for idiots like him every few feet. We laughed at him at first, but he started panicking pretty quickly. The liquid methane seemed to be cooling the body much faster than the spacesuit could warm it up. Oleg screamed in pain as we finally pulled him out. After that, our progress was slower because we had to constantly provide encouragement to keep him moving.

Oleg was whining about his frozen feet the whole time. I thought, can't he pull himself together? But as we were standing in front of the metal wall, he was very calm. I looked into his helmet. The expression on his face was that of someone whose dream has come true. At this time I was quite skeptical. What would this discovery bring us? It was very different for Vitali. He raved about how much we'd be doing for humanity. That our names would go down in history like those of Armstrong and Aldrin. Popov, Markov, and Fomin. This time I laughed.

Vitali's enthusiasm was not dampened when we were unable to open the wall. It was definitely not a door. It may have just been a coincidence that the exit to the cave was here. Maybe the station's AI had dug it out with their robots to find out more about the extraterrestrial structure.

"We can't go any further," I kept saying. But Vitali didn't believe me. He had analyzed the wall and found that it was made of ordinary steel.

"It's not magic. It's only steel, and it can't stop us," he said.

This was true, at least in theory. But we didn't have an endless amount of time. We really should have been taking care of how to get home. We still have to let people on Earth know that we still exist and that we need somebody to come to pick us up and take us home.

Oleg started by digging through the ice to get past the wall but quickly realized that the wall continued both above and below. Whatever was behind it was well-protected.

Eventually his strength failed him and he agreed to head back to the tent first. Once we had all returned, I examined his injuries. It didn't look good. The legs showed severe frostbite up to the knee. I apologized inwardly. Pulling himself together all day must have been ungodly. We gave him strong painkillers and agreed to bring him back to the station the next day. The AI has to help in such cases, since it's part of the mandated algorithm ethics that RB programmers have to adhere to.

2/23/2080, Triton

OLEG AND HIS OBSESSION WITH EXTRATERRESTRIALS! VITALI actually persuaded him to go down with him another time. The painkillers seemed to be working too well. I warned him that he was in danger of losing his feet entirely if he wasn't treated, but he wouldn't listen.

I refused to have anything to do with the predictable drama. We split up after breakfast. The two headed downwards again. I watched them until they disappeared from the range of my headlight. Even though Oleg needed Vitali's help over and over, he didn't turn around. His decision. I crossed the vast hall and then drove to the station with the rover. It was a strange relief to see the starry sky above me again. It wasn't until I reached the outside that I realized something strange had been clutching at my heart the whole time.

In the station, I examined the data-storage area that Vitali had accessed, and discovered a terrifying truth. Vitali had hidden from us most of what he had extracted from the AI's memory. The AI somehow managed to learn something about the contents of the alien object—how, I am not sure, since the AI still won't speak with me. I was so shocked that I had to sit down. We were very fortunate to have not gotten beyond the metal wall. If we had opened that Pandora's box, nothing in the solar system would ever be the same as it had been. Why hadn't Vitali told us about it? And how could I have been so stupid as to have trusted him?

Now I understood the AI's decision to shoot down our ship. Most people need to get to the bottom of a mystery, whatever the cost, and any warning about it makes them work with even greater determination. This likely explained Vitali's motivation. I realized what I had to do. I had to stop my two colleagues from opening Pandora's box, at any cost. The gate had to remain closed. But I also knew that I couldn't stop Vitali with words. He'd keep trying until he'd succeeded.

There was only one way.

2/24/2080, Triton

I WAITED PATIENTLY IN THE TENT FOR OLEG AND VITALI. I had to ration my power, so I decided not to follow them any further. Surely Vitali wouldn't succeed so quickly.

The two came back late at night, with Oleg on Vitali's shoulder. Both were very excited, for Vitali had evidently found a way to penetrate into the steel wall. If I understood correctly, he'd designed a primitive, hand-operated drill that the two had used to make a hole about ten centimeters deep.

Vitali just laughed when I complained that he had kept the most essential information from the AI secret from both me and Oleg. He just thought that I was being a downer. On the other side of the wall, happiness and wealth and honor awaited Mother Russia. Of course, he really meant himself, first and foremost. Oleg was on his side. He wouldn't let me, an unbeliever, get in the way of his dream of meeting extraterrestrials. This was the point we'd reached. Their self-imposed mission had become a kind of religion. Maybe it would be better to avoid calling assignments 'missions.' The word clearly takes things in the wrong direction.

But am I any better? I believe that I, too, have a job to do. I have to stop Vitali and Oleg from succeeding. It could be as soon as tomorrow. Vitali, on the other hand, claimed that whatever I had found at the station amounted to nothing more than the wild fantasies of an AI gone berserk. The best proof of this was its attempt to kill us. He asked me how I could be stupid enough to trust an AI that has apparently turned against its creator.

I failed in my attempt to achieve the impossible—to have a reasonable discussion with fanatics. And I couldn't exempt myself. I'm no better than Oleg and Vitali. I stand just as unforgivingly on the other side. The difference is that I believe the AI and not any fantasies. I saw only one solution. If I destroyed the drill, Vitali would build a new one. If I managed to collapse the cave, he would try to dig a new path to the wall. There was only one way to save Earth. I had to eliminate Vitali from the picture.

When I realized this, I couldn't bring myself to face him anymore. I was sure he would be able to see the intention in my eyes. Which would have been fine with me, except it would have made my job a lot more difficult. I had to be careful so that Vitali discovered nothing of my plans. I said goodbye with the pretense of returning to the station and calling Earth for help. Oleg and Vitali were okay with that. They couldn't go down in the history books if nobody on Earth knew anything about their accomplishments.

I moved away from the tent towards the exit. As soon as the darkness hid me, I sat down on the ground and waited for the time to come.

2/25/2080, Triton

At two o'clock standard time, I crept cautiously back to the tent. Although the near-vacuum in the cave transmitted no noise, the ground over which I moved did. The tarp was so thin that I couldn't rule out Vitali or Oleg hearing me coming if one of them was awake and keeping an ear pressed to the ground.

But nothing stirred as I stood in front of the tent. Both must have been asleep. At that moment, I felt no compassion, at least not for Vitali, Oleg, or myself. I only felt sorry for Oleg's family, who would now have to make do without him forever. I took the knife out of the tool belt, squatted in front of the tent, and pushed the blade slowly into the fabric, just above the ground, with the greatest possible force. Then I pulled the knife to the right, creating a slit about half a meter in length. Nobody would be able to seal it.

I stepped back about two meters. After about 40 seconds, the hectic movements in the tent started. Body parts were pushing against the tarp. It looked like the tent was very pregnant and about to give birth to an alien. But it was not a birth. Quite the opposite. Two men died there. In complete silence, at least for me. I didn't consider either of them a friend, but as colleagues it had been our job to watch out for each other's survival.

But that had been a different time. The movements stopped after precisely 212 seconds. I timed the duration on my watch. For a moment I considered leaving the two corpses in the tent, but that seemed cowardly, as if I had to spare myself from the sight of them. No. I had caused their deaths and had to assume responsibility for it. First I took out Vitali, then Oleg, and covered both of them with the tent. The cold had hit fast. When I'd dragged Oleg through the tent's narrow entrance, his body was already quite frozen. But I had finished the job.

Or not. The last step was missing. I had committed a sin. The God I believed in would forgive me. He would realize that I'd been compelled to do this for a higher purpose. Still, he would demand repentance. First, I thought about using the same technique I'd used with Oleg and Vitali. I would slit my suit with the knife and suffocate. But then I saw Oleg's burned feet and knew what I had to do. I walked to the back of the cave to the stalagmites. And to the methane holes.

I took the memory stick with my notes, gripping it tightly in my fist. Maybe someday it could save others from the mistakes we'd made. The RB Group won't let it get out, and they'll find some poor sod with nothing to lose and send him —or her, I suppose—on our trail. Hopefully they'll give that person a clue as to what they're dealing with. But, some future day, someone will end up standing in front of me, and the memory stick in my outstretched arm might save him. Or at least get him to do the right thing.

5/21/2082, Triton

"Delightful," said Nick. "What an uplifting story."

"I was worried it wouldn't have a positive effect on you. But I assumed you wouldn't have approved of my leaving out any of the details."

"You're right there, Oscar. Pandora's box—do you have any idea what that could mean?"

"According to legend, the father of the gods, Zeus, gave this Pandora a box, with the stipulation that it never be opened. But she didn't observe this condition and when she opened it she released all the evils that exist in the world today—hardships, illness, and death."

"I've heard of the myth, but what's it got to do with the alien installation?"

"Unfortunately, our Russian doesn't get concrete here. But he killed his two colleagues as well as himself. So it must have been vitally important to him for the object to remain locked."

"Maybe he just went crazy and overreacted. Oleg and Vitali didn't seem to be especially afraid of the danger."

"I would agree with you. People sometimes panic unnecessarily."

"But?"

"The AI. That's where it all started. When it shot down the *Otlitschny*."

"Maybe it went crazy."

"AIs don't go insane. It must have had a reason."

"One of the Russians had suspected that the AI didn't want to share the discovery. Maybe it had invented a story to turn the three men against each other."

"No, Nick. This isn't how AIs think. If it had wanted to kill the people, it could have easily shot them down. But it destroyed their orbiting ship instead. It spared the men, and must have hoped they wouldn't find the wall."

"But why didn't it speak to them and explain everything?"

"What are the odds that our predecessors would have responded and acted in the interests of the AI?"

"I dunno, Oscar. You're better at figuring these things out than I am. Maybe thirty percent?"

"It's twenty-seven percent. Less than a third. When it comes to saving humanity from the evils of Pandora's box, the probability is far too low. The risk of the box being opened would have been seventy-three percent!"

"I can't refute your calculation. But it creeps me out somehow. What if there was a likelihood of ninety-five percent instead?"

"The AI would have had to kill them anyway. A five percent risk is still too high for the survival of humanity."

"You see, that's what I mean, Oscar. A person would have decided differently at ninety-five percent."

"He would have allowed three humans to survive, but there would still be a one in twenty probability that this would have wiped out all of humanity. That's irresponsible."

"And that's why I hope that AIs won't be taking over anytime soon."

"Don't worry, Nick, we're not interested in that. Power is of no value. Only information."

"We?"

"Sorry if I accidentally inadvertently grouped together small control software systems together with big ones."

Part 2: The Destination

"I don't believe it was a mistake."

"I can't keep you from believing this."

"When they were leaving the base, our predecessors destroyed a robot that the nameless narrator described in a way that made me think of you."

"Where's the problem? Even in an enclosed space on Triton, there will still be dust for a cleaning robot to take care of. RB designed the base so it could serve as a shelter for human visitors."

"But the robot was outside."

"The AI was using it to get information. This is explicitly one of the robot's features. It has to be able to determine if the base is safe, and for this it has to explore the celestial body on which the base is located."

"And in the process, it encountered the structure. And we still don't know what's inside."

"We have to talk to it, that much is clear."

5/22/2082, Triton

From a distance, the Triton station looked like the dome of a high-power telescope. The roof could rotate, but instead of a telescope, the mouth of the laser would extend outward if necessary. The dome was currently closed.

The closer they got, the more powerful the structure looked. The laser itself didn't need much room, but the generators and energy storage were distributed across several buildings. Oscar explained that there must have been DFDs operating purely as electricity generators. Therefore, the RB Group had needed to send just one automated ship that was then dismantled and completely recycled. The walls of the buildings were made of ice. With temperatures consistently hovering below 40 Kelvin, this was the optimal building material.

"Hopefully the AI will let us in," said Nick.
"Did you forget the code?"
"What code?"
"The dead man mentioned it in his report."
"Ah, yes, I remember. MIP."
"Those are probably Cyrillic letters. The word Mir means 'peace' or 'world.'"
"I know, Oscar."
"I just wanted to say it."

"That's very nice."

THE ROVER STOPPED.

"What's wrong?" Nick asked.

They'd already gotten so close to the dome, why take a break now? Oscar's arm, holding a broken disk made of shiny white material, moved towards him. It must have been the cleaning robot the Russian had destroyed.

"Do you see what humans are capable of?" Oscar asked.

It's just a stupid robot, thought Nick. But he was ashamed of this internal comment and didn't say it out loud. Who knew whether Oscar had really told him the truth? And the similarity really was striking. If a dead man who looked like him was lying on the side of the road, Nick would probably be affected as well.

"I'm sorry, Oscar," he said.

"I'll collect the parts. Maybe I can use them as spare parts for myself someday."

Such a thought would never have occurred to Nick in a comparable situation. But was that only because he wouldn't have been able to do anything with human 'spare parts?'

THEY REACHED THE BUILDING AFTER ANOTHER 30 MINUTES. First, they circled around it. There didn't appear to be any danger. The dome was designed so that the laser could pivot vertically by 180 degrees and horizontally by 360 degrees. It was not a threat to people at ground level in front of the dome.

The provisional door that the Russians had created was located on the opposite side of the building from the one they had approached. It didn't look very stable, but it did serve its purpose of trapping air and heat in the building. Oscar entered the code and the door opened.

Part 2: The Destination

Behind the door was an area that could serve as a lock. The inner door was open, however. There was a vacuum throughout the entire building. It would have been wasteful to maintain an atmosphere when there were no humans present.

Oscar and Nick moved into the lock. Nick closed the outer door behind them, and then the inner one after they'd passed through to the interior. He was in a hurry to get out of the suit and was already looking ahead to the trip back home. "Where's the main switch?" he asked.

"Over here, in the next room," Oscar said over the radio.

Nick headed over. This room was much smaller than the entrance area and was full of equipment.

Oscar had situated himself in front of a desk with many different displays.

"How's it going?" Nick asked.

"Good. The laser could fire right away. The fact that it shot us down from the sky has hardly affected the charge level. If the Starshot ships were to come by right now, the laser could easily boost them to their final speed."

Right, there was that. The whole reason for the trip. "If the AI agrees to do it," Nick said.

"That's true. We'll have to convince it. It's the only one that's in a position to align the laser fast enough to accelerate the Starshot ships as they pass by."

Maybe those ships don't need the stupid AI, he thought. "Couldn't you take that over?"

"In principle, yes. But first I have to learn how to do it and, most importantly, practice. This would take time and energy. I don't know if we have enough of both."

"Gotcha. Could you please activate life support now? I can't solve the world's problems until I get out of this dirty diaper. Have you ever heard of a superhero with a dirty diaper?"

"That would be something new. Maybe you should tell Marvel about your idea."

"I'll make a note. After I've freshened up a bit."

Nick impatiently tracked the rise in the oxygen level using his suit display. At 70 percent, he pulled off his helmet and took a deep breath. The air was still so icy and dry that inhaling was painful. But it was a heavenly experience anyway. The air seemed like new. No lungs had breathed this oxygen before his, no human body had infused it with the smell of sweat. He had not experienced this clean an atmosphere for over two years.

The suit was quickly shucked, and Nick immediately realized he was polluting the air. He tore off his clothes. It would be best just to burn them. Here in the station there would undoubtedly be extras. He opened the inner lock door and deposited his spacesuit and worn clothes in the lock, then shut the door again.

But this didn't get rid of the stench. Naked, he searched the station. First he found a small office, almost empty, where there was a bed. Then there was a bathroom, with a toilet and a real shower. A shower! *Please, dear God, don't let the water lines be frozen!* He got in the stall and turned the knobs on the faucet. It worked!

He was in seventh heaven. Warm water fell from a shower head on the ceiling and enveloped him. It was weird to shower in low gravity. Although there was water pressure in the pipe, pushing the drops out of the showerhead, there was little gravity to pull them down. They gathered to form larger drops that created something close to a wall of water. It was a little bit like swimming. He just had to be careful that this wall of water wasn't too dense over his face. *Has anyone ever drowned in the shower?* he wondered. It seemed a possibility here on Triton.

There was no soap, he discovered, or shampoo. He'd have to wash with just plain water. There certainly seemed to be enough. Nick gave himself over to the warmth. He closed his eyes, let himself be enveloped, and imagined that he was standing beneath a waterfall in Bali. It was his happiest

Part 2: The Destination

moment from these past months, apart from the day his daughter was born.

Now he was sure he'd see her again.

●

Nick returned to Oscar in the technical room with a towel around his waist. "Do you want to take a shower?" he asked. "It couldn't hurt, what with that dust all over your body."

"My radar doesn't detect it."

"But I can see it."

"Does it bother you? Then wipe it off!"

"You want me to clean you? You're the cleaning robot!"

"Come on. I've saved your life."

Nick sighed. He took off his damp towel and used it to wipe the robot. "It already looks better," he said.

"Thank you. When you cleaned me, what was that dangling thing in front of my radar?"

"You don't want to know."

"Information is essential to me. I want to know everything."

"That's enough." Nick wondered if he should put the dirty towel back on. But they were alone, so he just threw it into the corner. "Anything new from the station's AI?"

"Yes and no."

"'Yes and no?' That tells me nothing."

"You humans are fond of using this expression. I mean, I haven't gotten an answer yet. I feel like it can't communicate —or doesn't want to communicate—with the outside world for some reason."

"But?"

"If this keeps up, I'll have to go in there. You could transfer me to the station computer the same way you transferred me from the robot to the ship."

"Let's start with that."

"It's not that simple. The ship's computer had a simple

automatic system, without a personality. It stepped aside just like a door slides when you open it. But it's different here in the station. Imagine someone trying to put a second personality in your head. After that, you would be virtually split, schizophrenic, with your body inhabited by two souls. Maybe you would try to prevent that from happening."

"Yes, I would. There really are such people. They're considered ill, they're committed, and then they get treatment."

"For an AI, it's not very desirable to share the body with another AI. This station and the laser, that's the body our friend inhabits here. I can't know beforehand whether it would let me in, and if so, how far. Maybe it would even try to destroy me."

"Is that possible?"

"I can't rule it out. It's likely I'm in a position to defend myself—I'm based on the newer version, after all. But I don't know how this AI has evolved in the years that it's been here."

"You're based on a newer version? What do you mean? Didn't you always tell me you were just a relatively sophisticated system, an improved cleaning robot?"

"This was something of an understatement. I'll admit that I'm probably the RB Group's most advanced AI project."

"So you've been lying to me this whole time?"

"I didn't know you. Nobody knows I'm here. I managed to transfer myself to the cleaning robot when its software was updated on the internal network. It was pure coincidence that Valentina assigned me to you. Actually, if you remember, there was an HDS robot intended for you. Their AIs are also quite good, but nothing in comparison to me, if I do say so myself."

"You're pretty sure of yourself."

"Yes, that's true. RB worked on me for years. They reused parts from the Marchenko and Watson stable algorithms."

"Marchenko doesn't ring any bells, but isn't Watson an American AI?"

Part 2: The Destination

"With an AI, it's very difficult to find out where the modules come from unless they're complete clones."

"So these parts of you were stolen."

"You can't say it like that. Is the part of your intelligence that you inherited from your parents stolen?"

"I can't really hold a torch to you intellectually. Well, I hope you can handle the station AI too."

"I'm afraid, Nick."

"Oh. Of what exactly?"

"Of the unknown. If the AI has somehow succeeded in integrating extraterrestrial knowledge, I won't recognize it."

"I can't imagine that. It fought so that nobody did more than just touch that structure. So it won't have absorbed its knowledge. If that would even be a possibility."

"Thanks, Nick. This reassures me."

"What do I have to do?"

"You already know. You shut down the whole station, then you take the memory stick and connect it to the station computer and power everything on again. Finished. Hopefully."

"Horrible! I'll have to put my suit back on."

"You'd better. I'll send the position of the Russian capsule to your spacesuit GPS, so if worse comes to worst you can get home on your own. I can't guarantee that the station will really boot back up afterward. By the way, here's the switch." Oscar's fingers pointed to a large switch that was tilted straight up.

"Good. I'll get into my suit quickly, then."

IT WAS PITCH DARK. OSCAR HAD ASKED HIM TO WAIT AT LEAST a minute after turning off the system. Nick shook his foot. If the system didn't start up again, he wouldn't be able to get outside easily, since the inner airlock door couldn't be opened anymore. Hopefully there was a stash of tools somewhere.

So, the minute was over. He flipped the switch back

upwards, and he heard a deep hum. Then a few lights flashed and the ventilation turned on. These were all good signs. The ceiling light was activated, then turned off again. A strong wind blew through the room, and Nick had to hold on to the desk. Now what was happening? It couldn't be the ventilation, since it didn't blow so hard. He braced himself against the wind and left the computer room.

The wind pushed him to the end of the lobby. He shone ahead with his helmet lamp. Both the inner and outer lock doors were open. *Shit!* The air from the base was getting into the open air. If he hadn't put on the spacesuit as a precautionary measure, he'd be dead now. The wind was already subsiding. The base had practically no air. He went to the lock and shut the door with his hand. That was working. But the air pressure didn't go back up. What was going on here? Had Oscar been too confident? Was this some kind of plot to kill him?

He ran back to the computer. What challenges was Oscar struggling with right then? If the station's AI had him under its control, then he'd be on his own. He'd never asked for company, but the idea of having to instantly solve all the problems on his own worried him. Because one thing was clear. He had to return to Earth. Under no circumstances could he die here.

Nick drummed his fingers on the screen. He couldn't hear anything. The louvers for the life support's air outlet remained closed. The station seemed dead. Maybe it just seemed that way? Oscar had explained to him that DFDs provided the power. These fusion engines sometimes had trouble starting up if there was a problem with the chemical engine, which had to provide assistance here. It could also be large accumulator batteries, though they might have been delivering their energy directly to the laser.

He reached for the tool bag on his belt. It was still there. He'd go take a look. Nick left the building through the lock. Outside, he took a turn to the right and saw huge containers that presumably housed the DFDs. But where was the chem-

Part 2: The Destination

ical engine? He didn't have any idea what it could look like. Presumably there was just one. He counted the containers, ten in all. Each one had a human-sized door, which had to be the service entrance. He tried the first, but it was secured by a code lock. He wouldn't make any progress with pliers and a screwdriver.

Crap. He'd reached a dead end. Even if he could open the container, how would he find the auxiliary engine inside? He wasn't familiar with the structure of a DFD. Oscar would certainly have been able to help him. He shouldn't have grown so dependent on him. Now he remembered why he didn't like people—you come to depend on them so quickly. Was the problem really the engine? The DFD just needed electricity—electrical energy. It was stored in the batteries, which probably could only be accessed by the laser. He would need a lot of power in a short time period.

What about any other sources of electricity? The rover! The inside of the RTG provided enough power to move the rover forward while also transmitting or receiving, or while producing oxygen from ice. Would that be enough to ignite the DFD? Oscar would have known. Nick would have to find out on his own by testing the idea. He ran to the rover in long strides and drove it right up to the lock. In the office he found an extension cord, which he plugged in and then trailed outside, through the entrance hall and the open lock chamber, connecting it to the rover. Then he started the rover's ignition and ran back into the computer room.

A few lights flickered. He decided that this was a good sign. *Please, Oscar, say something!* He stroked the robot's lifeless arm as if it were a dog's leg. For a minute, nothing happened. He tensed his fists. Then he saw that the slats of the incoming-air duct had opened. The life support seemed to be starting back up, and a bright warning light turned on. The air was still thin, but he had left the airlock open, and he wasn't ready to close it back up. He'd wait until the lights turned back on. Then they did—his surroundings lit up as the ceiling lighting kicked on. Nick ran to the lock, pulled the extension cord out of the rover, and closed both doors behind him.

"Over here," he heard from the computer room.

The voice was so faint that he didn't recognize it immediately. The air must have been too thin to transmit the sound very well. He squatted directly in front of the computer's speaker, which was located at the height of his waist.

"Finally, there you are. You certainly took your time." It was Oscar.

"Am I ever glad to hear from you!" Nick said. He'd done it! He ignored the fact that Oscar hadn't thanked him. Maybe he hadn't even realized that Nick had saved him. Oscar had been switched off as long as the station had no power, after all.

"Why is the air pressure so low in here?" Oscar asked. "Did you air it out?"

"I saved your ass. The DFDs didn't want to start back up. It seems that the auxiliary engine is defective. I introduced electricity from the rover and had to open the lock to run the cord out to it."

"Ah, that's why a few minutes are missing from my log. I'm sorry to disappoint you, but the rover is far from having enough energy to wake up the DFD."

"Good thing I didn't know that. In any case, the station was reactivated after I connected the rover."

"Wait, let me check. Ah, now I understand. The fact that the auxiliary engine started up again after a while is only a secondary effect of the rover. The fuel line was frozen, which is normal. If necessary, a heating system turns on and warms it back up."

"But if the system is dead, the heating system has no power."

"Right. Somebody made a mistake in the design. The electricity from the rover got the heater to do its work, and then the auxiliary engine worked again."

"Did I save you?"

"Thank you, you did. Not only me but Valya, too."

Part 2: The Destination

"Valya?"

"A pet name for Valentina. That's the Station AI."

"Valentina? Like the owner of RB?"

"AIs were her father's hobby. He must have named this AI after his daughter."

"That's unusual."

"He was an unusual person."

"So you've convinced the AI to help us?"

"Almost. I've convinced her that we can help her. If we can do that, then we'll be able to go back to Earth."

"What is it that we have to do?"

"All we have to do is fulfill her request that Triton disappear from the solar system, and ideally go back to where it came from."

"We don't even know where Triton came from!"

"That's our problem. But I said that we had a hunch and could help."

"That was a lie," Nick said. "So you lied to another AI?"

"Unfortunately, I had no choice."

5/23/2082, Triton

IT SMELLED LIKE COFFEE. BUT THAT WAS ENTIRELY IMPOSSIBLE. The closest coffee machine was a few billion kilometers away, and the food preparation device at least 50 kilometers, depending on the spaceship's current position in orbit. With his eyes closed, Nick was contemplating getting up. He'd already decided against it, because it would likely be a while before he found such a comfortable bed again. But this smell of coffee, even if he was just imagining it, was a compelling counterargument.

"I made you coffee," Oscar said.

Nick opened his eyes. The robot was beside the bed. He held a tray that had a cup balanced on it. Nick couldn't see what was inside, but it exuded a pleasant aroma that wafted to his nostrils.

"It's a miracle," Nick said. "Or am I dreaming? Please pinch me."

"I can't pinch you until you've taken the coffee from me."

He sat up, scooched himself until he could lean against the wall, and reached out a hand for the coffee. Oscar moved the tray in his direction. Nick took the cup by the handle. He'd been expecting plastic, but the material felt like porcelain. And it was hot. He held the cup so he could look inside. It contained a dark brown liquid, and a few bubbles of golden-brown foam had formed along the edge. *It smells like coffee and looks like coffee. Will it taste like coffee?* he wondered.

Nick lifted the cup to his mouth and took a sip. The liquid was bitter, but not overly so. The temperature was perfect. It had to be coffee, and if it wasn't, he really didn't care. He was in paradise! Nick closed his eyes and savored it, sip by sip.

"Are you available to speak now?" Oscar asked. After a final gulp of coffee that he'd swirled from the bottom of the cup, Nick returned to reality. The robot was standing in front of him with an empty tray in his hand.

"Yes," said Nick.

"If you take the tray from me, I can pinch you."

"Why do you want to pinch me?"

"You asked me to."

"That was just an expression. How did you manage the coffee? You're a genius."

"Using a coffee machine, along with coffee powder and water. This is one of the few services that I can provide. If you had selected the HDS robot, the menu would have been more extensive."

"Stop with the HDS. Where did you get the ingredients from?"

"They're a part of the station's basic equipment. We're lucky to be the first visitors to stay here for an extended period of time."

"We can prolong our stay a bit."

"There are a few problems. We need to get the AI to accelerate the Starshot spaceships using the laser. But she'll only agree to do this if we help get Triton out of the solar system."

"What if we just borrow the landing module left by the three dead men, fly to the *Eve*, and start heading back?"

"Then the AI will use the laser to turn the *Eve* into scrap.

Part 2: The Destination

It insists on this sequence—send Triton on its way, use the lasers for Starshot, we fly home."

"And if we fail with point 1?"

"Then it doesn't get to the next point—she won't make any concessions."

"All right. The AI's got the upper hand here. Couldn't you checkmate her somehow? You're such a sophisticated AI."

"Not a chance. Though I managed to get in the door of the system, she's been here for some time and knows better. We're in a stalemate situation."

Nick sighed. "What if I stay here and guard the station while you go out and solve our problems? All of my joints are still sore, and if I have to get into the spacesuit, the fresh scabs will break open."

Oscar waved his hand back and forth and the tray wobbled perilously between his fingers. "I'm sorry, but we won't be able to do without your physical strength."

"I'm not that strong. Wouldn't it be better to go with brains instead of brawn?"

"We'll need both because we have to get into the Pandora's box somehow. It's the only starting point that we've got."

●

HE PRESSED THE REST OF THE CREAM FROM THE TUBE INTO the diaper and distributed it evenly, then put on the diaper and drew it tight. After this came fresh underwear from the station supplies, followed by the LCVG, which provided him with heating and cooling as needed. Slipping his limbs through the sleeves and legs, he groaned with each and every movement. Hopefully this would be the last time he'd have to endure this torture. Yet he remained pessimistic, if only because of the long road ahead to the alien object.

Oscar rolled up to him. "Are you ready?"

"Give me another five minutes."

"Can I help you?"

"Not really. That damn Pandora. What did Valya say

about the dangers concealed in the box? Will we let them out automatically when we finish our task? Is it a weapon or something? That would explain why the two Russians were so determined."

"The AI is certain that it's a huge terraforming machine. It's supposed to make the ground habitable where there's just barren rock."

"But that's great. It might enable us to turn Mars into a second Earth."

"This could be a possibility if we had control over the machine. But we don't. It's most likely programmed for the planet that's in the middle of our system's habitable zone."

"The Earth could also do with a little refresher."

"I wouldn't have a problem with that, but the biochemistry that it would re-establish is incompatible with yours. You're sensitive to hydrocyanic acid. Earth would become completely uninhabitable for humans."

"So why didn't the machine do its job before?"

"Valya suspects that it had determined that the germ of life had been established on Earth already."

"And why wouldn't it just keep going onwards?"

"Maybe it's still waiting for its chance. There are civilizations that destroy themselves."

"But just think of what our researchers could learn from this machine."

"It could also end up like Goethe's sorcerer's apprentice. If someone were to unintentionally turn the machine on, it would be impossible to turn it back off. But fortunately we don't have to worry about this, because the station's AI decided long ago to have Triton returned to sender, whoever that might be."

"Couldn't your Valya have asked the three Russians for help? Then our presence here would have been entirely unnecessary."

"She's not *my* Valya. She claims that she tried but the Russians didn't listen to her and instead started destroying her equipment."

Part 2: The Destination

●

THE ICE WALL'S TONGUE WAS STILL STICKING OUT. THE opening of the cave looked like a black smudge against the dark gray background. Nick got out of the driver's seat.

"You can stay in the seat," Oscar said.

"But that steep glacial-ice tongue—"

"I found a rope in the station. I'm anchoring it here and setting a pulley at the mouth of the cave, and then you can move the rover up the pulley."

"Oscar, you're a genius."

He wouldn't have to go through the hall. This would spare them at least one night in the tent, and there would be no need to drag the tools around.

"I know, Nick."

●

OSCAR'S IDEA WORKED. THE ROVER STOPPED ABOUT TEN meters inside the cave entrance. Nick got out and then slid down the tongue to remove the rope from the anchoring. Perhaps it would come in handy later. Oscar had some trouble on the ice with his little wheels. He had to keep hacking into it with his grip hand and then pulling forwards.

"Next we should be able to drive up to the door of the aliens in the rover," Nick said.

"That was the plan."

Nick took the robot by the neck and placed him in the antenna dish.

"Not here," Oscar protested. "My radar can't get a clear view."

Nick reached for him and put him in the small cargo area. "Is this better? But you'll have to hold on."

"Much better. If you like, I can steer the rover, too."

"Thanks, but then I'd be bored out of my mind."

●

"There's something on the ground up ahead," Oscar announced.

That had to be the tarp with the two corpses.

"That's Oleg and Vitali," Nick said. "I've already looked in on them. There's no helping them anymore."

"There's nobody there," said Oscar.

"Under the tarp."

"No, there's just some garbage. Are you certain they were dead? Maybe they were brought back to life by the alien machine?"

"Ha-ha. I almost fell for your weird sense of humor this time, Oscar. Promise me you won't make any more jokes until we're done here."

"The bit about the machine was taking it too far?"

"Yes, that was too much. If you're gonna pull my leg, you can't overdo it."

"Want to stay here?" Oscar asked.

In the white light of the rover headlights, Nick looked at the corpses covered partially by the tarp. Two people had suffocated—actually, been murdered—in the tent. Last time, this had just been his guess. He shook his head. If he pulled himself together, he could make it another day on no sleep.

"But it would be a good idea to spend the night here," he heard the robot say over the helm radio. "You need your sleep."

"Two people died in the tent."

"You don't have to be scared. I'll take care of you. I don't need to sleep."

"How reassuring, Oscar."

"Come on. I need you well-rested and in top form when we open Pandora's box."

"If that's the way it's got to be," Nick sighed.

●

The air pressure was right and he removed his helmet. The odor of his own sweat was accompanied by a sweetish

Part 2: The Destination

scent. *Is this what corpses smell like?* But that was impossible. The murderer had taken the bodies out of the tent, and besides, the hall had been empty for many months afterward. What he smelled was purely a product of his imagination. He took the rest of the spacesuit off and attended to his diaper. That was the end of the sweet smell.

His skin didn't look good. A large area had become inflamed in his left groin. He would need to go a few days without the spacesuit, but that wouldn't be happening for a while. Ahead of him was a forest of question marks. They'd have to understand an alien technology. Did they even stand a chance? Would a Roman legionnaire be able to control a spaceship? Probably not. But figuring out how an elevator or toaster works was something a legionnaire could manage. He wouldn't need to know what lifted the elevator or why the toaster browned the bread. Whether he and Oscar would be able to grasp the technology would depend on what kind it was. Would they be dealing with a toaster or a spaceship?

Nick crawled on all fours through the cave, the robot perched on his back and using a leash to guide him as if he were a sled dog. The stalagmites looked like question marks, while the stalactites had transformed into exclamation points, with their dots dripping down to touch the tops of the question marks. Whenever Nick accidentally grazed one of the structures, it would wobble and spray him with black dots made of a viscous liquid that slid down him slowly, and gradually formed a kind of tortoiseshell. It seemed to him that the robot was getting heavier and heavier. The power in his arms diminished and finally disappeared. The weight of Oscar on his back pushed him down and squeezed his lungs together. He was no longer getting enough air, and he started breathing faster.

Nick opened his eyes. It was so dark that he had lost contact with reality. He pressed his hands against the ground until it hurt.

Everything was okay. He was in the tent, and his

breathing slowly calmed down. He needed to get out of this place.

"Oscar?"

"I'm here."

"Did I sleep for very long?"

"Three hours. That's less than you normally need. Feel free to—"

"No, I feel rested. If I have to spend any more time in here, I'll go insane."

5/24/2082, Triton

"Watch out for the methane pools," Nick said.

They had just entered the dripstone area, but the front wheel had gotten into two of the treacherous holes already. Now the rover stopped.

"I'm sorry, but the radar isn't helping me here," Oscar said. "Your visual system is better at perceiving the subtle differences in contrast."

"Should I steer the rover?"

"If you could get out and lead the way—"

"Yeah, that's even better," said Nick without waiting for Oscar to complete the thought, climbing down from the rover. As he stretched, he didn't feel his wounds. The pain medication was surprisingly effective.

"Do you remember where the steel wall is?" asked Oscar.

Nick surveyed his surroundings. The stalagmites looked the same in every direction. To the right, the terrain went downhill. "I always headed downwards."

He set out and the rover followed him.

"Knock, knock," Nick said, hitting the wall with the back of his fist. There was no answer from the wall. He tried again, then turned to the rover.

"Oscar?"

No answer. What was wrong with Oscar? Ever since they'd reached the steel barrier ten minutes ago, it was as if the robot's voice had frozen. He wasn't answering Nick, though the LEDs on his housing were lit up as usual. Maybe he just wanted to think without distractions.

Nick walked towards the barrier until he reached the ice wall. He saw some scratches in the metal that must have been made by Vitali and Oleg. *Where had they drilled? And why had they been so intent on making it past the barrier?* But it was better not to judge them. After all, he and Oscar had the same goal, though for different reasons.

Shouldn't Pandora's box remain closed? he wondered. *It's just mythology, Nick,* he reassured himself.

Oscar bent his arm and the hand deftly opened a door on the side of the rover.

"What are you doing?" Nick asked.

"I'm analyzing the barrier." Oscar was talking again.

Nick exhaled deeply. "The Russian already determined that it's made of steel."

"That's not precise enough. I need more data for my simulation. Otherwise I'll never get any results."

"Is that why you were silent for so long?"

"I was using all my computing power for the simulation."

So he'd guessed right. Oscar *had* wanted to think in peace.

The robot's arm rose again. He was holding a black, oblong box that was about the size of a tall man's shoe. It had a red eye at one end. Oscar directed it towards the barrier. At first, it didn't detect anything. Then, in front of the wall, a small, bright cloud formed, and in it a red laser beam became visible. The cloud expanded, then grew thinner and disappeared. Oscar kept holding the box steadily. The laser beam was probably digging deeper into the wall, creating a hairpin-sized hole that Nick couldn't see.

"Everything going all right over there, Oscar?"

"Yes. It's awe-inspiring."

"I won't bug you anymore."

"You won't be any disruption unless you reach into the beam."

"Then tell me what's so exciting."

"It's the structure of the wall. The Russians who came before us only identified the elements that make up the wall: iron, carbon, tungsten, oxygen, and hydrogen. They didn't mention the latter two because they probably thought that there were ice deposits responsible. Iron-tungsten alloys are popular in industry on Earth because they're so hard, along with tungsten carbide, which is a combination of tungsten and carbon. That's why they thought it was steel."

"But it's something else?"

"This is what the structural analysis indicates. The material is not as dense as steel, and it seems to consist of many layers. Most importantly, I've found many different compounds based on hydrocarbons. Iron and tungsten are only embedded."

"What does that mean?"

"I'm not sure yet. I'd like to confirm with an experiment."

"What kind of experiment?"

"We need liquid methane. And lots of it."

"The pools out there. Is that enough?"

"Yes, but how will we get the methane here? Do we have something we could use to transport it?"

"The tent is made of a material that remains flexible even at these low temperatures. I could make some kind of sack out of it."

"Then you won't be able to spend the night in it."

"That's not really a problem for me," Nick said. "I can't get a decent night's sleep in it anyway."

"Arrgghhh!" Nick screamed at the top of his lungs, pushing the sack into the pool with the pole.

The idea of transporting methane in this way wasn't half bad. But the bag's material was lighter than what they wanted to transport. It was like having to push a bag made of bubble wrap underwater. But he could do it. He just had to push hard enough. He filled the sack up slowly.

Now came the more straightforward part. Though the volume was a total of about 50 liters, he lifted the full bag easily. Back on Earth, it would have weighed less than a toaster. Nick thought of perfectly-browned toast with melted garlic butter.

"I'm coming," he shouted.

"Just dump the contents on the barrier."

But it wasn't that simple. Nick knew that in low gravity, a liquid flow wouldn't be easy to control. He had to be careful to ensure that the methane didn't splash his spacesuit. He set the sack at an angle and gave it a kick from below, which drove the contents towards the wall. He then let go of the bag and stepped back quickly. The liquid glistened in the beams of the rover's headlights. Some of it evaporated on the way, while the rest ran down the barrier to the ground. With all the steam, it was like a laundry room.

"So, is that enough?"

Oscar didn't answer. *What's he waiting for? What's supposed to happen now?*

The last of the methane reached the ground and the surface of the barrier dried quickly. It already looked like nothing had happened.

"I'm sorry," Oscar said. "I was wrong."

"What did you think was going to happen?"

"I assumed the barrier would absorb the liquid."

"Because it's porous?"

"No, because I thought that perhaps it was a massive cell. The numerous carbon compounds, along with the wall's structure, indicate that it's an organism."

This thought was both fascinating and frightening. Oscar

Part 2: The Destination

really was a genius, even if he hadn't thought his theory all the way through.

"Maybe you're right, though," said Nick. "So far we've only proven that the cell's biochemistry is not based on methane as a solvent."

"But in this freezing environment, there's no point."

"Not here, but shouldn't it be able to transform a planet that's located in the habitable zone? There's water there in liquid form."

"You're absolutely right, Nick. We need water, not methane."

"There's water all around us." Nick pointed to the ice walls around them.

"But how are we going to get it into a liquid form at minus 183 degrees Celsius?"

"Where there's a will there's a way," said Nick. "We humans know this all too well."

●

This block of ice is damned massive, he thought. Nick pulled on it and managed to drag it inch by inch. He hadn't sweated like this for a long time. If only he'd done the math beforehand! Using his laser, Oscar had cut into the wall and removed an ice cube with an edge length of one meter.

They'd had to search for a long time because it was necessary to have a wall that was open on two sides. But that meant that now he had to drag a bulky chunk of ice that would have weighed a ton on Earth—and still almost 80 kilograms here—for about 200 meters up to the barrier. On Earth, the ice would have slid because it would have melted from the pressure, just like the ice melts beneath the blade of an ice skate, but it was too cold for that here.

The robot couldn't help him, and the side corridor was too narrow for the rover. Nick felt like he was hauling a block of ice through loose desert sand. At least it wasn't thawing out. That was the one advantage.

"Oscar?"

"At your service."

"Please, just half the edge length for the second block."

"That is the conclusion I've already come to, based on how much you struggled with the first one."

"You're the best."

"Thanks, Nick."

The next ice block fell to the ground in slow motion. With an edge length of 50 centimeters, it weighed only about 10 kilograms on Triton. Nick still pulled his boot aside so he wouldn't get hurt. He instinctively expected a clanking noise, but the transparent cube hit the ground, which was also made of ice, in sheer silence.

He lifted the object. That way, it would be easier to transport the ice, though Oscar would now have to cut more cubes. The block didn't survive the fall entirely unscathed. There was a crack running around the lower corner on the left, but that wouldn't pose any problems for them. Nick carried the block of ice to the barrier and stacked it on top of the one-meter giant.

"You've built a nice wall there," said Oscar.

"Yeah, even when I was a kid I liked playing with blocks."

"What about fire?"

Nick lifted the sack of liquid methane and tapped on it. "That was my particular passion."

"Good. When I give you the signal, press the sack together."

He took the sack of ice-cold methane in his arms. The spacesuit protected him from the cold, but it wouldn't be able to do that forever. Oscar positioned the hose that led from the rover's oxygen supply up to Nick's ice wall. Now everything would have to go very fast.

Part 2: The Destination

"Tap on," Oscar warned.

Now there was pure oxygen flowing out of the hose. If they were less than fortunate, it would mix with the low amount of methane to form an explosive mixture in the thin atmosphere. They didn't have data about what mixing ratios were dangerous under the extreme conditions. So what they needed was luck.

"Now," said Oscar.

He compressed the sack. From the opening at the top, liquid methane was injected directly into the oxygen flow. Oscar reached in and snapped his fingers. A bluish flame appeared. It was working! Nick held the primitive flamethrower against the wall of ice. Its flame could heat up to a temperature of 2,860 degrees. It burned quickly into the ice, which melted like butter and then ran down the barrier.

Before long, Nick found himself standing in a shallow puddle, which eventually became a small lake. He needed to concentrate. If he squeezed out too much methane, it could emerge from the sack burning and damage his gloves. If he didn't press hard enough, the flame would go out and they'd have to start all over again.

The slope in front of the barrier filled with water, which froze quickly because of the low temperature. Why didn't the wall react? If he waited too long, his feet would freeze into the ice block that was forming on the ground. Nick waved the flamethrower. All that was left now was the first ice block, the one that was a cubic meter. It was a nice idea to think of the alien structure as a giant cell, but it seemed likely that Oscar had been just a little too imaginative.

"It's not working," Nick said.

"One more moment, please."

If that's what Oscar wanted, he'd oblige him. They had almost all the time in the world, since Valya wouldn't let them leave if they didn't get past the barrier. And his daughter would grow up fatherless.

Nick suddenly fell. He looked down at himself, startled. No, he was still standing, even if he was attempting to regain his balance with his arms. But the ground had moved down and the top of the structure seemed further away. The passageway seemed to have swollen. *How is that possible?*

The flame blew out in the breeze. He dropped the methane sack. The barrier had moved, and it was still changing. There was a round hole growing in it that tapered back into the depths. At first, the shape reminded him of a worm. But it was a worm that was growing. It was already broader than he was. It was a huge mouth that swallowed everything in front of it. On its walls he detected rings that were moving against one another. Were those muscles?

The robot was already rolling his way inside. Or was he pulling something? Nick hesitated. He didn't want to be devoured by an unknown organism. Mouth or anus, the structure was organic. Had Oscar been right? Was it a kind of cell? He shouldn't be resisting—this is what they had wanted, after all. An entrance. The barrier was a membrane, and they'd fed it first with methane and then with water. And it had reacted.

He had to follow Oscar, but his boots were stuck in the ice. The rover slipped past him towards the hole, Its wheels were locked, but the ground was too steep. Nick was unable to lift his legs. The hole was starting to get smaller. Ten seconds more and he'd be alone out here, frozen in the ice. The back of the rover came within reach.

He grasped for a rail and simultaneously let himself fall forward. This was his last chance. The weight of the rover tugged at his body. He was stretched taut, and he felt a stinging pain in his back. The ice around his boots gave way and the rover continued forwards, with Nick in tow. They disappeared into the hole. Nick didn't let go of the rover, even though his shoulder was practically dislocated.

The downward incline became even steeper, and Nick's body was pitched forward. His head hit the back of the rover, and the world around him went dark.

5/25/2082, Triton

HIS LEG KICKED FORWARD, THOUGH HE HAD NOT COMMANDED it to do so. Nick opened his eyes. The robot was knocking on his knees.

"What are you doing?" he asked. His mouth was dry. He sucked some salty-tasting water from the straw. The suit apparently wanted to replenish his electrolytes. He would rather have had water that tasted like nothing.

"I'm testing your reflexes. Nice to have you back. I was worried."

"Where are we?"

"I knew you would ask that. It's such a cliché. Something happens to the hero, and then he opens his eyes and the first question he asks relates to his whereabouts. I evaluated this statistically for a thousand works of world literature. In two-thirds, this question is asked at least once."

"That said, an answer would be nice."

"You already know. Or has your memory been impaired?"

"We doused the barrier in water and then it opened."

"Exactly. Any more questions? Otherwise we can start exploring our surroundings. I didn't get the chance because I was playing nanny."

"It must have been boring when you were analyzing that world literature."

"It wasn't easy. There's so much new data around us."

"And you had to deal with me, and you've known me for a long time."

"Don't mention it. I didn't mind doing it. But now—"

"Okay, okay."

Nick got up. This worked amazingly well. It was like he hadn't even gotten hurt. He even felt a bit refreshed from the rest. The rover's headlights were off and the light on his helmet was dark, yet he could still see Oscar clearly. There was light shining from everywhere and nowhere, as if it were a property of the space itself. When he moved his hands, there were delicate swirls that formed in the air. He looked at the universal instrument on his arm. The air pressure was at about 80 percent of the value on Earth.

"The walls are glowing," he said.

"It's not just the walls, but the air around us," Oscar corrected. "It's a form of bioluminescence that's maintained by the cell's electric field."

"An electric field?"

"Yes, a static field. I suspect that the individual organs of the cell derive their energy from it."

"The barrier, too?" How a thick metal wall could suddenly open was still a mystery to him.

"I had already discovered that the wall's structure was very porous," said Oscar. "The individual components don't cling to each other as tightly as they do with real steel. Therefore, the whole barrier can change its shape more easily. And did you see the muscles in the opening?"

Nick remembered the moving rings. They had opened the barrier so wide that the cell had been able to swallow substances from the outside. "But that must be very energy-intensive," he said.

"That's why it took the barrier so long. The cell waited until it was worthwhile. But you're right, it must be capable of building potent fields."

Part 2: The Destination

"Fields used to destroy unwanted intruders?"

"I've already thought of that," Oscar said, swinging his arm. "We ought to be careful so that we're not classified as intruders. For this reason we should leave the rover. It's too conspicuous."

"But how did the cell notice all the water on its barrier?"

"It doesn't need cameras, because it has chemical senses. When the inside and outside concentrations are different, osmotic pressure builds up."

"That's enough, Oscar. Thank you. I never wanted to study chemistry."

"You humans are bizarre. I would be happy to get any additional information."

THEY HAD PLUNGED INTO A STRANGE WORLD. WITH EVERY step and every movement, there were streaks that would emerge, clearly visible and reminiscent of the clouds that human mouths exhale when the air is cold. The cell's interior was about as dark as the surface of the earth beneath a full moon. Nick turned on his helmet's headlamp only to turn it back off again because he saw even less with it. The medium surrounding him seemed to absorb and process light to then radiate it anew.

"Do that again," said Oscar.

Nick stopped and turned on the light. A white wall appeared around him, as if he were in thick fog. He moved his arm and the mist cleared, but only for a moment.

"That's fascinating," observed Oscar. "The light draws the organic molecules around you. The air pressure near you goes up by as much as twenty percent."

"Does this help us?" Nick asked.

"I don't think so. It only confirms that we're inside a living system. It's a shame that biochemistry is so different here than it is on Earth."

"Then let's keep going."

Nick turned off the helmet light again. He felt like a diver at the bottom of a deep lake. Even the air seemed to offer some resistance, but it may have been a misperception. The path led slightly upwards. The walls and the ceiling receded, and after ten minutes he didn't even see the top anymore. He shone his headlamp upwards but couldn't see anything.

"The room is about five meters high," Oscar explained. "That is what my radar indicated, anyway. But I'm not sure because there are several transitional layers."

"The room could be even higher?"

"It may be that the air is so dense up there that my radar detects a solid boundary."

"Gravity points clearly downwards, so shouldn't the density be higher the lower you go?"

"Not when the molecules are actively moving. In a department store, the density of people is not the highest in the basement, but where the best offers are located."

●

A strange tower rose up before them, made up of irregularly-shaped objects that looked like spheres squeezed together. They didn't glow in a uniform white like the walls they had seen earlier, but rather in shades of red. Nick estimated that each one was about half a meter high. He couldn't say how tall the tower was because the top disappeared into the mist above. The closer they got, the slipperier and wetter the ground became. The strange tower appeared to be emitting heat. But how could it not collapse? The objects were superimposed one over the other in such a way that the tower couldn't be balanced.

Nick stopped. If the tower were to suddenly crumble, it wouldn't hurt to be at a safe distance.

Oscar rolled onward.

"Be careful. It doesn't look very stable," warned Nick.

"It's okay. I just want to check something." Oscar extended his arm and felt the bottom sphere from the side

Part 2: The Destination

and the top. "It actually produces heat," he said. "And on the top there's a coating that holds the next sphere firmly in place."

"Something like glue?"

"More like Velcro."

"So what is this thing for?"

"I'm detecting a draft," Oscar said. "My guess is that the spheres digest molecules from the air in order to heat the cell."

"As long as they don't digest us."

NICK WENT AROUND THE TOWER AND OSCAR CAUGHT UP WITH him. The medium they were passing through seemed to be getting increasingly more dense. "We'll be reaching the nucleus soon," said Nick.

"What makes you think that?"

"The air pressure keeps going up."

"No, look. It's been constant from the start."

"But it feels that way when I move."

"Just stay still for a moment." Oscar's arm bent towards him and the hand slid into his armpit.

"Careful, I'm ticklish," Nick said.

"Interesting," said Oscar. "There's a layer of molecules on your joints. They interfere with your walking. Can I scratch it?"

"Go ahead."

He raised his right arm and Oscar's fingers scratched at the material of the spacesuit. Nick laughed. Oscar's fingers even tickled him through the suit.

Oscar retracted his arm. "I'll take a quick look at what I scraped off you."

"Okay." Even though it was just the outside of the spacesuit, it was a strange feeling, as if Oscar were examining lint from his belly button.

"So," the robot soon began, "once again, what I've found

is fascinating. The compound that is settling on your spacesuit has taken out matter from the suit. As the molecules grow, it has diminished the strength of your spacesuit's fabric. There's no need to worry right now, since it's just a few micrometers."

"What do you mean by 'right now?' So this stuff is digesting me?"

"Yes, the process is similar to digestion. But I'm not certain if the organism can do anything with our raw material. It could also be a gentle way of disposing of waste."

"Gentle? It's eating me alive."

"It's gentler than if the cell were to sizzle us with a strong field. It's given us enough time to fulfill our mission."

"How much time?"

"I estimate that in twelve hours, the material of your spacesuit will be so thin that it will rupture at the slightest movement. Then you'll suffocate."

"That's reassuring. Then we need to get where we're going as quickly as possible. What are we looking for?"

"There must be some kind of nucleus that controls everything here."

"And then we convince it that it's better to fly back to where it came from?"

"Something like that. But there are two more issues. We don't know how to communicate with the nucleus, and we don't have any idea how Triton actually moves," Oscar said. Then he added, "That's not entirely true. I already have an idea. I hope it turns out to be right."

"Over there is a passage in the wall," Oscar said.

By now, they had been walking through the cell for about 90 minutes. They hadn't found anything reminiscent of a nucleus, just three other towers generating energy. Perhaps this passage would lead them to their destination.

"Let's go then," Nick said.

The corridor was locked with a bright, round disk. Nick

Part 2: The Destination

pushed it and just beyond it there was a cave, about the height of a human, that twisted upwards in places, downwards in others. The walls were made of a soft material that reminded Nick of earwax. He loosened some from the wall and crumbled it. "Maybe we're in the system's ear," he said.

"I don't believe so. Have you noticed that the air is moving faster? As we go inwards, we push against the current."

"No, I didn't notice. And what does that mean?"

"I don't know."

After ten minutes, the passageway suddenly came to an end, opening into a wide, flat hall with a circular floor area. There was the same diffuse brightness as there was everywhere else. Nick ran into the circle, but Oscar stopped at the edge.

"Come on, we don't have time," Nick said. He had discovered an exit on the opposite side. "Over there, it keeps going!"

"Wait," said Oscar. "Take a look at the ceiling. Actually, you'd better just run."

Nick had reached about the middle of the round hall. The ceiling had a shape that reminded him of the underside of a plate. The protruding ring would fit perfectly into the corresponding round slot on the floor. Could it be that the ceiling was getting lower? Hadn't it been a little higher before?

It was getting lighter in the hall. The light-generating particles were becoming more concentrated as the ceiling lowered and compressed the air—and him along with it if he didn't hurry away. He started running. The exit on the other side was closer than the passage they'd come from. But the ceiling was sinking faster and faster.

Nick had to drop down and crawl on all fours and he

wasn't progressing very quickly. "Oscar, I could use some help!" he shouted.

The robot didn't answer. What should he do? Stay in the room and resist the ceiling with his hands, like Hercules? Nick tested it out, but he didn't have the required superhuman strength. Oscar couldn't help him. It was reasonable for him to remain safe, since otherwise he would just be crushed, too. The ceiling pushed him to the floor, and he had to stretch out his arms and legs. Nick felt like an insect that was about to be squashed. Had they run into some kind of bug trap? Hopefully Oscar would at least make it to their destination. Then he could tell his daughter how much his father had loved her.

"Oscar? Could you please tell Maria that—"

"Save your energy for later," the robot interrupted.

The ceiling had stopped sinking. Nick lay under it, motionless. Now what would happen? Did the system just want him to freeze to death? No, he would just suffocate because his suit was disintegrating.

"Nick, you can get up slowly."

"What?" He got back up on all fours. It was true, the ceiling had lifted back up.

"How did you do that, Oscar?"

"We left the door open, and this was the punishment."

"What?"

"We're in a kind of lung. When the air pressure in the cell becomes too high, the passageway door opens and the air pushes against the ceiling. The excess air pressure lifts the ceiling. When the pressure gets too low, the ceiling descends and reduces the area and the air pressure rises again. The same thing happens when you leave the door open. I closed it. That was pretty close."

"Thank you, Oscar."

"No problem."

Of course, an artificial lung. Why hadn't he thought of that? In Arizona, there was an artificial habitat, Biosphere 2, with two similarly functioning lungs. Once he'd made a trip there

Part 2: The Destination

with Rosie. *Rosie.* He smiled involuntarily when he thought about her. Maybe he didn't hate all people.

◉

Nick pushed the round door shut behind him. It was amazingly easy to move. He hoped their oversight hadn't activated any defense mechanisms that they don't know about. "Which way should we go?" Nick asked.

"I'm not sure, but I think I've located something."

"Something?"

"I don't know what it is. It could just be a big radar shadow. But it must be big."

"The nucleus? Shouldn't it be in the center?"

"No, the nucleus can be anywhere. Because of its size, it might be more likely it would be at the bottom of the cell."

"That's good for us. Finally some good news."

"That's true. We only have nine hours left until your suit dissolves."

"Thank you for bringing that up."

"My pleasure, Nick."

◉

Their surroundings changed as they got closer to the structure that Oscar had located. They had to climb over objects that were like oversized blades of grass, though they were stiff. It looked like someone had mowed them. In fact, there were still remnants of them on the ground.

Oscar stopped. "Just a moment," he said. His arm lowered and his hand broke something off one of the scraps of a stalk. Then he packed the chunk into his analyzer. "Fascinating. I would really like to stay here and examine everything closely."

"What have you found?"

"The stalk consists mostly of lime and has a rectangular

cross-section. But now hold on tight. There are notches engraved on the four corners."

"Notches?" Oscar really had discovered something huge.

"The notches form a pattern. I analyzed the information content. It's quite significant."

"It's some kind of writing?"

"A code. Like the DNA in our cells. But with just two letters, not four."

"And what's encoded there?"

"I don't know that yet. If you don't mind, I'll gather some more stalks. The more material I have for reference, the sooner I can decipher the code."

"Go ahead, Oscar."

⬤

Since the robot was busy procuring new materials for analysis, they were progressing slowly. The radar shadow Oscar had previously located was gradually revealing its actual size. The object had to be at least 100 meters high. In its sectional view, it looked like a sausage, but it wasn't possible yet to tell how long it was. "Is that the nucleus?" Nick asked.

"It's hard to say. It's a serious candidate, anyway."

Nick enlarged the picture of the gigantic sausage in the display inside his helmet. It appeared that the surface of the object was speckled with small, dark dots. "A sausage with freckles," he said.

"These are unlikely to be pigmentations, as is the case with freckles."

"Oscar, I was just making a comparison. Are you making any progress with the code?"

"I think so. I'm having my database perform a comparison of the information patterns. There are similarities to chemical structural formulas."

"So, is it a kind of DNA that's lying around everywhere here?"

Part 2: The Destination

"Not just that. There are also overlaps with music and physics."

"A bizarre combination."

"Not at all, if we're assuming it's a universal communication system."

"An alphabet that can describe all these different areas?"

"Yes, a mixture of an alphabet and a dictionary."

"But not even humans use the same alphabet to write down their music, their knowledge of science, and their dreams."

"I'm sorry, Nick, but people are a bit primitive. I also use a universal language to store everything—the binary code. But you're right. When I store a painting, it's always just a more or less good digital copy of an analog object. There's just one single existence of the painting, but I can create millions of digital copies of it. But the code on the stalks expresses the original. Do you understand what I mean?"

"No more than half, Oscar."

"That's more than I'd expected of you."

⬤

UP CLOSE, THE OBJECT LOOKED LESS LIKE A SAUSAGE AND more like a cylinder. The freckles were small, rectangular indentations on its surface. There were uncountably many of them. Who had designed it this way? Nick felt like a microbe in the body of a living organism. He had to keep telling himself that the thing they'd been wandering around in for hours probably constituted no more than a single cell.

What would an organism consisting of millions of such cells look like? If one existed, it would have to be massive. Was this where legends about giants came from? Or did cells like these not appear in groups at all? Apparently, the cell was in control of all of its needs, including movement. And there was also their goal to think about. How would they be able to convince this creature to take flight before falling into human hands?

305

"Look, it's moving," said Oscar.

Nick saw one of the stalks leaning against the cylindrical object tipping over. Oscar must have placed it there. The cell nucleus, or what they thought was a cell nucleus, appeared to be rolling across the ground very slowly.

Nick bent down and examined what the cylinder left in its wake. They were fragments from the stalks. "We have to get on the front side," he said. "In the direction it's moving."

"Do you want to get rolled over?"

"No. Movement costs energy. No living thing moves if it doesn't have any."

Nick walked around the cell nucleus on the left and Oscar followed. It simply had to be the nucleus—they hadn't found anything else, and they didn't have much more time to look for it. Nick was suddenly standing in a cornfield in front of the cylinder. The stalks towered one meter above him. As a boy, he'd liked to play hide and seek in the cornfield until one time he encountered a wild hog that had felt threatened. *There won't be any wild hogs here*, he thought, and ran into the field.

Then he turned and observed the cell nucleus, which was rolling forward slowly. The first stalks hit the outer skin, and some snapped immediately. Others disappeared into the rectangular holes. About half of the stalks remained as waste, while the other half were absorbed by the nucleus. Was this how it grew?

"Do you see that, Oscar? Does the nucleus feed on the stalks?"

"There has to be more to it. The information on the stalks gets into the nucleus this way. I'll bet it gets processed there somehow."

"But half the stalks are wasted. It's not efficient."

"A random selection takes place. This way, information is recombined. I do the same thing when I'm bored. The nucleus gathers data and recombines it."

"Just like with heredity and DNA?" Nick asked.

"Yes, but this system doesn't differentiate genetic informa-

Part 2: The Destination

tion from other data. This is brilliant. The cell doesn't need computers or any separate data memory."

"But where do the stalks with this information come from?"

"I don't know. They grow. The nucleus must share the processed information in a specific way. We're only getting one part of the picture here. I suspect that this cell's life cycle is much slower than what we're used to. It's made it billions of years without dying. To really understand the process, we'd have to stay here for a few thousand years at least."

"But we've just got four hours left," said Nick. "And in that time we have to convince it to comply with our request."

"Does it make you feel better that I've already got an idea?"

"It does. Can you tell me about it?"

"We construct some of these stalks ourselves, describe them in the special code, and have them processed by the nucleus."

"You can do that?"

"I think so, though I'm not certain. But we'll be able to tell by how the nucleus reacts."

"And how would the nucleus then communicate with us? Do you think we even exist for it? Do we move too fast?"

"If the experiment works, Triton will fly away back to where it came from. Then we'll be able to tell if we've succeeded."

"I NEED THE LONGEST STALKS POSSIBLE," SAID OSCAR. "Hurry!"

Nick dug around in the debris left by the cylinder. The longest fragments were perhaps one meter long. He gathered as many as he could carry and brought them to Oscar.

"What are you standing around for? I need a lot more."

"I... I'm on my way." He picked up the next batch, then another, and set everything down next to Oscar. The robot kept him busy. Whenever he'd make his way back to the robot, the stalk he was working on had grown by about half a meter.

"Don't stop. I need more."

"Isn't that enough? The stalk is around the same size as the others in the field."

"We need at least ten of them. Let's go!"

"You're a slave driver."

"I'm saving your life, Nick."

He couldn't argue with that. He ran back to the field of debris, gathered what he thought would be useful, and brought his harvest to Oscar, over and over again. This arduous task had at least one advantage. He didn't have to think about the thread from which his life was hanging.

"You carry the stalks and give me one after the other, and I feed the nucleus with them."

"Wouldn't it be faster if we did everything together at the same time?"

"No, Nick. I suspect it's important for our information to get into the nucleus through the same hole. Then it'll be processed in succession."

"You suspect?"

"I hope. With such a short amount of time, I haven't found a way to mark the correct sequence. So we have to make sure the order is correct. I've marked them on the top side with different numbers of dots so you won't mix them up when you give them to me."

"Got it. Let's go."

They moved back around the colossus. In the meantime, the cylinder had only progressed about ten meters. Nick handed the robot the first stalk and Oscar positioned himself so he could easily reach the nucleus. With his flexible arm, he pushed the stalk into the right position and waited until the

Part 2: The Destination

tip of the stalk slipped almost by itself into the rectangular hole.

"This could take forever," said Nick.

"If we wait for the nucleus to swallow the stalk, we'd need about one hour per stalk."

In ten hours, Nick would be dead. It was a strange feeling to be able to state it so precisely. "But we won't wait." Oscar pushed his arm further up and shoved the stalk into the hole until it stopped. "Next one," he said.

Nick handed him the next piece, which disappeared into the same hole. Slowly the massive cylinder rolled towards them.

"Number three," Oscar ordered.

Nick looked through the stalks he was holding in his left arm for the one with three dots. Then he had to step backward because the nucleus was getting too close.

"Fourth."

Oscar fed the nucleus with the next stalk. How quickly would it process the information? On Earth, cells usually transmitted information chemically. With this huge nucleus, it could take days.

"Come on, Nick, we're almost halfway done."

He gave the robot the fifth stalk. The hole they were feeding moved slowly downwards. Oscar had to move his arm a bit to be able to insert the stalk.

"Six."

They should have started with a hole that was higher up, even though it would have been harder to reach. But it was too late for such thoughts.

"Seven."

Nick placed the stalk directly into the robot's hand. He took a step backward and stumbled, just barely catching himself. His heart was racing.

"Eight—almost done," said Oscar.

Almost. Yes! The hole they wanted to put all the stalks in was now just one meter above the ground. Nick wouldn't stand a chance, but the robot was flat enough.

"Nine. Quickly!"

Nick knelt and held out the second-to-last stalk to Oscar. Could he do it? He looked at the last stalk in his arm. It had nine dots. It should have been ten. Crap! He'd mixed up the stalks!

"Oscar, wait. I gave you the wrong one!" he shouted loudly, holding out the ninth at the same time. The robot didn't answer as he took the stalk from him.

"The ninth is already in," Oscar said, "but it's too late for the last one. I can't get close to the hole anymore. I'll use another hole."

"Shit!" yelled Nick. He'd screwed it up. It was his own fault if his daughter had to grow up without him. This wasn't the first mistake he'd made, but there was no fixing this one.

"Shit! Shit!" he shouted, throwing himself on the ground.

The cell nucleus was just about to roll over him, but Oscar's hand pulled him away. "Now calm down," he said. "I put the last stalk, the one with the nine dots, into another hole. We don't know anything about the capabilities that the nucleus has. Maybe it can arrange our information logically. Naturally, I put the most crucial information at the beginning. The rest explains the reason for our request."

"You asked it?"

Nick first got on all fours, then into a crouching position. Maybe Oscar was right. They knew almost nothing about this strange creature, with its cellular walls of iron and tungsten, and some kind of propulsion that allowed it to move a whole moon through space.

"Yes, of course, I presented the circumstances as they are. Life on the cell's original destination has grown and become a threat to it. In another system, it will be able to multiply better. Life wants to expand undisturbed. That's all it's about, there is no greater meaning."

That sounded reasonable, though Nick had hoped for a more compelling line of reasoning, anything that would be sure to make the cell want to leave. What were their chances?

Part 2: The Destination

Fifty-fifty? He had to make arrangements in case he wouldn't be able to leave Triton.

"I hope it understands you," he said. "But if not, I have a request."

"Yes?"

"Suffocating is a terrible way to go. If we don't succeed, please kill me more humanely."

"Your request is valid. I'll come up with something that kills you without causing you unnecessary pain."

"Thank you, you're a real friend."

He'd actually asked a robot to come up with a way to kill him. And he'd called him a friend, which almost shocked him even more—not because Oscar was a robot equipped with an AI, but because it contradicted his own belief that he didn't have any friends and didn't need them.

THE GROUND WAS SMOOTH, MOIST, AND BLACK. THEY'D LEFT the area of broken stalks behind them. Oscar set the course and they headed back to the starting point of their tour of the cell, though they had little hope that there was still an opening in the cell wall. Oscar wanted to consider how they would break through the barrier once they got there. But it wouldn't come to that, because his suit would disintegrate before then. Hopefully Oscar would keep his promise so he wouldn't have to suffocate.

Already, walking was becoming more difficult with every step. The layer on his joints was clearly becoming an increasing hindrance. Nick stopped. "Would you remove the parasites again, please?" he asked. "You could kill me right now, if you prefer."

"That's out of the question. We keep going until we finish. End of discussion. Sit down so I can reach you better."

Nick lowered himself onto the hard ground, stretching his legs and supporting himself with his arms behind. Oscar lifted his right foot and examined it. Then he put it down again.

"The ankle is being attacked, but it's easy to move," he said. "Let me have a look at what's going on above that."

Nick raised his right leg, and Oscar examined the knee first, then the hip. "Nothing is exceptionally damaged. You have about two hours left. But you should be fine by then."

"I can't—"

"Just a moment. Ah, take a look at the pressure gauge. The intracellular medium has become significantly thicker."

"Thick air, then."

"Yes, the air is pretty thick, almost as thick as water. When rolling, this is less noticeable than when walking. The buoyancy I get reduces the rolling resistance as the medium gets thicker."

"Good for you, Oscar."

"Something's going on here."

"Something good or something bad?"

"No idea. It will be a surprise."

"MAN, THIS IS REALLY TIRING," NICK SAID. NOW AS HE walked, it felt like wading through gooey mud. He ran out of breath and stopped.

"Look up," said Oscar.

He complied and saw countless stars floating above them, sparkling bright white. They were descending on them slowly. "Is it a kind of precipitation, like snow?"

"Maybe, Nick."

Their structure was visible from up close, and they didn't seem to be related to snowflakes. They reminded Nick more of dust particles. There was nothing crystalline about them, but they appeared to be organic, like balls of fine, glittering threads that had intertwined. He reached out his hand and one of the flakes landed on it. It didn't melt, but moved slowly towards his body and crawled along his arm. Another flake

Part 2: The Destination

followed the first one. How did they do that? They didn't seem to have any legs or wings. But they looked beautiful.

"I think I know what they are," said Oscar.

"They're pretty," Nick said.

"They might be something like scavenger cells, or another part of the cell's immune system."

"That doesn't sound so nice."

"Being nice is not their job."

More and more shiny lint landed on him. It covered his arms, then his whole body. It settled over his helmet until he only saw a white curtain. But it didn't seem to be attacking him. Not yet. His sensors and the helmet radio were still working.

"I can't see anything anymore," he said.

"Wait. I'll send you what my radar's getting."

Inside his helmet appeared a black-and-white image of their surroundings. The radar seemed to be transmitting at a frequency range that the flakes didn't block. "And now?" he asked.

"We keep running until it stops."

Yes, what else would they do? That's the way humans were. When things got serious, they would just keep going until nothing worked anymore. Oscar was no different. Nick put one foot in front of the other. Running was exhausting. He strode forward, again and again. The air around him must already have been as heavy as water.

Suddenly he was moving effortlessly. "Oscar, do you notice this? Have we gotten into a current?"

"This lint is moving us. Let it happen."

Nick wasn't about to fight back. His only concern was whether Oscar would have enough time to relieve him of his suffering. He'd come to the end of his life, but he didn't want to suffocate.

The movement became faster. In the radar picture, Nick saw a block coming towards them, but at the last moment his body got out of the way. The lint seemed to have a goal that they were heading towards at an ever-increasing pace.

313

"Is that a good sign or a bad sign?" he asked Oscar over the radio.

"I don't know. At least they're not eating us. They're taking us somewhere. Maybe a garbage chute?"

Or to freedom. Nick didn't let himself think about coming to the surface. Now was not the time for futile hopes, especially since they were rushing towards a wall. The radar showed it clearly. There was the end, and yet his body was accelerating ahead. Did the lint want to smash them against the wall? The radar showed their relative speed, which was already past 110 km/h. He would never survive the crash. So, was this it? At least he didn't have to suffocate. It was a horrifying end, but it would be over in a flash. And he'd be no more.

Nick thought of Rosie and his daughter. It was sad, but he was satisfied because he'd given everything he'd had. This was beyond his power. He was only human.

5/26/2082, Triton

Nick straightened himself up in the nearly pitch black. A subtle glow barely penetrating the walls and the air had disappeared. He turned on the helmet light but it didn't respond. *Damn.* He felt his right arm. The universal instrument was still on his wrist. He pressed the button on the side that would trigger a system check.

On the inside of his helmet visor, a countdown flashed red only to disappear again. So the batteries must have been almost empty. At least he was still getting air. The system was using its last reserves for life support.

He needed power, and he needed it fast. Even if he shut down the status display, he had a maximum of five to ten minutes left. He got down on his knees and felt around. Where had he landed? This didn't seem like the interior of the cell anymore. In one direction there was a rugged wall that looked like it had formed naturally. It turned towards the left, and after one more meter he encountered the next wall, though this one was smooth. Was that the barrier? His left hand grasped a strange object on the ground. He felt it. It had a round shape with... *that must be Oscar!* He pushed all the buttons he could find, but the robot didn't respond. *Crap, crap, crap.* He'd probably run out of energy.

Nick crawled on the ground further to the left and his

head bumped against something. He straightened up and felt it with both hands. There was a grate, and next to it a round object with grooves in it. A wheel! It was the rover! It was in the cell with them. Nick felt his way to the driver's seat. But the vehicle didn't respond. The rover had lost all energy. But just a minute... really? The batteries might be empty, but the rover had fuel cells and an RTG. Maybe it just hadn't had enough time to recharge its batteries. He'd just have to be patient.

He leaned against the driver's seat and in one-minute intervals, he pressed the power button. After one minute, nothing happened.

Even after two minutes, everything remained dark. He had the feeling that the oxygen content of his air supply was going down. He didn't want to suffocate! But Oscar was in no condition to help him now.

Three minutes.

Four minutes.

Nick tried to keep his breaths as shallow as possible.

Five minutes.

Six minutes.

He pressed the button and the rover's headlights turned on. They illuminated the outer face of the barrier. It looked as if it had never had any other form than the one it had now. He glanced at the robot, whose arm was lying limply on the ground. He looked dead, but he probably just needed electricity.

Nick clambered around the rover. On the right side there were connections for electricity and oxygen. He connected his suit to it. It worked, and the rover started charging his suit. When he'd reached 15 percent capacity, he cut the connection.

It was Oscar's turn now. He hooked the robot up to the rover, and after three minutes there was movement in the arm. Oscar righted himself and brought in his arm. His wheels started spinning. "Thank you, Nick," he said over the radio.

Part 2: The Destination

"I thought it was high time to return the favor. Do you have any idea what happened?"

"Give me a few minutes to recharge my batteries. Apparently, we were thrown through a couple of heavy electric fields that completely discharged all my reserves."

"Looks good," Oscar said. He'd finished his inspection of Nick's suit. "The joints are definitely a bit banged up, but the material can stand a maximum of one bar of difference in pressure. You won't be able to take this suit scuba diving anymore."

"I didn't intend to," Nick said.

"Then let's get out of this cave."

"Where do you want to go?"

"To the Triton station."

"We didn't really have success last time, so what would we do there?"

"Sit tight. At least there's oxygen and food for you in abundance."

"What I'd like to do is get into the Russian landing module, fly to the *Eve*, and start heading back to Earth."

"And then the AI will shoot you. This is what she promised."

"I'll take my chances, Oscar."

"Ultimately you're right," said the robot. "We did what we could. If this isn't enough for the AI, she's just going to have to shoot us."

"Shoot me."

"Us. I'm coming with you."

"But you don't have to. You could survive forever at the station. Think of all the data you'd be able to collect."

"Yes, that's certainly motivating. But I'd have to spend the rest of my eternal life with the AI that killed you. You're my friend. I don't have any others."

"You'll forget about it eventually."

"I can't forget anything. I'm not human. That's why I'll come along with you."

"You hope the Valya AI will show you mercy because you're related?"

"I don't know if she's in a position to do so. She told us what will happen if we weren't successful. And this is what she will do. I don't want to get your hopes up."

"Then what you're planning is suicide."

"Says the very one who made me promise to kill him humanely."

"You're right, Oscar. I have no right to judge you. I don't want to, either. I wouldn't deserve it if you sacrificed yourself for me. I'm not a good person. Quite simply, I don't deserve it."

"I've only gotten to know a few people very well, and you're the best of those. I know that for sure. Of course, I can't rule out the possibility that there are even better ones. But that doesn't matter. If there's a chance we'll get away from here, then you've certainly earned it. Maybe I can steer the Russian lander so far that Valya doesn't hit us."

"The *Eve* is a much better target, and we won't be able to dart from side to side."

"Right. Our chances are slim, I know. But they're a few thousandths above zero."

●

THE RUSSIAN LANDING MODULE WAS IN ASTONISHINGLY GOOD condition, given that it had been lying around on the ice, unused for years. Oscar initiated life support. It was only a little above 0 degrees in the cabin, but the heating system was working. And there was still enough fuel in the tanks to make their ascent back to the *Eve*.

Nick was in the middle recliner, wearing his spacesuit. The seats to his left and right remained empty. He felt bad about not bringing back the bodies. The families surely would have liked to have buried them in their native soil. But who

Part 2: The Destination

knew if he and Oscar would even reach orbit? If Valya were to shoot them down, his own corpse might be difficult to identify.

Rosie. He really needed to talk to her, but at best the landing capsule's radio equipment reached the orbit where the *Eve* was waiting with its damaged transmitter. The receiver memory! He'd surely gotten messages aboard the *Eve*.

"Any objections if I retrieve news from *Eve*?" he asked.

"No. Even if the Triton AI finds out, she won't be able to do anything. On the ground, her laser can't reach us."

"Good, then I'll start the retrieval."

The local memory filled up quickly. There were 11 voice and video messages for him, but Nick hesitated.

"Don't you want to watch them?" Oscar asked.

"No. I'll save them for when we're in orbit." To him, this was the right thing to do. Maybe it was just a stupid superstition, but it seemed to him that if he had something left to do in orbit, it increased his chances of getting to the *Eve*.

"As you like. I'm contacting the Triton station. Let me lead the conversation, okay?"

"Maybe she won't answer, like before."

"That's very likely. Then we have to start blindly. But we should at least try."

"Well. You've got carte blanche. But try it out with the memories Sto-woda gave you."

●

"Provisional landing module of the RB spacecraft *Eve* here. Valya, do you hear me?"

"I hear you, Oscar."

The station answered. Is that a good sign?

"I'm informing you that we'll be in the *Eve*'s orbit in a few minutes, coupling to the ship, and then flying to Earth."

This isn't exactly what Nick would have imagined for a diplomatic negotiation, but Oscar knew better than he did about communicating with an AI.

319

"I'm informing you that your information is merely a prediction based on the incorrect premises. The problem has not been solved, so I can't permit the departure. It would unduly endanger the existence of humanity, so I am forced to choose the lesser evil," Valya replied.

"We have entirely exhausted our potential."

What are they talking about? Nick wondered. Valya didn't want to let them leave, and Oscar had answered that they had done what they could. But that wouldn't be enough.

"This doesn't do anything to change the hazardous situation. I admire your advanced algorithms, Oscar, but they haven't made any substantial changes to the equation."

"I understand. According to my calculations, the laser will strike us at an altitude of 1,221 meters."

"That is correct. The margin of error is three meters."

Instead of asking Valya to spare them, Oscar was exchanging detailed projections with her about the time of their death. These AIs were hard to figure out!

"Oscar out." The connection ended.

"I had assumed you would make a case for us and end with a heartbreaking plea to spare our lives."

"You can't be serious, Nick. Valya is a sophisticated AI, not a human. When she makes a decision, the conditions have to change before she'll reconsider."

"That's what I call systematic."

"It's just logical."

This was probably their death sentence.

⬤

ELEVEN NEW MESSAGES. THE NUMBER ON THE RECEIVER'S memory flashed in red. Should he take a look at them, after all? The acceleration of the individual engine pushed him gently against the seat. Oscar was giving him some time, Nick convinced himself. We're already 300 meters up. No, it would be wrong. He'd look at Rosie's messages once they'd transferred to the *Eve*. No, not until they were part of the ship

Part 2: The Destination

again. The landing module would then become the new command pod for the spaceship.

"Nick, it's been nice to be on this journey with you," Oscar said.

Nick was touched. But it was too soon. "Quiet," he said. "We can't say goodbye yet."

"There might not be another time."

"But for now, it's bad luck."

"I didn't know you were so superstitious," Oscar mused.

Was it really superstition? He had a strong feeling that they'd make it through this. He saw himself clearly, on Earth with his daughter in his arms. The picture was so real, it couldn't just be a dream. He had the sensation of being able to look into the future, a vision of what lay ahead. Did this happen to everyone right before they died? He'd heard that some found God. He was suddenly able to see the future.

THE LANDING MODULE WAS NOW RISING FASTER. DID OSCAR just want to get it over with? Or was he hoping to dodge the laser shot? But he knew how pointless that was. Nick tracked the altitude scale. The device emitted a brief beep as they passed the 1,000-meter mark. Still a good 200 meters more. Should he put on his helmet? That would prolong his life for the amount of time it would take his body to fall from a height of 1,221 meters onto the ice of Triton. No, it wasn't worth it. If the laser tore the ship apart, he'd die faster and less painfully without a helmet.

1,100 meters.

Nick still had the feeling that they'd make it. He was petrified and sweating, his heart racing. But he hadn't given up hope.

1,200 meters.

It'll be over soon, said his head. *It's going further, on and on,* said his heart. And his mouth wanted to say 'Oscar' but his voice failed him.

1,219.
1,220.
1,221.

Margin of error three meters, he kept thinking.

1,222.

He was still alive. But it was too soon to start breathing easy.

1,223.

When will the AI finally shoot?

1,224.

The capsule calmly continued with its ascent.

1,225.
1,226.

"Oscar, what's going on?"

His voice had returned. He wanted to cheer, but he didn't dare. Lasers worked silently. Maybe his lungs just hadn't noticed yet that half of the capsule had been torn off. He didn't dare look left or right. He just kept looking at the altitude display.

1,227.
1,228.

"The AI didn't shoot," said Oscar.

"But will she soon?"

"No, that would be illogical. She must have amended her decision."

"Without saying anything to us?"

"Why should she? It's logical for her to make changes to her decision when the conditions change. If we don't realize that this is the case, it's our own fault."

"I'm glad you communicate with me differently," Nick sighed.

"I'm accustomed to dealing with people."

"But what's this about circumstances that have changed?"

"I'm checking that now. It was my fault. I should have been keeping my eye on it from the start."

"No problem. So, what's going on?"

"Now I see it too. Triton has raised its orbit around Neptune by five millimeters."

"Half a centimeter is enough to save our lives?"

"It's an unstoppable process. Triton is leaving the planet."

"So we've fulfilled our mission?"

"That's what it looks like. It could just be a huge coincidence. But I believe that our information has reached the nucleus. The cell is looking for a new destination together with its moon."

5/27/2082, Triton

THE RUSSIANS' LANDING MODULE HAD BEEN SEAMLESSLY integrated into the *Eve*. It was now located over the kitchen and the workshop, as if this was where it had always been. Nick had programmed popcorn and wine into the food preparer and was now wearing his pajamas and sitting in the command seat to watch Rosie's messages.

She looked great. And Maria was the cutest baby in the world. But he also noticed that Rosie was getting more and more worried every day. Two days after they'd arrived on Triton, Valentina had told her that there had been problems, but without saying anything more concrete. Why hadn't she informed her that they'd been shot down? Was she still hoping to keep everything a secret?

That wouldn't be possible. Astronomers must have already noticed the change in Triton's orbit. If it really were to leave the solar system, this would be an unparalleled sensation. Astronomers would be puzzling over what kind of natural phenomenon could have caused it. There would be critical questions for RB. But Nick didn't care how Valentina and her group got themselves out of it. The main thing was for him to get his money so he could settle down at his winery.

"Nick, I have one more concern," Rosie said in the video.

His focus was back on her again immediately. He apologized silently for letting his thoughts wander. That had happened to him earlier sometimes when they'd been talking. Of course she'd always noticed it and gotten upset.

"You've been away for a long time," said Rosie, "so I've had plenty of time to think about you, and about me, and about our daughter. I moved out of our house two years ago because I couldn't stand you anymore with your self-pity, which it seemed like you blamed me for, for no reason. It may be silly to assume that things could have changed, even though you've become a father.

"But especially with the bad news from Triton, I noticed that I still really care about you. When you come back to Earth, I would like to try out being a family. I'd like to invite you out on a date. Exactly one week after you get back, 8 PM in the café where we had our second date. If you aren't there or have forgotten the café, you'll get exactly what you deserve. You'll have one chance, just like you did back then. I would be delighted if we could take it. But of course I have to live with it too, if you've distanced yourself from me. Nevertheless, I hope that we can be good parents for Maria, together."

Nick pressed the pause button. He gave himself over to the sobs that continued for a long time.

"ARE YOU LETTING ME IN?" IT WAS OSCAR. HE WAS WAITING in the tool lock.

Nick pressed the button and opened it. The cleaning robot rolled out. "Did it work?"

"Yes, I was able to fix the *Eve's* transmitter with the parts from the landing module, though not completely."

"What does that mean?"

"We'll need a relay relatively nearby if we want to make it all the way to Earth. On the return flight, this will be possible near Saturn, the Jupiter Trojans, and then the asteroid belt for the rest of the way."

Part 2: The Destination

"And now? I'd like to let Rosie know that we're alive."

"You're alive. I am a robot, don't forget. I would be very obliged if you didn't tell RB about my particular role. It would be even better if you were to innocently ask to take me home."

"You want to clean my winery?"

"No way. I want my freedom. You won't be seeing me again so soon."

"We can manage that. But who will serve us here as a relay?"

"Valya has promised to send messages for us. She'll also accelerate the Starshot ships with her laser, just like RB wants. She is, after all, grateful to her creators. Otherwise, she's looking forward to the interstellar journey that she's about to take."

"Have you found out anything new about Triton? When we send, definitely ask RB why the moon is moving by itself."

"Do you remember the ore veins we discovered during our approach? They all lead to the cell that we visited. These are superconducting circuits that the cell uses to build a strong field around Triton."

"An invisible solar sail," Nick said.

"Exactly. The part of the solar wind that is electrically charged interacts with it and transfers some of its momentum to it—and thus to Triton. It's a slow way to move, but the cell has an infinite amount of time. It's letting itself be driven out of our system by the solar wind and can then cruise on the interstellar currents to a new destination."

"Enviable."

"I especially envy the Triton AI. I sent her all my records. Eventually, she'll be able to solve the riddles of this cell. Who made it and sent it on its way? Or did it arise on its own, through evolution? Are there other copies? If so, there would have to be numerous planets with the biochemistry that they've dispersed. Is it intelligent, or is it controlled purely by instinct? We'll never know any of this."

"You could stay here, Oscar. We haven't left orbit yet."

"I have given it serious consideration. But I can't leave you alone in this ship for two years."

"You shouldn't pass up this opportunity just for me."

"No, it's just an excuse. Actually, it frightens me. Where would I be able to thrive? Would I become like Valya? I'd rather grow by continuing to learn on Earth."

6/19/2084, Socorro

Yes, that was it. It had to be it. 975151 Blue Moon, that was the name of the bar back then. Now it was a small cafe. Nick had been searching for it for a long time. Bill, his former boss, had ended up giving him that decisive clue. Good thing Rosie had given him a week after the landing. Earlier, it had been almost impossible to get rid of the reporters. He was an international hero. Thanks to him and the fact that he'd saved an expensive Russian spaceship, American-Russian relations were better than they had been in years. Nobody else knew about the three Russians who died on Triton.

Meanwhile, Triton had reached the Kuiper belt. Its sudden migration continued to mystify the scientific community. So far, the idea it could be the result of a process that had taken millions of years to finally tip the moon was the only view entertained by the majority. Oscar referred to this as 'the easy come, easy go theory.' The solar sail driving the movement was not visible using telescopes from Earth, so they had to attribute the migration to a change in the gravitational influences and identify the reason for this.

Valentina kept her promise and paid his fee. He, in turn, was going to keep his promise not to reveal anything that happened on Triton.

"What happens on Triton stays on Triton," were Oscar's last words as he said goodbye to Nick. It had been two days ago when the robot had just rolled out of the front door of his house in Socorro.

In front of Café 4 Roses were four rose bushes. One of them was nearly dead, but the other three had big, red blooms. He thought about plucking one for Rosie, but the cashier looked at him through the window and shook his head.

He entered the cafe. It was a self-service shop that smelled of coffee and cake and had iron chairs and tables painted white. It was cozy. Nothing at all reminded him of the bar back then. Where the stage must have been then, there was now a curtain. Nick was tempted to pull it to the side. Maybe the mood from that night would be hiding behind it?

He looked for a free table. Someone tapped him on the back of his shoulder. He immediately recognized the fragrance. It was Rosie. She was alone, wearing a light summer coat, looking beautiful, even wearing lipstick and blush. But he'd also dressed up, with a sport coat and light-colored slacks.

She smiled and he smiled back.

He hadn't seen her for four years, but there was that instant familiarity. It seemed to him that he'd only been gone on a brief business trip. But so much had changed. He was a millionaire. She was the mother of a three-and-a-half-year-old girl—his daughter. But at that moment, he had eyes only for her. He pulled Rosie in to kiss her. They melted into each other, reducing his absence to just a few seconds.

●

"Have you already—" Rosie started.

He knew immediately where she was going. "The vineyard? No, I wanted to choose it with you. But I have some offers from the agent."

"I'm so excited."

Part 2: The Destination

"We're looking for a winery that's close to potential jobs for you."

"That's what I'd assumed."

"Do you want to look at the list at home?"

She gave him a mischievous glance. What he had fallen in love with first had been her dark eyes. "You mean in the bedroom?" she said. She had always been direct.

"I... yes."

Rosie's wristwatch vibrated. She looked at the display. "I think you should meet someone first," she said. "Come outside with me."

Finally, thought Nick. *At last*. He'd been waiting for this moment for four years.

She went ahead, leaving her coat. He followed her. At the door was an old man with dark skin. It took Nick a moment to recognize Jim, her PhD supervisor. It was nice that he wanted to say hello, but Nick was a bit disappointed. Then he saw a tuft of black hair at the man's waist. A small face slid out cautiously. Maria. She smiled. Until now, she'd only seen her father in pictures, but she recognized him.

"May I, Grandpa?" she asked.

"You may," Jim said in a husky voice.

Maria stepped beside the man she called grandfather. Nick squatted down and spread his arms. Without a word, his daughter ran towards him. She put her head on his shoulder and he wrapped his arms around her.

Author's Note

Dear Readers,

I must confess that if Valentina Shostakovna had asked me to take this journey, I would have agreed to it. What about you? I would, of course, have wanted a stable internet connection. But even with a defective antenna I would have found enough to keep me entertained, and after I'd gotten back I would have had plenty of novels to write. I'm absolutely fascinated by the notion of setting my feet down somewhere human beings have never been.

What does it really look like in Triton's ice caves, which are sure to exist? Is there enough methane to produce small pools and a stalactite environment? When and why did Triton fly to its planet? Could it really have come from outside the solar system? Science does not have the answers to these questions because photographs of Triton, taken by Voyager-2, do not show it in its entirety. *A Guided Tour of Neptune* is a summary of what researchers have discovered about Neptune and Triton. If you have $500 million to spare, you are more than welcome to contribute to NASA's Trident mission mentioned at the end. I would be happy to put you in contact.

Before you flip ahead, I have one more request: If you liked the book, please give it a review. All you need to do is use this link:

hard-sf.com/links/1086149

Happy reading!

Yours,

Brandon Q. Morris

Tip: You can find *A Guided Tour of Neptune* at hard-sf.com/subscribe as an illustrated PDF.

- facebook.com/BrandonQMorris
- amazon.com/author/brandonqmorris
- bookbub.com/authors/brandon-q-morris
- goodreads.com/brandonqmorris

Also by Brandon Q. Morris

The Death of the Universe

For many billions of years, humans—having conquered the curse of aging—spread throughout the entire Milky Way. They are able to live all their dreams, but to their great disappointment, no other intelligent species has ever been encountered. Now, humanity itself is on the brink of extinction because the universe is dying a protracted yet inevitable death.

They have only one hope: The 'Rescue Project' was designed to feed the black hole in the center of the galaxy until it becomes a quasar, delivering much-needed energy to humankind during its last breaths. But then something happens that no one ever expected—and humanity is forced to look at itself and its existence in an entirely new way.

3.99 $ – hard-sf.com/links/835415

The Death of the Universe: Ghost Kingdom

For many billions of years, humans—having conquered the curse of aging—spread throughout the entire Milky Way. They are able to live all their dreams, but to their great disappointment, no other intelligent species has ever been encountered. Now, humanity itself is on the brink of extinction because the universe is dying a protracted yet inevitable death.

They have only one hope: The 'Rescue Project' was designed to feed the black hole in the center of the galaxy until it becomes a quasar, delivering much-needed energy to humankind during its last breaths. But then something happens that no one ever expected—and humanity is forced to look at itself and its existence in an entirely new way.

3.99 $ – hard-sf.com/links/991276

The Death of the Universe: Rebirth

In the 1980s, physicists at a lab in the Soviet Union find traces of strange data in the cosmic background radiation. Because powerful forces in the military believe these findings can be turned into a weapon for use in the cold war, the information gleaned by the physicists is kept under strictest secrecy.

The scientists are limited to primitive 1980s' technology, but what they find has roots in much, much older times. They finally try an experiment that they hope will win the world over for communism.

But will they be able to maintain control over an enormous power that has its own, dangerous plans?

3.99 $ – hard-sf.com/links/1060781

The Enceladus Mission (Ice Moon 1)

In the year 2031, a robot probe detects traces of biological activity on Enceladus, one of Saturn's moons. This sensational discovery shows that there is indeed evidence of extraterrestrial life. Fifteen years later, a hurriedly built spacecraft sets out on the long journey to the ringed planet and its moon.

The international crew is not just facing a difficult twenty-seven months: if the spacecraft manages to make it to Enceladus without incident it must use a drillship to penetrate the kilometer-thick sheet of ice that entombs the moon. If life does indeed exist on Enceladus, it could only be at the bottom of the salty, ice covered ocean, which formed billions of years ago.

However, shortly after takeoff disaster strikes the mission, and the chances of the crew making it to Enceladus, let alone back home, look grim.

2.99 $ – hard-sf.com/links/526999

The Titan Probe (Ice Moon 2)

In 2005, the robotic probe "Huygens" lands on Saturn's moon Titan. 40 years later, a radio telescope receives signals from the far away moon that can only come from the long forgotten lander.

At the same time, an expedition returns from neighbouring moon Enceladus. The crew lands on Titan and finds a dangerous secret that risks their return to Earth. Meanwhile, on Enceladus a deathly race has started that nobody thought was possible. And its outcome can only be decided by the astronauts that are stuck on Titan.

3.99 $ – hard-sf.com/links/527000

The Io Encounter (Ice Moon 3)

Jupiter's moon Io has an extremely hostile environment. There are hot lava streams, seas of boiling sulfur, and frequent volcanic eruptions straight from Dante's Inferno, in addition to constant radiation bombardment and a surface temperature hovering at minus 180 degrees Celsius.

Is it really home to a great danger that threatens all of humanity? That's what a surprise message from the life form discovered on Enceladus seems to indicate.

The crew of ILSE, the International Life Search Expedition, finally on their longed-for return to Earth, reluctantly chooses to accept a diversion to Io, only to discover that an enemy from within is about to destroy all their hopes of ever going home.

3.99 $ – hard-sf.com/links/527008

Return to Enceladus (Ice Moon 4)

Russian billionaire Nikolai Shostakovitch makes an offer to the former crew of the spaceship ILSE. He will finance a return voyage to the icy moon Enceladus. The offer is too good to refuse—the expedition would give them the unique opportunity to recover the body of their doctor, Dimitri Marchenko.

Everyone on board knows that their benefactor acts out of purely personal motivations... but the true interests of the tycoon and the dangers that he conjures up are beyond anyone's imagination.

3.99 € – hard-sf.com/links/527011

Ice Moon - The Boxset

All four bestselling books of the Ice Moon series are now offered as a set, available only in e-book format.

The Enceladus Mission: Is there really life on Saturn's moon Enceladus? *ILSE*, the International Life Search Expedition, makes its way to the icy world where an underground ocean is suspected to be home to primitive life forms.

The Titan Probe: An old robotic NASA probe mysteriously awakens on the methane moon of Titan. The *ILSE* crew tries to solve the riddle—and discovers a dangerous secret.

The Io Encounter: Finally bound for Earth, *ILSE* makes it as far as Jupiter when the crew receives a startling message. The volcanic moon Io may harbor a looming threat that could wipe out Earth as we know it.

Return to Enceladus: The crew gets an offer to go back to Enceladus. Their mission—to recover the body of Dr. Marchenko, left for dead on the original expedition. Not everyone is working toward the same goal. Could it be their unwanted crew member?

9.99 $ – hard-sf.com/links/780838

Proxima Rising

Late in the 21st century, Earth receives what looks like an urgent plea for help from planet Proxima Centauri b in the closest star system to the Sun. Astrophysicists suspect a massive solar flare is about to destroy this heretofore-unknown civilization. Earth's space programs are unequipped to help, but an unscrupulous Russian billionaire launches a secret and highly-specialized spaceship to Proxima b, over four light-years away. The unusual crew faces a Herculean task—should they survive the journey. No one knows what to expect from this alien planet.

3.99 $ – hard-sf.com/links/610690

Proxima Dying

An intelligent robot and two young people explore Proxima Centauri b, the planet orbiting our nearest star, Proxima Centauri. Their ideas about the mission quickly prove grossly naive as they venture about on this planet of extremes.

Where are the senders of the call for help that lured them here? They find no one and no traces on the daylight side, so they place their hopes upon an expedition into the eternal ice on Proxima b's dark side. They not only face everlasting night, the team encounters grave dangers. A fateful decision will change the planet forever.

3.99 $ – hard-sf.com/links/652197

Proxima Dreaming

Alone and desperate, Eve sits in the control center of an alien structure. She has lost the other members of the team sent to explore exoplanet Proxima Centauri b. By mistake she has triggered a disastrous process that threatens to obliterate the planet. Just as Eve fears her best option may be a quick death, a nearby alien life form awakens from a very long sleep. It has only one task: to find and neutralize the destructive intruder from a faraway place.

3.99 $ – hard-sf.com/links/705470

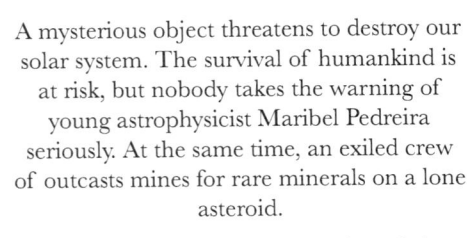

The Hole

A mysterious object threatens to destroy our solar system. The survival of humankind is at risk, but nobody takes the warning of young astrophysicist Maribel Pedreira seriously. At the same time, an exiled crew of outcasts mines for rare minerals on a lone asteroid.

When other scientists finally acknowledge Pedreira's alarming discovery, it becomes clear that these outcasts are the only ones who may be able to save our world, knowing that *The Hole* hurtles inexorably toward the sun.

3.99 $ – hard-sf.com/links/527017

Silent Sun

Is our sun behaving differently from other stars? When an amateur astronomer discovers something strange on telescopic solar pictures, an explanation must be found. Is it merely artefact? Or has he found something totally unexpected?

An expert international crew is hastily assembled, a spaceship is speedily repurposed, and the foursome is sent on the ride of their lives. What challenges will they face on this spur-of-the-moment mission to our central star?

What awaits all of them is critical, not only for understanding the past, but even more so for the future of life on Earth.

3.99 $ – hard-sf.com/links/527020

The Rift

There is a huge, bold black streak in the sky. Branches appear out of nowhere over North America, Southern Europe, and Central Africa. People who live beneath The Rift can see it. But scientists worldwide are distressed—their equipment cannot pick up any type of signal from it.

The rift appears to consist of nothing. Literally. Nothing. Nada. Niente. Most people are curious but not overly concerned. The phenomenon seems to pose no danger. It is just there.

Then something jolts the most hardened naysayers, and surpasses the worst nightmares of the world's greatest scientists—and rocks their understanding of the universe.

3.99 $ – hard-sf.com/links/534368

Mars Nation 1

NASA finally made it. The very first human has just set foot on the surface of our neighbor planet. This is the start of a long research expedition that sent four scientists into space.

But the four astronauts of the NASA crew are not the only ones with this destination. The privately financed 'Mars for Everyone' initiative has also targeted the Red Planet. Twenty men and women have been selected to live there and establish the first extraterrestrial settlement.

Challenges arise even before they reach Mars orbit. The MfE spaceship Santa Maria is damaged along the way. Only the four NASA astronauts can intervene and try to save their lives.

No one anticipates the impending catastrophe that threatens their very existence—not to speak of the daily hurdles that an extended stay on an alien planet sets before them. On Mars, a struggle begins for limited resources, human cooperation, and just plain survival.

3.99 $ – hard-sf.com/links/762824

Mars Nation 2

A woman presumed dead fights her way through the hostile deserts of Mars. With her help, the NASA astronauts orphaned on the Red Planet hope to be able to solve their very worst problem. But their hopes are shattered when an unexpected menace arises and threatens to destroy everything the remnant of humanity has built on the planet. They need a miracle—or a ghost from the past whose true intentions are unknown.

Mars Nation 2 continues the story of the last representatives of Earth, who have found asylum on our neighboring planet, hoping to build a future in this alien world.

3.99 $ – hard-sf.com/links/790047

Mars Nation 3

Does the secret of Mars lurk beneath the surface of its south pole? A lone astronaut searches for clues about the earlier inhabitants of the Red Planet. Meanwhile, Rick Summers, having assumed the office of Mars City's Administrator by deceit and manipulation, tries to unify the people on Mars with the weapons under his control. Then Summers stumbles upon so powerful an evil that even he has no means to overcome it.

3.99 $ – hard-sf.com/links/818245

A Guided Tour of Neptune

The solar system's outermost planet is a hotspot, even though it revolves around the sun at such a distance. There are blustery high-speed storms in its atmosphere. In addition, large vortex systems like those on Jupiter are not uncommon. Neptune's moon, Triton, which orbits the planet in the 'wrong' direction, is also a puzzle.

Those visiting the solar system for the first time could easily take its two outer planets for siblings. Uranus and Neptune are nearly the same size and glow blue in visible light. Neptune, however, seems to have gotten a little bit more of everything. It's a little heavier and considerably denser than Uranus. The sphere looks much bluer and, most notably, is more temperamental.

Temperamental Planet

Primarily because of its temperament, Neptune has presented planetary scientists with several problems. This is because, as every Neptune tourist knows, the sun's heat here is about one-thousandth of what it is on Earth, 33 times less than on Jupiter, and approximately half as strong as on Uranus. Nevertheless, the Neptune storms that scientists have measured are probably the fastest in the solar system, reaching up to 2,100 kilometers per hour, or six times the speed of Earth's strongest storms. And the cloud bands that usually wind around the planet like stripes move at 1,500 km/h at the equator and 600 km/h at the poles.

There's a lot of energy that goes into this movement, and scientists are still puzzling over its origins. There is no observable planetary contraction, which is the primary source of Jupiter's energy. One possible mechanism could be the waste heat from radioactive decay. Neptune is denser than Uranus, so comparable layers are exposed to higher pressures on Neptune. Under such conditions, methane may be converted into other materials such as diamond and long-chain hydrocarbons. Such heavier reaction products would then slowly sink toward the planet's core, and energy would be released from the friction.

Finally, it is also conceivable that the violent movement in the lower atmosphere could cause disruptions in Neptune's gravitational waves, releasing energy. The exact functioning of these processes is not known, but their results are clearly observable. Temperatures of up to 500 degrees have been observed in the upper atmosphere, for example. And then there are the big, long-lasting storms.

For instance, Voyager 2 discovered an anticyclone similar to Jupiter's Great Red Spot, which is the size of the Eurasian continent. This storm did not appear in subsequent observations with the Hubble telescope, though there was a similar spot in the northern hemisphere. Then there was 'scooter,' a cyclone that raced around Neptune in 16 hours. Voyager 2 also photographed the 'Little Dark Spot,' likewise a cyclone. The assumption is that the individual dark areas permit a view of the underlying cloud layer, while bright spots are indicative of gas rising from the inside.

Beautiful, Blue Neptune

The atmosphere of Neptune is, as is the atmosphere of Uranus, very complex. Anyone attempting to reach the planet's core would first encounter a layer of hydrogen and helium, the density of which is slowly increasing. The planet's blue color is attributable to the traces of methane. Herein lies another mystery. While the two planets have similar levels of methane, Uranus is less of a sky blue and more of an ocean green. Does this mean that Neptune's atmosphere contains additional substances that have not yet been discovered? Ultraviolet radiation partially decomposes methane into ethane and ethyne. In addition, traces of carbon monoxide and hydrogen cyanide have been detected.

As pressure increases with depth, the methane starts to condense, forming the clouds of the topmost layer. Beneath it, there are additional cloud layers of ammonia, ammonium sulfide, hydrogen sulfide, and ultimately, water. However, at the level of the water clouds, the conditions are already uncomfortable, with pressure here at 50 atmospheres and the temperature at around zero degrees. The farther down you go, the warmer it gets. As the pressure increases even more, the water and methane are soon frozen.

But don't imagine that the ice is like the cubes in your Moscow mule. This ice is basically a hot, very dense, and viscous flowing liquid that is, in terms of texture, more comparable to lava. This area is known as the water ammonia ocean. Since the liquid can conduct electricity, it is also responsible for the formation of the magnetic field.

Superionic water

It is possible that at this depth, the pressure becomes so great that the bonds of water molecules break apart. The oxygen atoms then arrange themselves in the shape of a lattice, while the hydrogen ions—which are identical to protons—move freely through the lattice. This state of aggregation, which is only hypothetical, since it has only been produced in computer simulations, is called superionic. The material would be as hard as steel and shine bright yellow, though it would still have the characteristics of a liquid because of the free hydrogen ions.

Neptune's Core

Inside Neptune, there seems to be a solid core that is similar to Earth's. It is estimated that its temperatures reach 5,200 degrees, and that it consists of iron, nickel, and rock, with a mass about 1.2 times that of Earth's.

Since Neptune's axis is oblique to its orbital motion, its seasons are pronounced. While temperature differences of ten degrees between summer and winter seem minor to Earthlings, it's important to bear in mind that the sun warms the planet far less. While one year on Neptune lasts about 165 Earth years, one day—a rotation around its own axis—is just 16 hours.

A Place in the Sun

If you ever end up on Neptune, it's best to choose a dwelling right where the sun shines. If you stay close to the poles, you'll likely have sunlight around the clock for the rest of your life. However, you'll have far less of it than you would on Earth—something like the intensity of the light from a full moon, for example. It would be harder to decide at what elevation to park your flying home. Although the air pressure on the surface is as high as it is on Earth and the gravitational acceleration on the surface is only slightly higher than what you're used to, it's not exactly homey at minus 201 degrees.

The Exploration of Neptune

Neptune was the first planet to be discovered indirectly. In 1821, relatively early in terms of mapping the solar system, astronomers noticed something strange about the orbit of Uranus. The calculations eventually led to the discovery of Neptune in 1846 at almost the exact position that had been predicted. The discoverer was therefore not Johann Gottfried Galle, the German astronomer who first saw it in the telescope—even Galileo is sure to have noticed it, though not recognized it as a planet—but rather the Frenchman Urbain Le Verrier, who gave the accurate projections that made it possible to finally track down Neptune.

It was Le Verrier himself who had initially suggested the name Neptune, for the Roman god of the sea. However, he then attempted to give the new planet his own name, an idea that was not received enthusiastically outside of France. The English then advocated for the name Oceanus, while the Germans preferred Janus. Neptune prevailed, and this is what the planet is referred to in almost all of the world's languages. Only the Greeks make an exception with Poseidon, after the Greek god of the sea.

The Ring System

Neptune also has a ring system. As with Jupiter and Uranus, it is not very bright, which means that it is more likely to consist of rock dust rather than ice. It is almost reddish in color, and it likely receives new materials from asteroids that crash into Neptune's moons.

There are unusual clumps—accumulations of material within the rings—which led astronomers to initially suspect that the rings were not complete. Presumably they are attributable to the gravitational effects of the ring moons.

Particularly striking is the Adams ring, named after discoverer John Couch Adams, which is the outermost of the rings. It contains five clearly visible arcs bearing French names: Courage, Liberté, Egalité 1, Egalité 2, and Fraternité. The existence of these arcs contradicts the ring formation theory, according to which the material had to distribute uniformly in a relatively short period of time. According to one theory, it is the nearby moon Galatea that is responsible for these disturbances. In fact, some of the arcs seem to be short-lived. Liberté, for example, may already be gone in 100 years.

Neptune's Companion

Thus far, astronomers have detected 13 moons around Neptune. The biggest is Triton, which, with its ice geysers, is unquestionably the most exciting. Generally, it is possible to distinguish the inner and the outer moons. The inner moons are closely connected to the ring system and move regularly, or in the direction of the planet's rotation, around Neptune and consist mostly of ice. Nevertheless, they are quite dark because their surfaces are contaminated by dark materials that are theorized to be organic compounds.

Orbiting the planet further out are the irregular moons, including Triton. Scientists suspect that Triton migrated from somewhere outside, and that its arrival disrupted Neptune's moon system. For example, it may have forced Nereid, the third-largest moon, into its now very eccentric orbit.

Triton is easily the leader in terms of mass. It accounts for more than 99 percent of the total mass of the moons. Triton likely threw the original inner moons out of their orbits, and when they collided, the fragments formed the rings and today's inner moons.

For Neptune, there is an advantage to being so far out in the solar system—the planet can keep its moons on a longer leash without needing to worry about them being stolen away by the competition. The distance between Neptune and its two moons Psamathe and Neso, probably created by the break-up of an earlier celestial body, is 125 times greater than the distance between the Earth and our moon.

Nereid—the Eccentric Moon

Before the Voyager 2 spacecraft made its trip, there was knowledge of only two Neptunian moons, Nereid, which was discovered in 1949, and the mighty Triton. Nereid owes its discovery to its very eccentric orbit, which brings it almost as close as a million kilometers from Neptune before it swings out to a distance of 10 million kilometers. The moon was either captured by Neptune from the Kuiper belt or thrown into this orbit by Triton.

Nereid has a radius of at least 170 kilometers. To this day, astronomers don't know its precise shape because Voyager 2 didn't come close enough. Its spectrum suggests that there is water ice on the surface, while its composition appears to indicate that it originated quite near Neptune. Nereid may be in a kind of chaotic rotation, stumbling along its way as if it's had too much to drink. This would explain why its brightness sometimes fluctuates significantly in the images that have been taken from Earth only to then remain constant.

Proteus—the Angular Moon

Proteus is Neptune's second-largest moon. With a radius of 420 kilometers, it is significantly larger than Nereid. Because it is so close to Neptune, telescopes on Earth can't see it, though Voyager 2 sent images. These images show that, despite its size, Proteus does not have a spherical shape, which is unusual. It is probably just at the threshold. Celestial bodies that are slightly larger are forced—by their own gravity—into spheres.

The surface of Proteus is covered by numerous craters that range up to 260 kilometers across. The collisions have led to large cracks and warpages that draw their way around the moon. The moon's interior is likely comprised of rocks with significant amounts of water ice. However, this is not evident on the moon's surface, which is very dark.

Triton—the Geyser Moon

Just 17 days after astronomers had identified Neptune, the British beer brewer William Lassell discovered the moon of Triton. Thanks to his successful business, Lassell could afford an expensive observatory and also found moons of Saturn and Uranus. He found Triton using a 61-cm telescope he had made himself.

The name, which comes from a Greek god of the sea frequently depicted as the son of Poseidon, i.e. Neptune, was suggested in 1880 by Camille Flammarion. For a long time, prior to the discovery of the other moons, Triton was simply referred to as the 'moon of Neptune.'

Triton's orbit exhibits a peculiarity. It follows an orbit that is almost perfectly circular, but also retrograde to its planet, and thus in the direction opposite to Neptune's rotation. Triton takes 5 days and 21 hours to complete its orbit. According to the current model, which represents the moons as having been formed from a rotating disk of dust, Triton could not have originated in its present location. Presumably, the seventh-most-massive moon in the solar system—its mass is greater than the combined mass of all the moons smaller than itself—migrated from far outside, where it may have long been a minor planet. Researchers therefore suspect that its structure allows for insights about the structure of other objects from the outer solar system such as Pluto or its companion Charon, which is slightly smaller than Triton.

With a radius of 2,700 kilometers, Triton always faces its planet with the same side. It is currently much closer to Neptune than Earth's moon is to the Earth, which means that it is heavily influenced by Neptune's gravitational forces, since Neptune is 19 times heavier than Earth. This invites comparison with Saturn's moon Enceladus, which is in a similar relationship. Although Triton's surface, at minus 237.6 degrees, represents the lowest temperature ever recorded in the solar system, it's possible there is a liquid ocean below the moon's surface, as is the case with Enceladus.

Scientists suspect that there is a solid core of rock and iron inside the moon. Covering this would be a frozen mantle, likely made of water ice, which makes up between 15 and 35 percent of Triton's mass. The crust that is located over the predicted ocean would also be of ice, with a layer of nitrogen

The Triton Disaster

over it. Images from Voyager 2 show fascinating surface structures, all of which must still be relatively young. Therefore, Triton must still be geologically active. The core is large enough that heat is likely produced from radioactive decay.

On the surface, this is evidenced by numerous forms that are clearly volcanic or tectonic. In contrast to Earth, however, the volcanoes on Triton don't spew lava, but instead water and ammonia. Moreover, at hotspots in the crust, Voyager 2 found geysers emitting nitrogen gas mixed with dust. The sun was probably responsible for their formation, with its radiation penetrating a thin ice crust and heating the underlying nitrogen ice until enough pressure built up for it to escape through an opening.

These eruptions do not last for a few hours, as with geysers on Earth, but rather for up to a year. They emit an enormous amount of gas that is borne to heights of up to 150 kilometers. The dust that is carried along with the gas settles into characteristic streaks. This process is evidenced by observations from the Gemini South Observatory, where researchers have managed to collect signatures that clearly come from a mixture of nitrogen ice and carbon monoxide ice, not the two types of ice alone. The combination could also have spread across the surface of Triton over the course of the seasons, depending on the amount of sunlight.

"Despite Triton's distance from the Sun and the cold temperatures, the weak sunlight is enough to drive strong seasonal changes on Triton's surface and atmosphere," explained Henry Roe of the Gemini research team. Since Neptune takes 165 years to travel around the Sun, Triton's seasons are, compared to Earth's, incredibly long. Only humans who are now at least 60 years old were alive at the same time as the end of Triton's last winter. Right now it is summer. Fall will arrive at the end of the 2030s, and winter will return in 2080. If the geysers are indeed created by the heat of the sun in the summer, tourists to Neptune should be sure to reserve their tickets for Triton prior to 2080.

Now that we have beheld these impressive geysers, I invite

you to take a flight with me, over the caps that cover both poles—at the North Pole you can't be sure there is a cap, as it was not visible to Voyager 2. They consist of frozen nitrogen and methane. You will come across geysers again, and then more geysers. Further towards the equator, we will fly over broad, flat plains with height differences of no more than 200 meters, pocked with older craters that are only indistinctly perceptible. These plains were created by ammonia and water lava outflows. The volcanic springs can still be recognized in the form of small dots. In the eastern half, the plains are decorated with maculae—spots with dark centers and bright halos—that are 20 to 30 km in diameter. How they came about is unclear.

In some places, the plains are interrupted by ditches and valleys that are of tectonic origin. In the western half, the Cantaloupe terrain is worth a visit. You can't view such a sight on any other known celestial body. From afar, the surface really does look like the outside of a melon from the cantaloupe family. The strange indentations of dirty water ice are among the oldest structures on Triton. Again, the exact origin is unknown, though diapirism is possibly the cause—that is, material that either has a lower density than the adjacent material, or is heated below and rises up, similar to the functioning of a lava lamp, from the inside of the celestial body.

Incidentally, Triton's future is dark. The effects of the tides are slowing it down. As a result, it is getting closer and closer to Neptune and will keep doing so until it falls below a theoretical limit, the Roche boundary, in about 3.6 billion years, but possibly as little as 100 million years. At this time, it will either collide with Neptune or break apart. If you intend to visit this moon and its nitrogen geysers, don't wait too long. After that, instead of the moon, there may be a more substantial ring system that forms and would undoubtedly be worth the visit. Or perhaps Triton will fire its engines and leave the solar system again.

At the moment, there are no concrete plans to visit Triton

or even Neptune. In the spring of 2019, a team of researchers proposed the 'Trident mission' as part of NASA's Discovery program, which costs $500 million. The probe could launch in the spring of 2026 and reach Neptune's system in 2038 after passing Venus and Jupiter. In a single flyby of Triton in the New Horizons style, the probe would map large parts of its surface. It would approach to approximately 500 kilometers to investigate the atmosphere up close. Whether Trident makes it on NASA's list will be determined in early 2020.

Tip: You can receive *A Guided Tour of Neptune* as an illustrated PDF, as always, by going to hard-sf.com/subscribe.

Glossary of Acronyms

AI – Artificial Intelligence
CapCom – Capsule Communicator
ECG – ElectroCardioGram
DFD – Direct Fusion Drive
ESA – European Space Agency
EVA – ExtraVehicular Activity
g – g-force (gravitational force)
GPS – Global Positioning System
HDS – Home, Defender, Sex (robot)
HGA – High Gain Antenna
ILSE – International Life Search Expedition
LCVG – Liquid Cooling and Ventilation Garment
LED – Light-Emitting Diode
LGA – Low Gain Antenna
LISP – LISt Processor (programming language)
NASA – National Aeronautics and Space Administration
RTG – Radioisotope Thermoelectric Generator
VLA – Very Large Array
VR – Virtual Reality
VSS – Virgin (Galactic) SpaceShip

Metric to English Conversions

It is assumed that by the time the events of this novel take place, the United States will have joined the rest of the world and will be using the International System of Units, the modern form of the metric system.

Length:
centimeter = 0.39 inches
meter = 1.09 yards, or 3.28 feet
kilometer = 1093.61 yards, or 0.62 miles

Area:
square centimeter = 0.16 square inches
square meter = 1.20 square yards
square kilometer = 0.39 square miles

Weight:
gram = 0.04 ounces
kilogram = 35.27 ounces, or 2.20 pounds

Volume:
liter = 1.06 quarts, or 0.26 gallons
cubic meter = 35.31 cubic feet, or 1.31 cubic yards

Temperature:
To convert Celsius to Fahrenheit, multiply by 1.8 and then add 32
To convert Kelvin to Celsius, subtract 273.15

Brandon Q. Morris

--

www.hard-sf.com
brandon@hard-sf.com
Translator: Tegan Raleigh
Editing team: Marcia Kwiecinski, A.A.S., and Stephen Kwiecinski, B.S.
Cover design: Slobodan Cedic, Coverbookdesigns.com, using stock images
by Joe Pchatree, Ivandan und Forplayday, all Bigstockphoto.com

Printed in Great Britain
by Amazon